I0607462

CHANGING FORTUNE
COOKIES

CHANGING FORTUNE COOKIES

AUNTIE CLEM'S BAKERY #14

P.D. WORKMAN

PD WORKMAN

Copyright © 2021 by P.D. Workman
All rights reserved.

No part of this book may be reproduced in any form or by any electronic or
mechanical means, including information storage and retrieval systems, without
written permission from the author, except for the use of brief quotations in a book
review.

ISBN: 9781774680490 (IS Hardcover)
ISBN: 9781774680506 (IS Paperback)
ISBN: 9781774680483 (IS Large Print)
ISBN: 9781774686102 (KDP Paperback 2 ed)
ISBN: 9781774686119 (KDP Hardcover)
ISBN: 9781774683415 (Lulu Paperback)
ISBN: 9781774680469 (Kindle)
ISBN: 9781774680476 (ePub)

ALSO BY P.D. WORKMAN

FIND MORE BOOKS AT PDWORKMAN.COM

MYSTERY/SUSPENSE:

Auntie Clem's Bakery

Culinary & Pet Cozy Mysteries

Gluten-Free Murder

Dairy-Free Death

Allergen-Free Assignation

Witch-Free Halloween (Halloween Short)

Dog-Free Dinner (Christmas Short)

Stirring Up Murder

Brewing Death

Coup de Glace

Sour Cherry Turnover

Apple-achian Treasure

Vegan Baked Alaska

Muffins Masks Murder

Tai Chi and Chai Tea

Santa Shortbread

Cold as Ice Cream

Changing Fortune Cookies

Hot on the Trail Mix

Fateful Plateful

Cut Out Cookie

AND MORE AT PDWORKMAN.COM

*To those who are willing to help
and those who are waiting for it*

~

CHAPTER 1

*E*rin invited Mary Lou into the house and, at first, it looked like the older woman was going to refuse. She hadn't been happy with Erin recently. This latest development wasn't going to make her more likely to forgive Erin for past mistakes. But then Mary Lou nodded her head, patted her gray bob, and entered. Erin motioned toward the couch, her brain spinning, trying to sort things out.

Vic stood in the kitchen doorway, her long blond hair tied back in a ponytail, her mouth open slightly. She knew how Mary Lou felt about them lately, so she was surprised by Mary Lou coming into the house. Vic looked at Erin, her brows coming down.

"Erin? What's wrong? Is everything okay?"

"No." Erin shook her head. She couldn't explain it. She pointed at Mary Lou for her to explain to Vic. "Tea? I'm going to put on the kettle." She passed Vic in the doorway and started to get the tea things ready. She turned on the electric kettle and gathered teacups, an assortment of tea bags, and the other items she needed.

"What is it?" she heard Vic ask Mary Lou, her tone anxious and uncertain. "Did something happen? Is it Roger?"

But it was not about Mary Lou's husband. As far as Erin knew, he was still safe in the facility where he had been held since he'd been arrested for murder and assault. Not jail, but somewhere they would, hopefully, be a little more compassionate and be able to handle his brain injury.

Nor was it about Campbell, Mary Lou's older son, who had been in some trouble in the past.

Erin listened for Mary Lou's answer, but she didn't explain to Vic. She probably handed Vic the same paper that she had shown to Erin. The Bald Eagle Falls weekly newspaper, which had included a news article written by Mary Lou's younger teenage son, Joshua. But the article had been cut out and there was a sticky note in its place.

If you want to know where your son is, maybe you should ask Erin Price.

The kettle started to whistle. Feeling numb and distant, as if she were enclosed in a bubble, Erin poured the steaming water into the teapot and then took the tea service out to the living room. She set it on the coffee table and sat on the couch beside Mary Lou. Not too close—she didn't want to impinge on Mary Lou's personal space—but close enough that they could talk and Mary Lou would know that Erin was there to help and support her. Vic sat in one of the easy chairs across from her, looking as pale and horrified as Erin felt. Mary Lou herself, appearing composed as she always did, smoothed wrinkles in her pantsuit and didn't immediately help herself to a teacup. The newspaper lay folded on the table in front of her.

"Can I pour for you?" Vic offered. "What kind would you like?"

Mary Lou seemed far away. It took her a few extra seconds to process Vic's question and focus on the tea bags in the basket.

"Earl Gray," she said eventually. "Thank you."

Vic busied herself with preparing a cup for Mary Lou, then passed it across to her. She poured for herself and Erin, and let Erin choose and add her own teabag. They sat there, looking at each other. They looked like three friends gathered for a gossip session. But that wasn't how it felt.

"I don't know anything about where Josh is," Erin told Mary Lou. "I hope you know that. I don't know what this note means, but... I don't know anything about where Josh is or what he is doing. I haven't seen him since he came to Whitewater Junction to interview me."

That had been days before. She remembered his coming to her hotel room, notepad in hand, eager to act the part of a mature reporter. Erin assumed that Joshua had gone home after that interview, had carried on his life as usual through the remainder of the cooking contest. And he had, of course, handed in his report to his English teacher and submitted it to the newspaper.

And then...? What had happened? And why did the note say that Mary Lou should ask Erin, when she knew nothing of Joshua's whereabouts?

"He isn't home?" Vic asked the obvious.

Of course Josh wasn't at home, or his mother would not be concerned about a note that implied something had happened to him.

"No. He was home yesterday... everything was normal. I thought... everything was even better than normal. But something happened. This morning... he didn't come down for breakfast. When I looked in his room to wake him up... he wasn't there." Mary Lou's gaze sought out Erin's. "His bed hadn't been slept in."

Erin's stomach clenched into a tight ball. She felt like she was being strangled. What could have happened to Joshua? If his bed hadn't been slept in, he hadn't just gone for a walk or to visit a friend or pick up a cup of coffee that morning. Something had happened to him the night before. He had left the house without Mary Lou being aware of it and he had not returned.

"Have you called the police?"

"No." Mary Lou shook her head. "I haven't talked to anyone. I just... I called him on his phone, but there was no answer. The newspaper was on the table and when I saw the note... I was going to call you, but... I just came over."

"Yeah. This is really crazy. But I... I don't know where he is..." Erin trailed off. She didn't know how to explain the note. Someone was trying to throw suspicion on her, but she hadn't had anything to do with Joshua's absence.

"But maybe if you thought about it, you would have some idea," Mary Lou said. "Even if you haven't seen him or heard from him, you must know something about what is going on. Why would the note say that if it wasn't anything to do with you?"

"But it isn't. I don't know anything."

"Where would he go? You two have been involved in everything going on around here. You must have some idea."

Erin felt lost.

"What about Cam?" Vic suggested. "Maybe he went to visit his brother. And this note is just... I don't know. Some kind of cruel joke."

Mary Lou had her phone in her hand. She stared at it as if it were something foreign to her. Or might blow up any minute.

"Have you called Campbell?" Erin asked. It was probably the first thing Mary Lou had done.

"No. He won't be up yet. He stays out late. Sleeps half the day. He wouldn't wake up."

"But if Joshua is with him... they must know you'd be looking for him. Or if he's not, won't Campbell want to help look for him? He would want to know right away."

Mary Lou shook her head. "There's no point, Erin. I said he won't wake up. I can't ask him or tell him anything if he is asleep and doesn't answer his phone."

Erin understood this, but still felt like Mary Lou should at least try.

"If he really is missing, we should call the police," Vic said.

"Yes," Erin agreed. "The earlier they can start looking for him, the better the results."

"I don't think they'll look if it hasn't been forty-eight hours, will they?"

"No, they'll look sooner than that," Erin assured her. "If you think something has happened to him, you should tell them right away. The first few hours can be critical. We don't want to lose them."

"I don't *know* that anything has happened to him. This could just be... a joke. Someone being silly. He's a teenager. They do stupid things without realizing what the consequences could be."

"But if he was just out with friends, wouldn't you be able to get him on the phone?" Erin pointed out.

"Maybe. Maybe not. There are a lot of places in these mountains where you can't get a signal. If he's out of range of a cell tower, or in a canyon, or spelunking, I wouldn't be able to get him."

"Spelunking," Erin repeated. Just thinking about being underground in a cave was enough to take her breath away. Still. "He wouldn't go into a cave without friends, would he? And without letting someone know where he was?"

"N-no..." Mary Lou drew the word out and, even though she said he wouldn't do it, she immediately contradicted herself. "Like I said... he's a teenager. And teen boys do all kinds of crazy things without understanding the dangers. As you well know." She gave each of them a hard stare. Erin looked down at her cup, her face hot with embarrassment. "You try to tell them something they need to be careful of, a decision that could bring them to harm, and you just get 'I'll be fine, Mom. I promise.' As if they can control the consequences." Mary Lou took a sip of her cooling tea. "I don't know how many times I've told them you can't choose the consequences. You can only choose your actions."

Erin looked at Vic. "Well... we can look around town. See if he's at the school or any of the regular hangouts. We can't check out all of the caves in the area, of course, but maybe Willie could drive by a couple of the more popular ones. See if there are cars parked outside."

Vic nodded. "If you aren't sure yet if there's really a problem and want to look for him first, we can help with that."

Erin remembered the search party for Roger when he had wandered off on his own. It was different for Roger because of his brain injury. He wasn't just a teenager off having a good time. He was easily confused and could have hurt himself. The whole town had shown up to help look for him and to comfort Mary Lou. Should they send out the call for help with Joshua?

But Erin could see that would not go over well. If Mary Lou made a big fuss about his being missing and it turned out that he'd just taken a day off to mess around, the police and everyone else would be irritated, Mary Lou and Joshua would be embarrassed. Tensions between them would increase instead of decreasing.

"Do you want us to help look?" Erin asked Mary Lou.

Mary Lou sipped her tea and looked around, a small crease between her eyebrows. Then she finally nodded. "Yes. I suppose so. We can at least do that."

Erin and Vic nodded their agreement. Auntie Clem's Bakery was covered for the day, so they were free to spend the day as they wished. Erin had been planning to do some business planning and later to run some errands, but those things could be put off. If Joshua was missing, it was an emergency. She needed to be flexible and concentrate on what was most important.

"With this mention of you," Mary Lou said, motioning to the newspaper lying on the coffee table, the sticky note incongruous in the sea of black print, "do you think... that he's back in Whitewater?"

Erin looked at Vic. She didn't feel like driving back to Whitewater and, once she got there, where specifically would she look? But the notes said to ask Erin where he was. That implied that something Erin had done had resulted in Joshua's disappearance. And lately, all she had done was to be a judge at the cooking contest and to help solve Beryl Batcombe's murder.

A murder that Joshua had been asking questions about.

In Whitewater.

"I guess," she said reluctantly. "If it has something to do with me... that's really the only thing unusual that I have done lately. And Joshua interviewed me about it."

Vic nodded her agreement.

"I don't have a vehicle, though," Erin realized. "Willie took his truck and Terry took his."

"You should have gone with Jack to look at cars when they were here," Vic pointed out. "They had their eye on a few good deals."

"I know. But there was so much going on with the contest and everything else." And Erin hadn't wanted to go with Jack. She'd felt pressured before even getting near a car lot. She didn't want to be pushed into anything. She would buy a new car when she was ready.

On her own. Without someone else pushing her into it and spouting facts and figures at her.

"Is Terry actually using the truck?" Vic asked. "Could we borrow it?"

"I'll check." He was often on foot patrol around the town, his truck just parked in the lot at the Town Hall, where the police department was housed. It was only a short walk to get there from Erin's house.

CHAPTER 2

*M*ary Lou raised her hand to stop Erin as she slid out her phone and looked down at it to dial Terry.

"What are you going to tell him?"

"That I need the car to go to Whitewater and…" Erin trailed off. She could see the warning in Mary Lou's eyes even before she said anything. "And… you don't want me to say anything to him about Joshua?"

"I've told you before that you need to watch what you say to him. If I wanted the police involved, I would call them myself."

"Okay." Erin looked at Vic. "Then I guess… tell him that I decided that my errands might take longer than I had originally planned, so I want to get started. And after we check out Whitewater, we'll have to run into the city to take care of them, so it doesn't look suspicious."

Mary Lou gave a brusque nod.

Erin swallowed. "Okay." She didn't like the subterfuge, but it was really just a lie of omission. She really would do her errands as she told him.

"Should we split up?" Vic asked. "I suppose I should stay here and look around; we can cover more area if we split up."

It was a sensible plan of action, but Erin bit her lip and shook her head. "I'm not sure... I don't want to go by myself."

Vic cocked her head. She raised her eyebrows in query. "It's just for a few hours. You wouldn't be staying there alone."

"I know. But since the accident, I don't really want to drive the highway by myself. I can, but... I just would feel better if I had someone with me. So that if anything happens..."

Nothing would happen, of course. Just because she had been followed and forced off the road once, that didn't mean that it would ever happen again. It was a once-in-a-lifetime occurrence.

Not something that was going to happen to her again.

"Oh, hon," Vic leaned across the coffee table and touched Erin's arm. "I didn't realize."

Erin squirmed. She wasn't looking for pity or even just attention. She wasn't doing it to be the poor, damaged little girl. She'd filled that role too many times in the past, the only survivor of the rollover that had killed her parents when she was just a child.

"I *can* go by myself," she asserted, looking at Mary Lou. "It's just... safer with two people in the car."

Mary Lou nodded. "If you could see if there's any sign of him in Whitewater Junction, that would help," she said, without comment on Erin's weakness and the inconvenience it caused. "I think I should stay here, in case he comes home, or in case... I don't know. The police call me with news."

Erin was about to ask why the police would call Mary Lou if she didn't report Joshua missing, but then bit back her response.

If they found Josh's body, Mary Lou meant. If they found him injured or dead, Mary Lou would be the one they called and she would want to be close at hand. Erin tried to blink back tears and not let the lump in her throat change her voice.

"Yeah. If he's in Whitewater, we'll find him."

If he were in Whitewater.

If he were alive.

If someone hadn't kidnapped him and hidden him away somewhere.

Erin managed to borrow Officer Terry Piper's truck without giving away that she was running over to Whitewater to see if she could find a missing teenager. There had been a couple of awkward pauses during the call. Like he knew that Erin was keeping something from him. Like he was trying to figure out how to ask her what was really going on but was afraid to ask.

Or maybe she just imagined it.

"He said it's fine," Erin told Vic. "He and K9 are just out on foot patrol, and he'll either walk home or get Stayner to drop him, depending on how he's feeling at the end of his shift."

"He's been doing better lately," Vic contributed. "It's nice to see him looking bright-eyed again."

It had been a difficult few months, a hard recovery after Terry had been attacked, hit over the head, and choked out. The damage went a lot deeper than she had expected. Nothing like TV cop shows where people got knocked out all the time and seemed to go on with barely even a headache or moment of vertigo. Things had been much worse for Terry.

But he had seemed to be doing better the last few days. She could only hope that he would continue to feel good and not relapse back into migraines, insomnia, and nightmares. And the irritability and mood issues.

"We'd better head out pretty quickly," Erin suggested. "If we're going to look for Josh and try to get our most urgent errands done, we can't waste any time."

"Yep," Vic agreed. "We'll be quick as two winks. Do you want me to make some sandwiches so we don't have to stop for lunch later?"

"Good idea. I'll check the animals' bowls"—she had two pets at home, Orange Blossom the cat and Marshmallow the rabbit—"Then, why don't I walk over and get the truck while you make the sand-wiches. I'll make sure it's gassed up, and then we'll head out."

"Sounds like a plan," Vic agreed. She shook her head and *tsked*. "Poor Mary Lou. If we end up finding Joshua and this was just some kind of joke or ill-conceived teen prank, I'll whup that boy myself."

Erin had seen Vic's father try to beat her. He did not approve of her being transgender or getting together with a man from a rival clan —and she knew that Vic was only blowing hot air. There was no way she could do the same to another teen, no matter what he had done.

"I don't think it is a prank," Erin said. "I can't see Joshua doing something like this. He loves his mom and he knows all the stuff that she's been through. He wouldn't do something that might hurt her more just as a prank."

"No. I don't think so," Vic agreed. "Okay. I'll see you in twenty minutes or so."

After checking the food and water dishes, Erin grabbed her purse and headed over to the police department at a brisk walk.

Erin didn't run into anyone who slowed her down on her way to the Town Hall, so she was able to get Terry's truck and top off the gas tank in the allotted time. She picked Vic up at the house, and they were on their way to Whitewater.

Erin didn't want to keep going over the same ground when they hadn't found out anything yet. They could speculate all day long on where Joshua had gone or why he had disappeared, but they wouldn't know until they'd had some time to turn up some clues. Erin looked around for other things to talk about as she drove the highway. She didn't want to admit how anxious she was about being followed again, and she wouldn't be calmed just by listening to the radio. She needed something that took enough of her attention that she wouldn't constantly be thinking about the cars and trucks on the highway behind her.

It was a busy highway, not like the secondary road she'd been on the day that she'd been forced into the ditch. Nothing was going to happen to her out in the open where everybody could see.

"I did a few trials of recipes for the fortune cookies," she told Vic. "A few other people have done gluten-free fortune cookies. Mostly based around tapioca starch or cornstarch. They are pretty simple, actually. Just a matter of rolling or pressing them, cutting them into a circle, and then folding them while they're still warm. Then they get crispy when they cool."

"I always wondered how they baked them with paper inside," Vic laughed. "Because you would either have to bake them at a really low temperature, or the paper would light on fire. And I'd never even seen a scorched fortune."

Erin smiled and nodded. "I always wondered too. It's a bit of a letdown to realize that they insert the fortune and fold the cookie after they are baked. Removes some of the mystique."

"Won't it be great for the Chinese restaurant to offer gluten-free fortune cookies for their clientele? It's such a nice touch. I can't wait to see Peter Foster try his first gluten-free fortune cookie."

Erin was determined to keep her smile from fading, so she kept it firmly in place even though it made her sad that Mrs. Foster had decided Peter would not be visiting the bakery in person any time soon. Like Mary Lou, she was upset with Erin for mentioning Peter's name during a police investigation, resulting in Peter being inter-viewed by the police. Not just once, but twice.

It wasn't Erin's fault that he'd been a witness in both cases. He'd told her key clues that had led to her figuring out what had happened, but which also led to his being questioned.

It wasn't like he'd been a suspect, like Joshua. It was understood right from the start that the little boy had only been a witness, and one who didn't even realize what it was he had seen.

"I thought we should do some kind of care basket for Mrs. Foster," Erin said, changing the subject. "She'll be having that baby any day now, and it would be nice if she didn't have to be on her feet coming around to the bakery for a couple of weeks. We could take or deliver her the things that she normally comes around for... bread, muffins, after-school snacks..."

"What a great idea," Vic enthused. "You're always coming up with such creative plans."

"You don't think she would be offended, do you? Thinking that I was saying she wasn't capable of looking after her own family, or that I was just trying to get closer and interfere with things..."

"Of course not. It's a lovely thing to do. No one could find fault with you for helping a customer out during a challenging time."

"Okay." Erin wasn't always sure. People did seem to find fault with her for the littlest things. Even when she was doing something she thought people would approve of, doing something nice for someone just to be nice, they would criticize or put some kind of negative spin on things.

"Don't worry about the old gossips," Vic said, reading her mind. "Some people are negative no matter what. You're not going to change that. You have to just ignore them and live your life."

Erin nodded. "Yeah. I will. I just feel sometimes like I missed out on a bunch of etiquette lessons because of the way I was raised. There are all of these little rules that I never picked up on."

"That's just the south for you. And small-town living. There *are* a bunch of special rules. But you can never do them all, so you have to just develop a thick skin about the rest of them."

CHAPTER 3

elcome to Whitewater Junction.

Erin slowed as she approached the town limits sign. She had not expected to be returning to Whitewater any time soon. She had thought that when the contest was over and she had returned to Bald Eagle Falls, it would be the last time she'd be there for a few years. It wasn't exactly the center of civilization. It was the opposite way from the city, so she would always be traveling away from it. There were no tourist sites and, with everything that had happened during the contest, she had been glad to see it in her rearview mirror.

But now they were back again.

"Where should we go?" Erin asked. "The hotel?"

"I suppose… if Joshua intended to stay here, he would have to book a room, right?"

"I don't know… it just seems like such a bizarre idea, him coming back here on his own and staying by himself. Would they let a minor book a room by himself? Wouldn't they want an adult's signature on the register and some kind of guarantee that he wasn't going to have wild parties and mess things up?"

"If he had his own credit card, I don't know if they would ask how old he is."

"You had to show your driver's license, didn't you?"

Erin thought back. "I don't even remember. There was so much going on. I think that with the contest having booked all of the rooms, I didn't have to do anything but claim one."

Vic considered. "Yeah, maybe. I know when I first left home… there weren't a lot of places that I could have stayed. But I didn't have a credit card or any money, really."

"Most of these places don't let you stay for free," Erin agreed, smiling slightly.

"No, for some reason, they don't."

Erin pulled the truck carefully into the parking lot of the hotel away from the other vehicles so that no one would open their doors into it and mess up the paintwork. It wasn't like it was pristine anymore. Terry had driven over plenty of gravel roads and got other chips and scuffs on it. But Erin didn't want to contribute any damage. They walked into the lobby.

There were promotional signs up from the cooking contest. Actually, it had been a 'cooling' contest, using carbon dioxide to make fizzy drinks and ice cream treats—a very unique idea.

There were two big boards on easels displaying the three winners' faces in each of the classifications and the large cash prizes they had received. Eugene Bath, the man who had won the grand prize in the beverages section, Bella Prost, one of Erin's part-time employees below him, followed by a woman named Louisa David, who had received Clayton's third-place position when he had been arrested. And on the board for the ice cream winners, Doc Edmunds in first place, followed by two people Erin didn't know, Deidre Robinson and Hannah Clark.

Erin recognized the girl at the registration desk. They had spoken to each other several times during the cooking contest.

"Anita, hi." Erin smiled at her. "Long time, no see!"

"Erin Price. What are you doing back here so soon? Do you need a room?"

"No, I'm just here to see Joshua Cox. What floor is he on?"

"I didn't think there was anyone from the contest still here," Anita mused, tapping on her keyboard and squinting at the computer screen. "Joshua Cox... hmm... how is that spelled?"

"C-O-X." Erin had a sinking feeling. Of course it wasn't going to be that easy, but she had hoped.

"No, I don't see anyone by that name still registered here..." Anita tapped something else into her search parameters. "In fact, I don't see any registrations in that name at all. Would it have been under the name of one of the sponsors or someone else?"

"No, I don't think so," Erin admitted. "Is there somewhere else he might have stayed? This is the only hotel, right?"

"Yeah, unfortunately. There are a couple of B&B's or holiday rental places. I don't know, did he tell you he was going to be staying here?"

"Maybe I misunderstood," Erin said. She brandished her phone. "I'll give him a call."

"Okay. Let me know if you need anything else." Anita went back to answering phones and doing other work. Erin grimaced at Vic and they headed back toward the truck.

"Where else?" Vic asked. "Should we just drive around? It doesn't seem like we're very likely to turn him up that way."

"We might as well check B&B's. We're here anyway. And maybe... I don't know. The tourist center. Chamber of Commerce. The library. Anywhere else he might have gone if he was doing more research here."

"But why would he stay here? He'd already turned in his article for the paper."

"But he could have been researching something further. Maybe... he ran across something he thought was suspicious or interesting and wanted to do some more research."

"Like what? I think we pretty much got everything the first time around. Theft, murder, corruption. Do you think there was something else?"

"Well... no... I don't know what else he would be investigating. Maybe just more background, a more in-depth article on Beryl and what she had done. Or something about Clayton and his family."

"Yeah… Clayton's family." Vic thought about that. "I didn't really think about the fact that he must have family around here."

"If the reason he did what he did was because of the way his family had been taken advantage of, then he must have someone around here."

"He could be the last of the line, and that's why he thought it was all up to him to do something about it."

"But if he's a member of one of the old mountain families here, then he's related to everyone else. Not closely, maybe, but cousins, second cousins…"

"Yeah. How about the library, then? Josh might have gone there. They must have some genealogical records, histories of the local families."

That sounded like a good idea to Erin. She had not spent a lot of time in the library when she had been there, just stopping in to look at a few recipe books and get away from the crowds. The librarian had seemed friendly enough.

The library was quiet, just a couple of people reading or browsing through shelves. Nothing like the bustle that Erin had seen at big-city libraries. It was a cozy little place. That had attracted her when she had been trying to get away from the contest for a few minutes and to sort things out in her mind.

The librarian working at the computer at the circulation desk looked up when they walked in and smiled an invitation. Vic and Erin approached.

"We're looking for a friend," Erin said when they got close. "I think he might have stopped in here to do some research. A teen boy from Bald Eagle Falls…?"

"Oh… what was his name? James?"

"Joshua."

"Joshua." She nodded. "Yes, he was here a couple of weeks ago. While the contest was on. A budding young reporter."

"Yeah." Erin was relieved. It hadn't occurred to her until she walked in that she didn't have a picture to show the woman. How were they supposed to find Joshua without a picture of him? "Is he around today? Or yesterday?"

"With everything shutting down, it's been mighty quiet. He hasn't been around. I assume he went back to Bald Eagle Falls." She raised her brows. Obviously, Joshua would go back home after the contest was over. Why would he stay?

"Well, he's not back, that's why we're looking for him. Do you know... where else he might have been going? Did he say that he had some other research he needed to do...?"

"I haven't seen him lately, I'm sorry. I think everyone is done with that now. All of the excitement... it turned out to be kind of an embarrassment. The contest was supposed to generate so many tourism dollars for the town, lots of positive publicity that would last even after it was over... but all of the negative press has not been good for us. I don't see it being much benefit, to tell the truth. You can bet the town council will think twice before approving something like that again."

Erin rubbed the back of her neck. She wasn't sure why she felt guilty. Her role in the contest had been completely innocent. Chef Kirschoff was a friend, he'd asked her to be a judge, and she'd agreed. Everything had happened so quickly after that.

Erin hadn't been responsible for anything that had happened, of course. She had helped identify Beryl's killer. But she felt like she'd been the cause of the problems in Whitewater instead of just an innocent bystander.

"Yeah, it's too bad the way everything blew up—turned out," she corrected quickly. Her face heated. She avoided looking at Vic, who she knew would be trying not to laugh. "We just thought... Joshua was going to do a follow-up story. Or maybe some background on Beryl or on... you know, Clayton... and I figured he would come back here."

The librarian shook her head. "No, sorry. I can't help you there."

"Can you think of where else he might have gone? If he wanted to get some background on Beryl's or Clayton's families?"

"We have a section on histories of the old Whitewater families."

The librarian looked toward the shelves where they were situated. "I would expect him to come here. Aside from that... maybe an amateur genealogist in town. Or if he knew one of the older people, who might remember some of the history that wouldn't be in the books."

"Can you think of who he might go to?"

She shook her head.

"Does Clayton have any kinfolk around here?" Vic suggested.

"Some distant cousins, maybe. The Hinchey line has pretty much died out. Times are difficult. People move their families into urban centers where they can get jobs and get into good schools. And the kids don't come back here."

"He doesn't have any grandparents? Great aunts?"

"No." The librarian shook her head slowly. "No one who comes to mind."

Perhaps that was the reason that Beryl had thought she could get away with stealing from the old families. She figured there would be no one left to complain.

"Well... thank you for your time," Erin told the librarian, disappointed.

The woman gave a sympathetic smile and went back to her work. Vic and Erin walked slowly back to the truck.

"One more down," Vic said bracingly. "It's only one place. We can still check with the Chamber of Commerce, pop into the coffee shops with Wi-Fi, maybe check with the paper. They must have a weekly."

"Yeah, that sounds good," Erin agreed, trying to be cheerful about it.

After all, they hadn't found out anything negative—no hint of any violence. Joshua just hadn't been to the library. There were plenty of other places he could be.

If he were even in Whitewater.

And he probably wasn't.

CHAPTER 4

*T*heir search petered out after a couple of hours. Neither could think of anywhere else to go, and no one they had talked to had seen or heard from Joshua. Some of them knew him from when he had been doing the research for his school project. Vic downloaded a picture of Joshua from Facebook to show people who didn't recognize him from their description. But no one had seen him recently. It would appear that Joshua hadn't gone back to Whitewater Junction after all.

They even drove around for a while, methodically covering all of the streets that crisscrossed the town. As if they might see Joshua walking down the road or be inspired by a storefront. But there was still no sign of him.

On their drive into the city, they focused on lists of what they needed and how they would tackle the various stores. They worked out an efficient plan of attack to get done as quickly as possible and return home to Bald Eagle Falls.

They were, Erin knew, avoiding the real issue.

They hadn't gotten a call from Mary Lou saying that she had found him or that he had called.

He wasn't in Whitewater. He wasn't anywhere obvious in Bald Eagle Falls.

It would be a lot more challenging to find him in the city. They couldn't just drive all of the streets there. It was a small city, but it was still too big for two people to search in one vehicle.

They shopped like they were on a mission. Like that was the more important thing. As if everything would magically fall together if they could get everything done, like the pieces of a puzzle fitting together.

When they were finished their errands and eating the second round of sandwiches, they avoided looking each other in the eye and admitting their failure.

"Should we see Campbell while we're here?" Vic suggested. "He might know something. Joshua might have gone to him."

"I'm sure Mary Lou must have called him by now," Erin pointed out. "He'll be out of bed and able to answer his phone. If she wanted us to go see him, she would have let us know."

Besides, Erin remembered the last time they had gone on a search in the city. Not looking for Campbell, but for his girlfriend Brianna. That had turned out to be a dangerous proposition. Erin had no desire to go back to any of the flophouses they had searched for Brianna. Or to run into anyone from the Russian mob. That was off the table.

"I suppose," Vic agreed with a sigh. She wadded up her sandwich wrappers to throw them out. "I'm worn slap out. I don't think we could manage much more today anyway."

Erin nodded. She needed to get back home. She needed to see Terry and to make sure that she was prepared for the next day at Auntie Clem's Bakery. She would only have a little while to relax, and then it would be time for bed. Bakers had to rise before the rest of the world to get the daily bread in the oven.

Erin wasn't quite sure how to handle their report to Mary Lou. They could make a call to her on the way back to Bald Eagle Falls. Or they could go back to Erin's and ask Mary Lou over. But calling her seemed way too impersonal, and making her come to them after she had spent the whole day stressed out and waiting for Joshua seemed cruel. They had exchanged a few quick texts during the day to report. Still, Erin thought it was important to see Mary Lou face-to-face and go over everything they had done, in case something turned out to be important. She didn't think they had discovered anything of consequence, but Erin knew that the outcome of an investigation could hinge on the tiniest of details. Sometimes just a gut feeling about how it all fit together.

"Do you think it's okay to go by her house?" Erin asked Vic tentatively. "I know that she might not want us there... but I don't want to drag her out somewhere else."

"We can go by. If she doesn't want us there... she can tell us so."

That didn't make Erin feel much more confident about going to Mary Lou's house. But it seemed like the only reasonable solution, so once they arrived at Bald Eagle Falls, she pulled to the curb in front of Mary Lou's house. They walked up to the front door and knocked.

Hospitality in Bald Eagle Falls dictated that if someone was expecting you or had opened up their home to you, it was fine to simply knock on the door or 'yoo-hoo' and walk in. But while Mary Lou had previously welcomed them, she had not been keen on them lately, so Erin didn't think it would be a good idea. Vic apparently agreed, because she didn't push the door open and walk in ahead of Erin. She stood to the side and slightly behind Erin. Erin hoped that was just reticence and not concern that Mary Lou might welcome them with a shotgun blast.

It was a few minutes and a few more knocks and a doorbell later that Mary Lou finally came to the door. She looked Erin and Vic over, her face pale and drawn, looking like she had been sitting up for days waiting for Joshua to come home. Erin's heart hurt. She wanted to take her former friend in her arms and give her a comforting hug. But she refrained, waiting to see whether Mary Lou would even allow them in or be interested in hearing what they had to say.

"Nothing?" Mary Lou asked dully.

"No," Erin confirmed. She was prepared to leave. That was really all Mary Lou needed to know. Erin's search had not come to fruition, Joshua had obviously not returned on his own. It was up to Mary Lou to take the next step.

Mary Lou sighed, rubbed her hand over her face, then turned slightly and motioned the other women in. Erin led the way, Vic trailing behind her. Erin had a strong feeling of deja vu on entering the front room. She remembered arriving there on Thanksgiving, seeing the cops outside taking Campbell away, walking in to find Joshua there comforting Mary Lou.

Joshua should have been there with Mary Lou. But he wasn't.

They sat down and looked at each other, silently working out who would speak first.

"We went everywhere we could think of in Whitewater," Erin offered. "And when we couldn't think of anywhere else to look, we just drove up and down the streets. *All* of the streets."

"Was there any sign he had been there? Any hint at all?" Mary Lou asked.

"No. No one had seen him since he did the research for his report on the contest. People remembered him. The librarian. Other people he had talked to when he was tracking information down. But they hadn't seen him for the last day or two. Nothing since he wrote the article, I guess."

"He's been at home since then. He didn't say anything about going back to Whitewater or doing a follow-up story. He's been at home... going to school and doing homework..." Mary Lou shook her head. "He's been here. Everything was normal. And then, just... gone. How could he be gone?"

"I don't know." Erin looked at Vic, raising her brows. "He never said anything to you either?" They were, at least, closer in age than Erin and Joshua. Both still teenagers, even if Vic was legally an adult.

"No. I haven't seen him at all. We weren't close friends." Vic wasn't even from Bald Eagle Falls. She had probably seen less of Joshua than Erin had. But Erin didn't want to reveal to Mary Lou that Joshua had been by to talk to her more than once since Erin had been told to stay away from him and not involve him in any more police investigations.

That wasn't Erin's fault. She had never contacted him or encouraged him to talk to her against his mother's wishes. He had just shown up, and would not be dissuaded by any of her arguments.

23

"Well, that's it, then," Mary Lou sighed. "I was hoping it would be something simple… that you were right and he just wanted to get some more research done. Off being an intrepid reporter." Her eyes moved to the newspaper that she had previously brought to Erin's house, which now resided on her dining room table. "Except for that."

"It could still be something innocent. Maybe he just… lost track of time."

"For an entire day?" Mary Lou snapped. "No. He didn't just wander off in the middle of the night and forget to come home."

"No." Erin looked down, her eyes suddenly swimming.

"Are you going to call the police?" Vic asked.

"It looks like I don't have any other choice now," Mary Lou said. She squeezed her lips together tightly, trying to keep her own emotions under control. "I guess I'll do that now. The two of you can see yourselves out."

"Don't you want us to stay with you?" Erin protested. "At least until the sheriff gets here?"

"No." Mary Lou's words were clipped. "I will be fine by myself. You have had a long, unproductive day. You'll want to get some rest tonight. I know I won't."

Erin forced herself to her feet. Her legs were shaking and she hated to leave Mary Lou like that. She must have been screaming inside. Erin couldn't imagine how terrified she must be about what had happened to Joshua. If Erin could feel so worried for someone who was nearly a stranger to her, she couldn't imagine how badly Mary Lou must be taking it.

But Mary Lou didn't crack. She watched Erin and Vic head back toward the front door, looking down at her phone to make the call she had been dreading making all day. The call that would mean she could no longer deny being worried that something had happened to Joshua.

Something terrible.

CHAPTER 5

*J*osh awoke groggily. He lay still for a long time while waiting for his brain to start working and to join the real world again. After a while, he wondered what time it was and if his alarm was going to go off soon. It seemed like he always hit that floaty, unreal feeling just a few minutes before his alarm went off. If he looked at his clock, then he would be awake, but if he could just maintain that floatiness, he could get a little more sleep. Or at least a little more rest.

Then he started wondering what day it was. Maybe it wasn't even a day that he had to get up early. He still had to get himself out of bed on Saturday and Sunday, but he was allowed to sleep in for a couple of hours. His mother said that she understood that teenagers needed more sleep, but he had to do his part and go to bed in good time. He couldn't just stay up all night and then sleep all day just because it was the weekend.

He liked it when he woke up early on a Saturday morning and realized he could go back to sleep for a couple more hours. It was a great feeling.

But he wasn't feeling great.

He couldn't remember what day it was.

Maybe that in itself told him that it was a weekend. He wasn't a big drinker, but he had gone to a couple of parties where alcohol had been snuck in. Or he had dipped into Campbell's stash when Campbell was still living at home. He didn't particularly like alcohol and was just as happy to leave it alone. Especially if it left him feeling so rocky in the morning. Who needed that?

It was still longer before he started to wonder *where* he was.

He was still so close to sleep that he couldn't be sure, but nothing in his environment felt familiar. He wasn't in his bed. There was a bad smell. There were strange noises that were both close and far away at the same time.

It wasn't his house.

CHAPTER 6

*E*rin and Vic drove back home in silence. What else was there to say? They had done their best to help Mary Lou, but they had failed. Neither had any idea where Joshua was, or why Erin had been named in the cryptic note left in Mary Lou's paper.

A day that should have been a calm, relaxing, regenerating day had ended up being dark and depressing.

And she wasn't allowed to tell Terry about it. Mary Lou had made it abundantly clear that Erin was never to bring Joshua or Campbell up with Officer Terry Piper. Not ever. Not a casual comment in passing. Not pillow talk. Not saying she was worried about him.

Not telling anyone that he was missing.

That wasn't Erin's place. She needed to just stay out of it and mind her own business.

She pulled Terry's truck in front of the house, and she and Vic got out slowly.

"I'll see you in the morning," Vic offered.

"Sure. It will be good to have a normal day at the bakery tomorrow."

Except Erin didn't feel good about it. She felt horrible. She would be working, baking, pretending that there was nothing wrong, knowing that Joshua was missing and that Mary Lou's heart was breaking.

While Erin walked up to the front door, Vic took the sidewalk around to the back, where she had a loft apartment over Erin's garage. Erin hadn't even thought to ask whether Willie would be home. Or would Vic be sitting over there all by herself stewing about what had happened to Joshua and if he was okay?

Just like Erin would be stewing, even if Terry were home.

She raised her hand to unlock the door, but it opened in front of her. Terry smiled and took a couple of bags from her.

"You must have had a successful time in the city," he observed. "You were later than I expected you to be."

"Um… sorry about that," Erin apologized, without answering his comment. She carried the rest of her bags into the house and put them down. Orange Blossom meowed loudly, rubbed against her legs, and then started thrusting his head into the various bags, checking to see if she had bought him any treats. Or just because he liked to stick his head in bags.

"Nothing for you, sir," Erin told Blossom, scooping him up and cradling him in the crook of her arm. "How is my furry baby today?"

He meowed, objecting to being treated that way. Still, when she didn't release him, he chirped and yowled and huffed at her like he was telling her all about his day. Erin encouraged him with little noises and questions, as was her usual routine. She stood on her tiptoes to kiss Terry in greeting without letting Orange Blossom go, squashing him between their bodies. He complained loudly and squirmed away. Erin let him go, putting her arms around Terry to give him a squeeze.

"Thanks. I needed that," she said, putting her head on his chest and relaxing in his arms.

It was nice to see him on his feet at the end of the day. So many times recently, he had been knocked down by a migraine by the end of the day, unable to enjoy himself or the time they had to spend together.

"How was your day?" she asked him.

Terry released her from his grip. Erin stooped to pet Marshmallow, the brown and white rabbit patiently nibbling at her toes.

"And hello to you too."

She and Terry made their way over to the couch to cuddle.

"Do you need anything?" he asked. "A drink? A cookie?"

K9 was sleeping beside the couch, and Erin saw his head jerk up at the suggestion of a cookie. He looked hopefully in Erin's direction.

"Oh, you said one of those words. Now you're going to have to get everyone a cookie."

"Fine with me. I want one too."

Erin sat down and let him do the honors. Terry gave K9 one of Erin's gluten-free doggie biscuits, fished treats out of Orange Blossom's treat can and slid them across the floor for him to chase, and got a couple of small carrots out of the crisper for Marshmallow. He opened the freezer to check out the supply.

"Chocolate chip or ginger snap?"

"Chocolate chip. Today has definitely been a chocolate chip day."

Terry got a couple of chocolate chip cookies from the freezer and put them on a plate to be microwaved.

"Been a long day?"

Erin nodded. "Yeah. Kind of."

"Well, you did it to yourself with all of that shopping."

"Uh-huh."

Half a minute later, the microwave beeped and Terry brought the melty-chocolate-chip cookies out to the living room. They each took one and tried to eat them over the same plate so that no crumbs or drips of chocolate would get into the couch and carpet.

"Sorry," Terry said through a mouthful of cookie. "I should have brought two plates."

Erin just laughed.

~

She should have known that the idyllic moment wouldn't last. She wasn't going to be able to forget about the rest of her day that quickly. Terry sat back as his phone started to buzz and pulled it out of his pocket. He thumbed the fingerprint unlock button and his eyes moved quickly over the words on the screen.

"Uh-oh."

Erin's stomach clenched again, and she regretted having just topped it off with chocolate and sugar. "Is everything okay?"

He looked at her, thinking about what he could tell her, and decided that he wasn't free to give her any information yet. "No... I'm going to be needed."

"Will it take long?" Erin asked, pretending she didn't know exactly what it was. "You already put in a shift today; you don't want to push it with your health."

"I put in a half shift," he corrected. "And I'm feeling okay. I can put in a few more hours."

"Not too long, though, right? You can't pull an all-nighter. You need to make sure you get enough sleep."

He evaded her concerns. "I don't know how long it will be tonight. I won't stay any longer than necessary, but I am needed." Terry stood up, licking chocolate off his fingers. "I'll put this in the sink."

Erin didn't say anything as she watched him get ready to go. K9 was on his feet and prepared to follow, recognizing Terry's body language and eager to work.

She carefully avoided saying anything that would indicate she knew he was going to Mary Lou's house and that Joshua was missing.

It wasn't a lie.

She just wasn't allowed to tell him that she already knew what was going on. As soon as it became public knowledge—and gossip spread quickly through Bald Eagle Falls—then she wouldn't have to pretend she didn't know anything about it.

But even then, Mary Lou wouldn't want her talking to Terry about Joshua.

Erin didn't see how she was going to be able to avoid it.

CHAPTER 7

$\mathcal{T}$erry hadn't returned before it was time for Erin to go to bed. She hadn't expected him to. She didn't know how long to expect him to be, but she assumed he would need a few hours to start the preliminaries of the investigation. Talk to Mary Lou, ask her everything he could think of about Josh. Maybe drive around town to talk to his closest friends or to check out places where they might hang out.

When she got up in the morning, he wasn't in bed beside her and he wasn't asleep on the couch. Erin glanced at the door and could see that his shoes were still gone, as was his truck.

She was going to need to have a word with Sheriff Wilmot about letting Terry work that long. If he crashed and couldn't work again for a week, it would be their fault for exceeding the number of hours that the doctor had said he should work during the transition period.

She did her best to put her anger and worry aside and get ready for the day. She loved her job and needed to be in a good mood for her customers.

She talked to the animals, made herself tea and toast, and checked her lists for the day, adding an item here and there. Terry was obviously not there to drop them at the bakery. Looking out the back, she could see Willie's truck on the gravel pad beside the garage. She texted Vic to see whether they had a ride. They would need to leave a few minutes earlier if they were going to walk, and she would leave her shopping bags at home and only take the necessities that they needed for that day.

Vic texted back that Willie would drop them off. Erin took a few more minutes to load up the dishwasher, change the water bowls, and check one more time to make sure she had everything ready to start the day at Auntie Clem's.

~

Josh was a little less groggy when he awoke again. He tried to move around but found that his arms wouldn't move. His shoulders hurt. A lot of things ached, but his shoulders and his head were the worst. Whatever he had drunk, it had really bothered him. He'd had way too much.

He tried to move again. If he wasn't at home, then he needed to wake himself up and get home. Before his mother awoke and discovered him gone.

He didn't know what he had done. Had it been Campbell? Had they gone out together? He'd been calling Cam, trying to set something up. But Cam hadn't been eager to get back to Bald Eagle Falls and Josh didn't want to get in trouble for driving into the city. Mary Lou was already irritated about his going to Whitewater to do interviews on his own. She said he shouldn't have gone without a responsible adult to make sure he didn't get himself in trouble.

But what was going to happen? He was doing news interviews. On a public contest. It wasn't like he was doing anything dangerous.

He groaned, trying to get his arms into a more comfortable position, but he couldn't move.

He knew in his heart that Mary Lou had a point. There *had* been a murder in Whitewater associated with the contest. And he had previously shown that he didn't have the best of judgment as far as the criminal element was concerned. So she was right; he could have gotten himself in the crosshairs of the murderer by approaching the wrong person or saying the wrong thing.

But the culprit had been found. And Joshua had never even met Clayton.

It was kind of disappointing, actually. He had hoped to be able to break a story that would be picked up by syndicates across the country. Or at least to provide the background, the story behind the story. He had been conditioned by Disney movies and Marvel comics to think that a teenager could make a difference. Could break the big story.

But of course, the world didn't work that way. He had known that all along, but he had held on to the fantasy. Nothing else in his life had gone like a Disney movie, so why did he think that his investigative reporting would?

At the bakery, everything proceeded as usual for the first few hours of the day. They got the initial morning baking done and opened up the shop. People drifted in with their coffees to go and picked up muffins or pastries. Moms stopped in either on the way to school or after dropping their kids off. Then there was a lull, and Erin and Vic took a break for their early lunch. There was a tap at the back door.

Erin unlocked and opened the door, and found Terry there. He looked tired, but he didn't have the heavy-lidded, haggard look he got when he had a migraine.

"Hey." Erin gave him a peck. "How are you doing? You just getting off now?"

Terry nodded. "Yeah, I just thought I'd let you know. In case you try to reach me and I'm too far gone to wake up for the phone."

"Thanks. I can't believe you worked this long. You must be wiped."

"I am. But I'll sleep until you get home. It will be okay."

"You need to be more careful. You know you're not supposed to be working those hours."

"It was an emergency. I really did have to be there." He hesitated. "Have you heard…?"

"Not yet," Erin admitted, though she was dying to talk to him

33

about it. News of Joshua's disappearance hadn't yet reached Auntie Clem's, and she couldn't talk about it with Terry until it did.

Terry sighed. He cupped the side of her face with his strong hand for a minute and ran his thumb along an escaped tendril of hair. "Okay." He gave her no clues. He wouldn't tell her anything about his investigation that wasn't already public knowledge, so they would both just keep dancing around the topic and saying nothing. "I'll see you tonight." He looked past her and sketched a wave at Vic. "Hello and goodbye, Vic."

Vic smiled and waved. Terry gave Erin one more kiss and then left, K9 following close at his heel.

CHAPTER 8

"*H*ere it comes," Vic said in a warning tone.

Erin looked at her to see what she was talking about and followed Vic's gaze through the front door. Melissa was coming down the sidewalk at a quick clip. In a moment, she was through the door, the bells ringing wildly and her brown curls dancing and swinging around her face.

"My, what a day!" she exclaimed, placing a hand dramatically over her heart.

Erin and Vic both put on innocent expressions, waiting for her to break the news.

"What's going on?" Vic prompted.

"As if she hadn't had to put up with enough already," Melissa said, shaking her head in pity.

"Who?"

"Mary Lou."

"What happened?" Erin asked. "Did something happen to Roger?"

"No, not Roger. As far as I know, he's still doing just fine. No, the latest news is that Joshua is now missing."

"Josh?" Vic repeated innocently. "What happened to Josh?"

"No one knows. And believe me, we have been investigating

intensively ever since the call came in." Melissa was only a part-time admin at the police department, but one would never guess it by the way she talked. To hear her tell it, Erin would have thought that she was a high-ranking detective, not a typist and file clerk.

Vic leaned closer to Melissa, and Melissa drew in so that their heads were close together. "Nobody knows anything?" Vic asked. "What happened? He just took off?"

"There was a note," Melissa said ominously. She straightened her posture and nodded solemnly.

"A ransom note?" Erin asked. Even though she knew there had been no ransom note, her heart still beat faster at the thought.

"No, not a ransom note. A note saying that..." Melissa looked around dramatically as if she were afraid someone would hear her. When in reality, she was probably making sure that everyone was paying close attention. "A note saying that if she wanted to know where Joshua was, you know something about it." She looked pointedly at Erin.

Erin had known that it was coming, but she couldn't stop her body's automatic reaction, her face getting hot. She dabbed at her cheek with the back of her hand, wishing she could hide her flush. How many people would take blushing as an admission of guilt?

"I didn't have anything to do with Joshua disappearing," she said. "I don't know anything about it!"

"Well, you can expect a visit from the police today, I'll tell you that. I'm surprised they haven't been here already."

Erin cleared her throat. "They know what time I work and where they can find me."

"They certainly do," Melissa laughed. "I'm sure they'll keep in close contact." She waggled her eyebrows suggestively. Erin's face heated even more.

"I need to check some cookies," she advised, turning her back on Melissa to hide in the kitchen.

"I don't think this is something to kid about," she heard Vic say as she left.

"Oh, I don't think there's really anything to worry about," Melissa said breezily. "Just teenagers pulling a prank. You know how they are. Well, you still *are* a teenager. Maybe you're in on the whole thing."

"I may be a teenager, but I'm not a kid," Vic retorted. "I wouldn't do something like that. And Josh and I barely know each other."

"I don't really think you have anything to do with it," Melissa assured her, still not adopting a more serious tone. "And neither do the police. But they're not convinced that it is a real disappearance."

"A *real* disappearance? What would make it not real? If they found him in his bedroom?"

"No, I just mean, there isn't necessarily anything sinister or criminal about it. Not if it's just kids fooling around."

"What would make them think it was just a joke?" Vic asked.

Erin fanned her face, but she didn't want to miss too much of the conversation or observing Melissa's face and body language, so she returned to the front of the shop as if she'd finished checking on the fictional cookies.

Melissa's eyes closed slightly, looking like a contented cat. She stepped closer and peered into the display case. "The writing on the note. It looks like a teenager's writing." She again paused for dramatic effect. "It looks like Joshua's writing."

Erin caught her breath. Joshua's writing? What kind of sense did that make? Why would Joshua have written a note like that? And then disappeared? What reason would he have for making his mother worry about him or pointing the finger at Erin? He had apologized to Erin several times for the way that Mary Lou treated her. He didn't want Mary Lou to be mad at Erin, so why would he do something that would make Mary Lou even more upset? And after all that his mother had been through, he wouldn't want to make her suffer more.

"Joshua didn't write that note," Vic said firmly.

Erin nodded.

"Mary Lou said it looked like his writing," Melissa persisted.

Erin looked at Vic. She ran the previous day's events through her head. Had Mary Lou known that Joshua was up to something? Had she thought that it was just some big prank? She shook her head. Mary Lou had been concerned. She was worried that something had happened to Joshua. She had worried about staying close to home in case the police found his body. That wasn't a parent who thought her son was just off on a jaunt enjoying himself.

"No," Vic agreed. "No way."

Melissa raised her brows. "I'm just telling you what they have found out. It's the truth. How you interpret it…"

"Someone might have a similar handwriting style to Joshua's," Erin said. She bit her tongue before adding that the writing had been messy. It could have been any teenager's. It wasn't like they were being taught penmanship in school anymore. She didn't know how a forensic expert would have been able to tell anything from looking at that little square sticky note.

Someone might have been attempting to mimic his handwriting style. Or Josh could have been forced to write the note himself.

"Just because it looks like his handwriting, that doesn't mean that it is," she told Melissa. "Or that it means it's a prank."

Melissa shrugged. "I guess we'll find out."

"Yes."

Melissa picked out a brownie for her snack and a loaf of rosemary bread to take home for supper.

"You and Mary Lou have been pretty close lately," she said to Erin. "I'm surprised she didn't call you as soon as this happened."

Melissa, on the other hand, had not been as supportive of Mary Lou as she could have been following Roger's incarceration and Campbell's arrest. Many of the friends that Mary Lou had thought she would have been able to depend on had been silent over the past year. They had stopped going to her house, defending her, or inviting her out with them. Erin knew that she'd felt isolated, betrayed by the people she had thought were loyal friends.

"Matter of fact," Melissa went on, not waiting for Erin to respond. "She didn't even call the police right away. You would think that if your child disappeared and you were concerned about what might have happened to him, you would at least call the police to make a report."

"I'm sure she was concerned," Erin said coolly. "But maybe she was concerned about gossip. Or that the police department wouldn't take her concerns seriously. It sounds like not *everybody* who works at the police department thinks this is something to be concerned about."

Melissa either didn't feel or else intentionally ignored the barbs. "Maybe she thinks he's old enough that she doesn't have to worry about him anymore. Or maybe he's gone to stay with Campbell, and she didn't want to admit both have wandered from the fold."

"I don't think Cam has wandered from the fold," Vic objected. Erin was an atheist, so she let the younger woman take that one. "Just because Cam has moved out on his own, that doesn't mean that he's turned away from God."

"Drinking, drugs, immorality... who knows what he's been doing." Melissa tapped her card against the reader to pay her bill and took the proffered bag from Erin.

"You don't know anything about what Campbell has been doing. And if you're listening to gossip and making judgments based on that, how Christian is that?" Vic demanded. "Didn't Jesus say not to judge people? To welcome them and love them—"

"He was arrested for dealing drugs!"

"He was framed! You know that."

"But if it wasn't credible, if people didn't think that he could have been doing it, because he *was* involved in drugs, then they never would have charged him. They would have known it was planted and that Campbell didn't have anything to do with it."

"That's ridiculous."

Melissa raised her eyebrows. She turned back toward the door, her expression saying that she had done exactly what she'd come to do. Not to tell them that there was a child in danger and to get the town's assistance in starting a search and rescue for him. To revel in the fact that she once again had firsthand knowledge of a crime that had taken place in Bald Eagle Falls. To incite drama and speculation. To be in the spotlight and have other women in Bald Eagle Falls envying her position.

Erin didn't say anything as Melissa smiled goodbye and left the bakery.

CHAPTER 9

$\mathcal{V}$ic cussed under her breath, something she was usually far too ladylike to do.

Erin looked at her. There were a couple of other customers waiting to be served, so they couldn't talk about it yet. Erin wouldn't stoop to gossiping about the situation with the other customers.

One of the waiting customers was Mrs. Peach, Erin's next-door neighbor. She hobbled forward to the counter and checked the goods on display.

"You don't think there's anything to all of this, do you?" she questioned. "I would hate for anything else to happen to Mary Lou Cox and her family. They've already been through so much."

"I know," Erin agreed. "It's more than one person should have to go through." If she'd believed in God, she would have had a word with him about it.

"Could I get the raisin bread?" Mrs. Peach pointed. "No, not that one, Miss Victoria, the one to the left. My left. It has far more raisins than the others."

Vic picked up the loaf that Mrs. Peach wanted with her gloved hands and put it into a bag.

"Anything else?" Erin asked.

"I don't know about all of this nonsense about a note. Does that sound right to you? I wonder if there even was a note. That girl has been known to exaggerate at times," she took a look in the direction Melissa had gone, back toward Town Hall.

"It really isn't any of my business," Erin pointed out.

"You ask that handsome policeman of yours," Mrs. Peach advised sagely. She pointed at the blueberry muffins. "Are those fresh today, or are they from a couple of days ago?"

"They're fresh today, Mrs. Peach." Erin tried to ignore the comment about her handsome policeman. He wasn't going to share anything about the investigation with her, and Erin was going to have to take care not to reveal to him how much she had known before he even started.

"I'll have… six of those. If you can put them in a box for me so that they don't get crushed."

"Can you carry all of that?" Erin asked as she packaged Mrs. Peach's purchases. "I've told you before that if you want to just tell me what you want ahead of time, I'll set it aside for you and take it home. You don't have to come all the way here and carry it home."

Mrs. Peach smiled and shook her head. "I'm not that infirm, dear. I can carry my own bags. If you had a furniture store instead of a bakeshop, things might be different. But I can carry my own bread and muffins."

"Well, you know you can change your mind and ask any time. If it's ever more convenient for you to just have me bring something home for you."

"I like to be able to come in and see what I'm buying. And to make sure that it is all fresh."

Erin shook her head. "Everything is fresh, Mrs. Peach. I don't sell day-olds unless it's labeled that way."

"You never know," Mrs. Peach advised. She paid for her purchases with cash money and left, wobbling a little, but perfectly capable of carrying her own bags.

In a few minutes, the bakery was empty of customers. It was the lull between lunch and school letting out, so it would likely stay just a trickle until parents started to arrive to pick up their children from school.

"Can you believe Melissa?" Vic whispered. "I can't believe that she would be so... blatant about spreading her speculations around. And she and Mary Lou used to be best of friends. I can't believe she's spreading that garbage around about Joshua not really being missing and that Campbell is... some kind of drug lord now. Why don't they fire her?"

Terry had complained more than once about how Melissa gossiped and spread around the information she learned while working at the police department.

"I don't know why they don't do anything about it," she admitted. "It isn't like they don't know. There must be other people they could hire in her place."

"They have a duty to keep things confidential," Vic said, shaking her head. "What if Mary Lou sued them for spreading stuff around?"

Erin nodded. She liked Melissa. But the police department really should do something about her. It was getting more and more blatant.

"I'm going to put together a basket for Mrs. Foster. You can handle things out here?"

Vic looked around pointedly at the lack of customers. "I don't know, Erin. You really want me to just jump into the deep end like this?"

Erin grinned at her and went into the kitchen.

The Foster family was growing. The new baby would be number five. That was a lot of work for a mom. She would be tired and sore after the baby came—she was undoubtedly tired and sore waiting for the event—and it would be nice if Erin could help her out a little bit. A few care baskets for those initial weeks, so that Mrs. Foster didn't have to spend as much time on her feet and running around town.

And Erin secretly hoped—maybe not so secretly—that she would be able to repair the rift between herself and Mrs. Foster. And she would start bringing Peter and the other children to the bakery again. Erin loved little Peter especially. He was very mature and well-spoken, advocating for himself and his celiac disease. Maybe arguing a bit too much with his mother, who was doing the best she could to ensure that he was both safe and polite and respectful. It wasn't an easy thing for anyone raising kids in the present state of the world. Erin didn't know if it were something she would ever take on herself.

She packed bread and muffins, bagels, cookies, and some of the granola bars that Peter particularly liked for school. It was hard for a kid who was so sensitive to gluten. Before Erin had opened Auntie Clem's Bakery, he had been limited to less-than-stellar loaves of commercial gluten-free bread from the grocer and boxes of stale gluten-free cookies. If the grocery store didn't get anything in, Mrs. Foster would have to drive into the city to pick up what she needed. Or make something from scratch. Not easy for a mom of four. But otherwise, Peter had to avoid baked products altogether.

Since the opening of Auntie Clem's Bakery, Peter had been able to explore a whole new world of gluten-free baked goods. Erin was his new best friend.

But Mrs. Foster was understandably wary of her son getting so close to a stranger. She taught him about boundaries, but Peter was inclined, like any other little boy, to break the rules when he was out of his mother's sight and hearing. An observant little fellow, he had provided key clues to a couple of important police investigations lately. Something that would have been commendable in an adult, but Peter's being interviewed by the police had produced considerable anxiety for his parents.

And Mrs. Foster blamed Erin for that anxiety. If she hadn't said anything to the police…

Erin sighed as she wrapped everything carefully. It was depressing to have so many of the Bald Eagle Falls parents upset with her.

Unlike Peter, many of the other children had not just been witnesses.

Erin breathed slowly in and out as she looked at the Foster house. She hadn't been there before. She wasn't surprised to find the lawn littered with children's ride 'em toys, the paint peeling from the siding and porch railings, and the gardens somewhat overgrown. People in Bald

Eagle Falls were not wealthy, and having that many young children was enough to overwhelm any mother.

Willie looked over the seat into the back of the king cab, raising his brows at Erin. "We're here."

His face was reassuring. She remembered how leery she had been of him when she had first arrived in Bald Eagle Falls and he had offered to help her with her groceries. She had taken him for a dirty homeless man. She hadn't known back then that his skin was perhaps permanently stained by the mining and processing he did on his own. Now that she knew him, she didn't even notice. It was only brought to her attention when other people saw him for the first time and treated him like a second-class citizen.

"Yeah. I'll just be a minute."

Erin still didn't move. She knew what she needed to do, but she was nervous of the reception she would get. Mrs. Foster wasn't expecting her and might not be happy to see her, even if she was there bearing gifts.

Vic gave Erin a reassuring smile. "Just this one thing, and then you can go home to Terry and relax for the evening."

Erin nodded. She took one more deep breath, pushed the anxiety away as best she could, and climbed down out of the truck. She rang the doorbell, listening for the sound of the bell on the other side of the door so that she would know it worked and she didn't have to knock or press it again. She heard children playing, a dog barking, and footsteps approaching the door.

There was a scuffle and some yelling, Peter's voice over the girls', insisting that he was in charge and they had to let him answer the door. Then the doorknob turned and Peter peeked cautiously around the door.

His face broke into a grin. "Miss Erin!" He pulled the door open the rest of the way. The little girls stood back and looked out at Erin, uncharacteristically quiet.

Erin smiled back at Peter. It was good to see him again. But she knew she wasn't supposed to be visiting with him. "Is your mom available?"

"She's having a nap," Peter informed her.

If she had slept through the sound of the doorbell and the children fighting to see who got to answer the door. Erin was surprised that Mrs. Foster hadn't been right behind the children.

She was surprised that the children were allowed to answer the door while Mrs. Foster was lying down. Or maybe they weren't supposed to.

"I brought some things from the bakery." Erin handed the basket to Peter. "You put that in the kitchen and none of you open it. It's for your mom."

Peter took the basket and peered at the goodies through the plastic wrap. "But this isn't all for Mom," he protested. "It's for me."

"I don't want you eating cookies or anything else before dinner and ruining your appetite. You aren't to open it until your mother says so."

Peter opened his mouth to argue with her. He could negotiate like a lawyer. Erin raised her finger at him, trying to look stern.

"Peter. You listen, or I'm not going to bring any more. You aren't to open it. Your mom will open it when she wants to."

Peter rolled his eyes and shook his head a little, giving Erin attitude. "I wouldn't ruin my appetite. Mom says I have a hollow leg. I'm always hungry."

"No arguments. You aren't allowed to open it."

"But if Mom says. Then I can."

She could just see him sneaking into her darkened bedroom and whispering to her as she was in a state between sleeping and waking, trying to get her to say yes to him so that he could open the basket of goodies.

"When she's up from her nap and wide awake. Then if she says you can. Until she's up, you're not allowed."

Peter huffed, but he couldn't hide a little smirk from her, acknowledging that she was on to him. "Okay," he said with a note of exasperation. "Fine."

CHAPTER 10

*S*he felt much lighter with the job out of the way. Now, as Vic had said, she could go home and relax for the rest of the evening.

She opened the front door quietly, not wanting to wake Terry up. She walked in and closed it behind her, punching the security code into the burglar alarm so it wouldn't start shrieking. Terry was not sleeping on the couch in front of the TV. That was a good sign. If he'd been restless or had a migraine, that was usually where she would find him.

Orange Blossom jumped down from the back of the couch, yowling at her. Erin picked him up and cuddled him and asked him about his day. He was eager to tell her all about it. She had been astonished when she had first rescued him, at how loud he was. She was used to it now, and he wasn't quite as noisy now that he was no longer a kitten but a more mature, settled adult. But she still winced at how loud he was when Terry was sleeping.

"Let's get you a treat and put something in the oven," she whispered to Orange Blossom. "Then maybe you'll be quiet so that Terry can sleep."

But as she got Orange Blossom's can of treats out of the pantry and grabbed a couple of cans of food to make them some supper,

Erin could hear Terry moving around and K9's dog tags jingling in the bedroom in the far corner of the house.

In a few minutes, he wandered into the kitchen, rubbing his eyes.

"Hey," Erin greeted. She kissed him when he got close enough and searched his face for signs of how he was feeling. Had she woken him up too early? Had he gotten in a few solid hours of sleep before she had arrived home? "How was your sleep?"

Terry nodded. "Not bad. How was your day at work?"

"Fine. The usual. Except, of course..." she trailed off.

Terry waited, not contributing his own details.

"We heard about Joshua's disappearance," Erin told him.

Terry nodded. His arms were still around her body, resting and holding her casually close to him. "I figured you would by the end of the day."

"It's so terrible for Mary Lou," Erin said. "I wish that everything would just go right for her. Joshua would get on track, Campbell would come back home or at least get himself straightened out, and they would find something that would work for Roger. For her to have to deal with all of this stuff, one thing on top of another, it's just not fair."

"Tell that to Joshua," Terry said, shaking his head.

"You don't really think that it's just a prank, do you? When Mel—when I heard that—I just couldn't believe it. Joshua wouldn't do something like that to his mother. He loves her. He's good to her. He tries to help her out and to do the things she wants him to. He wouldn't do something like this."

"We don't know yet. There isn't a lot of evidence one way or another."

"You don't think he wrote that note himself."

Terry grimaced. He sat down at the table. "I can't really say what I think or discuss any details about the evidence. Let's just say... we have yet to establish that a crime has been committed."

"But you are looking for Josh, right? You're not just blowing it off."

"Anything that involves minor children needs to be taken very seriously. Yes, we do end up having to deal with pranks, especially with kids Joshua's age. We're not just blowing it off… you know I was investigating all night and most of the morning today. I wasn't just going through the motions."

Erin nodded. She busied herself with opening cans and trying to pull together something that would be both tasty and good for them. Baking was her forte; she was not as good with the main course, especially when it was just the two of them at the end of a long day at the bakery.

"I know. I didn't mean that you're not doing what you're supposed to. I'm just saying that… if you start with the wrong assumption, you might go the wrong direction."

"Investigative bias," Terry agreed. "I know. We try to be careful of that."

Erin didn't say anything for a few minutes. She wanted to know all of the details of the investigation, but she had to be just as careful about what she asked as he did about what he revealed to her.

"Do the police really think that he might have written the note himself?"

"It's a possibility."

"He wouldn't do that."

"I have to look at all the possibilities. It is possible he wrote it himself. It's also possible that someone else wrote it, either trying to imitate his writing or just someone with similar writing. It's not a very big sample. Not a lot of points to compare. And kids these days… they don't handwrite anything. It's all on the computer. So there aren't a lot of samples of Joshua's handwriting to make a comparison."

"You haven't asked me if I know where he is." Erin turned from her pots and leaned against the counter, looking at him.

"Come sit down."

She joined him at the table. Terry took her hand.

"Do you know where Joshua Cox is?"

Erin shook her head. "No."

"How did you know what the note said? Melissa?"

"I don't reveal my sources," Erin said with a smile. He could interpret that as he liked. He would probably assume that she was trying to protect Melissa. Not that she was trying to avoid telling him anything that was Mary Lou's business. Mary Lou had apparently not told him that she had talked to Erin and Vic about it a full day before talking to the police. And if Mary Lou didn't tell them that, Erin couldn't very well reveal it. That would make Terry suspicious of Mary Lou. They didn't need to investigate Mary Lou. They needed to spend their time tracking down the real culprit, whoever that was.

"I don't know why someone left that note," Terry said slowly. "I don't think that anyone seriously believed it would throw suspicion on you. No one thinks that you snuck off in the middle of the night and met Joshua or did something to make him disappear."

"Good. Because I didn't." Erin pulled her hand out of Terry's grasp. She was too anxious to sit still. She got up and checked the pots on the stove, giving everything a quick stir. She opened the fridge and started to pull out the makings of a salad. She was trying really hard to eat salad at every meal. Or at least, at every dinner. Marshmallow hopped over and started to nibble at her pant leg. He knew the rustle of vegetables in plastic just as well as Orange Blossom knew the sound of his can of kitty treats.

"Hello, bun. How are you doing?" Erin murmured to Marshmallow. She cut off a few vegetable ends for him. She bent down and scratched his ears after giving them to him. She washed her hands and continued assembling the salad.

"I think that something really did happen to Joshua," she told Terry. "I don't think it's just a joke."

"It seems like it's been going on a bit long if it was just intended to be a joke," Terry agreed. "Any sensible person would understand there is a big difference between pretending someone has been kidnapped for a couple of hours and making them disappear for a couple of days."

"Yeah. And Josh wouldn't participate in something like that. Maybe someone else would cover and say that it was just a joke because they didn't want Mary Lou to know what really happened, but… Joshua wouldn't do that. He knows how much Mary Lou worries about him."

"Sometimes that's exactly the reason kids rebel. They find it suffocating, parents always worrying and trying to make sure that nothing happens to them."

"Well… yes. I think Campbell is more like that. He needed to get out of there… to find a way he could make his own decisions."

Terry nodded.

"Did Mary Lou—or you—did anyone get ahold of Campbell? To see if Josh was with him, or if he knows what Josh's plans were?"

"Mary Lou spoke with him on the phone. Stayner was going to drive into the city to have a chat with him this afternoon." Terry worked his phone out of his pocket and tapped through a few screens. "No messages. I guess I'll find out later what the results of that trip were. But if Josh had been found, there definitely would be a message on my phone."

And word would have quickly spread through Bald Eagle Falls too.

"I'm really worried about him. What do you think happened?"

"We don't have enough information to make an educated guess at this point. Maybe nothing."

"But he might have been kidnapped. Or hurt. You don't have any evidence that he *wasn't* either."

"There are no indications that anything violent occurred."

"No?"

"No."

That was a little reassuring. If someone had come into the house and kidnapped Josh, then there would surely have been some sign of that. Someone couldn't just grab a teenager and cart him off without knocking a few things down.

"So you think… he just walked away, under his own power."

"That is the most logical explanation. But why? And what happened next? Where did he go?"

"Maybe he met someone…" Erin tried to visualize it. It wasn't that long since she'd been a teenager herself. And she had been around a lot of other teenagers, kids who had very different personalities from hers. Who had grown up with different rules and had different experiences from hers. "A girlfriend. A party that he knew

Mary Lou wouldn't let him go to. Even just... feeling restless and going out for a walk..."

"Exactly. There are lots of different possibilities, and not all of them would suggest that something happened to him."

"He could have planned to drive into the city with someone. Or Campbell might have been coming over for a visit."

Terry's lips pressed together.

If Joshua had gone somewhere to meet with Campbell, then they should know that by now. Campbell would have told Mary Lou when she called him, or Stayner would have found out when he went into the city to talk to Campbell.

But Joshua had apparently not gone to see his brother. Or if he had, then things had fallen apart and something had happened.

"Do you really think that it's just something innocent? That he'll show up again and everything will be okay?"

Terry considered, scratching his stubbly jaw. "We don't have enough information yet to make that kind of judgment. If it was just a prank, then it is surprising that he hasn't shown up again yet. It's been two days. But if he ran away for another reason, it could still be voluntary."

"But why would he?"

"You never know all of the reasons someone might choose to run away." He gave her a half-smile. "I'm sure you've seen that, living in foster homes. You must have known a few runners."

"Kids that run away chronically, sure. But that's not Joshua. He isn't a troubled kid who has grown up in half a dozen different homes or has had to fend for himself or defend himself against an abuser. He's a kid living with his mom, who he's always lived with. She has a good job and looks after him. He goes to school and was trying to get his grades up again. He's not involved with a gang or drugs."

"But you are a casual outside observer. How much of that do you *know* to be true?"

CHAPTER 11

*E*ven though she didn't want it to grow from a discussion to an argument, Erin wanted to defend her position. She knew Joshua. She knew Mary Lou. She knew that Mary Lou gave Joshua a good home.

But what did she really know? The way a family looked from the outside was not necessarily an accurate representation of what was really going on. Abusers could act sweet and caring in public. Molesters could be upright citizens, making good money and acting like responsible parents. They could be women as easily as men.

Mary Lou was tough, Erin knew that. She wanted Joshua to shape up in school and to get back on track. Campbell had come from the same home, and he had dropped out and moved to the city, essentially running away from home, before turning eighteen. He was possibly into the drug culture and was close enough to street life and organized crime that Beaver—Federal Agent Rohilda Beaven—used him as a confidential informant.

Erin didn't know how bad things had been when Roger was still living at home, but she didn't imagine living with a confused, increasingly violent parent had been fun for either of the boys. They had worked hard to help support the family and take care of their father, a lot to expect from a couple of teenage boys.

"Well, you don't know what goes on behind closed doors," Erin admitted. "I don't think that Mary Lou was too strict with him, but... she's not an easy woman to get along with. But we at least know that he wasn't running with a bad crowd or involved with drugs."

Terry raised an eyebrow. Of course, he might know details that Erin did not. He wouldn't be in a position to tell her if he knew that Joshua had been caught with drugs or was suspected of being an addict or dealer. He had dropped out of his sports teams and extracurricular activities. His marks had plummeted. He'd spent a lot of time at home alone. All classic signs of a kid involved in drugs. Or human trafficking. Or both.

"I'm sure he wasn't," Erin protested. She had seen his honest reactions when they had gone looking for Brianna. Joshua had been shocked at what he saw in the city, at the state of the girls they had talked to. If he were taking drugs, it was still at a recreational level. He hadn't seen addiction like that before. "And he was working on bringing his marks up. He was in Whitewater to do interviews for the paper. It wasn't drugs, it was just everything else that had happened in their family lately. All of the disruption. The stuff with Roger and Campbell."

Terry got up from the table to grab some dishes and set the table. He took a jug of water from the fridge, stood staring into the open fridge for a few long seconds, then closed it, returned to the table, and arranged things the way Erin liked them.

"I heard from Mary Lou about him going to Whitewater. You saw him while he was there?"

"Yes. He came to talk to me. To 'interview' me for background on the contest and... on Beryl. He was more interested in what happened to Beryl than in the cooking contest."

"Of course," Terry nodded. "I would be too. Cooking is interesting," he allowed, "but not nearly as compelling as someone showing up dead in a freezer."

Erin shrugged.

"But why do you say 'interview,' like that." Terry used his fingers to put air quotes around the word.

Erin hadn't meant to use that inflection. It had just come out that way. "Well… because I didn't really want to be interviewed for his article. If he wanted to know things about the contest, that was great, it would be good publicity for the contest and for us. But he wanted to ask me about finding Beryl and what I thought… and I really didn't want to talk to him about it."

"Ah." Terry nodded. "Makes sense. How much did he manage to worm out of you?"

"He was good," Erin admitted. She smiled at Terry. "Not as good an interrogator as a policeman, of course…"

"I wouldn't expect so. Though some reporters would give the police a run for their money. Have you read Joshua's article?"

"No. How was it?"

"Good. He did a nice job on it. Didn't come off as a kid's school essay. Good clear language, well thought out. He's not an investigative journalist, but he made a good start."

"I'll have to read it." Erin usually flipped through the copy of the Bald Eagle Falls weekly paper that was delivered to her, but with everything that had been happening, she hadn't yet had the chance.

Josh really needed to get home. He needed to wake up, get himself out of bed or off of whoever's couch he was sleeping on, and get home. If his mother had already woken up and discovered him missing, he would be in big trouble. There would be a lot of explaining to do.

Or not very much explaining, since he couldn't remember for sure what had happened or where he was. But he would have to come up with something.

Josh opened his eyes. They were gritty and blurry, and he couldn't really see anything around him except darkness and darker shapes in the darkness. It was still night. So maybe he still had time.

But his body told him that it wasn't night. There was a part of his consciousness that was growing increasingly alarmed each time he woke up. It had been too long. It couldn't still be night. He had known several wakenings ago that dawn was coming.

He groaned and tried to move. As before, he couldn't seem to move anywhere. His arms and legs did not respond the way that they should. He'd really gotten messed up on whatever he had indulged in. Had it been a party? He was beginning to think that someone had roofied him. That would explain why his memory was so patchy.

The thought both relieved him—because it meant that he hadn't chosen to get so screwed up—and made him more anxious. He felt violated and anxious. It made him angry. Who would do something like that to him? One of his friends, thinking it was a good prank? Someone else who had wanted to steal from him or get something out of him? The joke was on them, since he was dirt poor and didn't even have a dime in his pockets.

He didn't think that it was to take advantage of him physically. That didn't happen to guys.

Did it?

He tried to sort out the sensations of his body, worried. But he couldn't sort out all of the sensory inputs. It was dark, that he knew for sure. He couldn't move his hands to take out his phone and look at the time or at his camera roll in case he had recorded something.

He kicked his feet, trying to turn his body over and look around. Nothing would move the right way. He thrashed around in the blankets, unable to control his position or to right himself.

"Stop that," a hoarse whisper came out of the darkness.

Josh froze. He scanned the layers of darkness for a human figure, but could not see anyone and could not turn over to check the rest of the room. "Who's there? Who are you?"

"The person who's in charge here. The person you need to listen to."

He couldn't build a picture of the owner of the whisper. It wasn't a voice he recognized, but he wasn't sure that meant anything, because it was just a whisper, with no tone or pitch. He couldn't tell whether it was male or female, old or young. He didn't detect any particular accent.

"Where am I? What time is it?"

"None of that matters."

Joshua tried to clear his throat. His mouth was dry as a bone. He needed a drink. Not alcohol, just water. He was dehydrated. Maybe that was why his head hurt so much. He tried to move again.

"I can't... I'm tangled up here," he told the voice, embarrassed. He tried to get free of the blankets once more. "I'm just trying to get up..."

"You're not tangled. You're tied."

Josh stopped moving. He tried again to find the dark figure in the shadows. "What?"

"You are restrained."

Joshua tried to move his hands, and finally figured out why they were not moving the way they were supposed to. They were bound together. Any time he tried to move one of them, the other was dragged along with it. He moved his feet slowly, and found that his left foot followed his right when he tried to move it to the side.

He fought the restraints. Tried to bring his wrists up to eye level so he could look at them. He couldn't get them up to his face or see the restraints that held him. He couldn't feel what they were, but didn't hear any jangling, so assumed it wasn't handcuffs. Maybe zip ties or duct tape. Who would do that? Was it a joke?

"What's going on? Why am I tied up?"

"So that you can't leave."

Joshua couldn't help himself. He fought the restraints, trying to rip his hands away from each other, to kick out with his feet to hit something. He tried to squirm around to turn over but couldn't.

"Quit fighting."

"Let me go! What are you doing? This is kidnapping! You can't tie someone up! This isn't funny."

"Nobody's laughing." There was a strange noise, and Joshua wondered if his captor was, in fact, laughing in a whisper. "This isn't meant to be funny."

"You can't go around kidnapping people. Where am I?" Joshua blinked, trying to bring his surroundings into focus, but still all he could see was darkness and shadows. It wasn't home. He had known that for a while. But he couldn't figure out where he was.

"Stop thrashing around."

Joshua kept kicking and trying to turn over. What was the whisperer going to do? He couldn't stop Joshua from trying to escape his bonds. Josh wasn't going to be quiet and compliant and do whatever his captor told him to.

There was movement nearby. Behind him. He couldn't turn his head all the way around to see. He tried anyway, straining. The noise moved closer.

"Who are you? Tell me what's going on!"

A cloth fell over his eyes. Josh tried to pull away from it, but it was tied tightly around his head, snagging bits of hair and pulling them tightly into the knot of the blindfold.

"No! No, I'll listen to you. You don't need to blindfold—"

He shouldn't have opened his mouth. The gag went in next. A round ball of cloth that felt and tasted like rolled-up socks, and then a rope of something that went into his mouth, pulled tight around his head so that it pulled his lips taut and his jaw slightly open. But it kept the packing material in his mouth and prevented him from opening and closing his mouth to speak. Josh tried to protest this treatment, but he couldn't get anything coherent out.

"Next time, maybe you'll stop when I tell you to," his captor whispered.

There was a pain in his thigh.

He felt dizzy and lightheaded.

And that was all.

CHAPTER 12

Their dinner was a quiet affair. Both were thinking about Joshua Cox and what might have happened to him. Erin hoped that it wasn't something awful. She hoped that the note had just been left by his friends to cover for his absence when he had gone off to see a girl or on a road trip or one of the many other things that a stressed-out teenager might do to escape his life for a few days. Maybe Joshua didn't even know about the note left behind. He wouldn't have caused Erin extra grief, but the same would not necessarily be true of his friends at school. Who knew how many of them had been affected by Erin's investigation at Christmas. There might be several who resented the attention she had drawn to them and the school even if they hadn't been implicated in the police investigation.

"I should call Mary Lou," she said, as she scraped her fork along the bottom of her plate. She licked off the last of the gravy. "Did she have anyone over there with her, when you were there?"

"Women were coming and going." Terry rolled his eyes. "Do you know how hard it is to run a police investigation when women are coming in with casseroles every few minutes? It's not the forensics I'm talking about. We kept things sealed up until the techs were done looking for evidence, but the constant interruptions. Trying to ask all of the important questions while people keep knocking on the door, ringing the bell, or yoo-hooing, and walking in on the interview."

Erin shook her head, suppressing her smile as much as she could. She was surprised that Terry hadn't taken Mary Lou to the police department where he could question her without interruption. Only maybe she hadn't wanted to go there. He couldn't force her to leave the house and she probably didn't want to leave in case Joshua showed up or one of his friends stopped in with news.

"Well... I'm glad that people are trying to look after her, but I'm not sure casseroles are what she needs."

The last Erin had seen, at Thanksgiving, Mary Lou already had a freezer full of food contributions. And with it just being her and Joshua, they probably hadn't made much of a dent in it.

And now it was just Mary Lou, and she didn't eat very much, trying to watch her weight. One casserole would last a couple of weeks.

"You can give her a call. She'll probably go to bed early; she was pretty tired last I saw her. Not that you stay up late anyway."

"She probably sat up waiting for him all night."

Terry nodded. "She had police there all night, so even if she had wanted to go to bed, it would have been difficult."

Erin licked off her fork once more, sighed, and put it down on her plate. "I'll call her once I've cleared everything away, then."

"Leave the dishes. I can do that. Go call now, then it's done and you won't spend the rest of the evening worrying about her."

Erin left Terry in the kitchen and went to her bedroom to make the call. She shut the bedroom door and sat down on the bed. She wished she were more eager to make the call. She wished that she knew ahead of time how it would go over. The dinner sat like a lump of lead in her stomach.

But procrastinating wasn't going to make it any easier. Erin forced herself to unlock her phone and pull up the contact entry for Mary Lou. She tapped it and listened to the ringing. Mary Lou might already be asleep. If she hadn't slept for two days, she might have fallen asleep in front of the TV or while trying to do something else. Or she might have talked with enough well-meaning people that she really didn't want to deal with anyone else.

Erin wasn't sure whether to leave a voicemail. As the phone continued to ring, she tried to script a message in her head. *I was just calling to see how you are... let me know if you need anything...* Everything sounded so lame. The woman's son was missing. What was the appropriate response to a disaster like that?

There was a soft click and Mary Lou's well-measured tones. "Erin. Hello."

"I'm sorry. I hope you weren't sleeping."

"No."

"Do you want me to come over and sit with you? I can tidy up if the police left anything in a mess, or figure out what to do with all of the casseroles."

"No. I don't want anyone else here tonight. It's been like Grand Central Station."

"I could come tomorrow and help with whatever you need."

"I only need one thing, and that is to have my son back."

Erin swallowed. "I wish I knew where he was. I wish I could help with that."

"The note says to ask you."

"I know... I don't know why it says that, because I have no idea. If I did, I would tell you. I swear."

"I don't think it literally means to ask you where he is," Mary Lou said in a studied tone. "I think it means that this has happened because of something you did."

"I didn't—" Erin broke off. How could she be sure that it hadn't happened because of something she had done? Actions had consequences. Not always things that could be foreseen or controlled. Every action sent out little ripples over a growing area. And Erin had thrown some pretty big rocks into the pond. "I don't know what I could have done that would have had any impact on Joshua. I really don't."

"Well, we know that's not true. You had him hauled into the police station."

Erin cleared her throat. Mary Lou knew that what she was saying was an exaggeration. It wasn't Erin who had interrogated Joshua. It wasn't her fault. Not really. It was Harold who had mentioned Joshua and his friends to Erin.

Do you know about them?

He hadn't asked if she knew Josh, but if she knew about him. And Erin had been left to wonder what Josh and his friends were doing that she should know about. She had mentioned it to Terry, and Terry had been the one who had invited Josh in for questioning. That wasn't her fault.

Rocks thrown into the pond.

"And you were the one who went with him into the city. I still don't know what happened there, but I have a pretty good idea that it wasn't the innocent little trip that you and Vic would have me believe."

"I didn't go with him. We ran into him in the city…"

"But you took him to those places. Looking for Brianna."

"I went with him," Erin corrected. She was in the right on this one. She had tried to talk Joshua out of it, and when she hadn't been able to dissuade him, she had gone along to help keep him safe and out of trouble.

"You have shown a shocking lack of awareness of what is appropriate behavior and what could have serious consequences. You should never have let Joshua search for Campbell."

Erin's temper rose at the unfairness of Mary Lou's comment. "I'm not his mother. I couldn't stop him from doing anything. I went along to try to keep him safe and that's the best I could do. What would he have done if I told him he couldn't go look for her? He would have laughed in my face."

"Then you call me. You let me know what's going on. You don't just let him rush headlong into something dangerous."

"Okay, fine. I didn't do that. I guess I should have. But that doesn't have anything to do with him being missing. That was months ago."

"I told you I didn't want you to have anything more to do with him."

Erin rubbed her face tiredly. "I know. And I didn't."

"You didn't talk to him in Whitewater?"

"Well... yes, I did. He came to my hotel. I didn't seek him out. And when I asked if you knew where he was, he said you did."

"I don't know what's going on with Joshua. I don't know where he is or what he's doing. I don't know why he's disappeared. But if it had anything to do with you..."

"It's nothing to do with me. I didn't have anything to do with him disappearing. The last time I saw him was when he was working on the article for the paper. I never saw him or talked to him again after that."

There was silence for a few moments. "Very well," Mary Lou said finally. "If you hear anything... I expect you to tell me. Not Officer Piper; me. His mother. And if you do anything to interfere, anything that puts him in further danger..."

"I wouldn't do anything. I won't. And I hope... I hope he turns up again soon, and that everything is okay."

"So do I."

Mary Lou hung up. Erin put her phone down, put her arm over her eyes, and tried to resist the urge to burst into tears.

CHAPTER 13

*E*rin was getting ready for bed when she heard Terry answer the door. She hovered near the bathroom doorway, listening to identify the visitor. It didn't take her long to figure out that it was Stayner, the newest member of the Bald Eagle Falls police department. He had been contracted when Terry was unable to work, and they had managed to make room in the budget for him to stay on for an extended period. He was young and didn't have a lot of experience. Erin hoped that he was a quick learner. She found him abrasive and too quick to jump to judgment. He was opinionated and, she thought, sexist, though he had never come right out and told her that her place was in the kitchen. Or the bakery. It was just a feeling she got from him.

But Terry and the sheriff said that he did good work. Yes, he was rough around the edges, but that would improve with experience and a good teacher.

"Ten to one, he's on a binge," Stayner told Terry in the living room. "It's a waste of our time and resources. He'll show up again when he sobers up. Mom is overreacting."

Terry's response was softer, and Erin hoped it was something along the lines of 'Mary Lou is not overreacting. She waited a full day before reporting him missing, and he's now been gone for two days. No one knows where he went.'

"His friends know where he is," Stayner said. "Mark my words. Probably his brother too. He acted all shocked and concerned, but I know the way these kids act. He knows exactly where Joshua Cox is."

Erin moved out into the bathroom, closer to the living room. She didn't want them to see her, didn't want to have to deal with Stayner's 'I know better' bluster, but she wanted to learn what she could.

"What did Cam have to say?" Terry asked.

Erin heard the squeak of springs as Stayner sat down to continue the conversation. "He said he hasn't talked to Josh for a few days. And when they did talk, Joshua didn't give any hint that he was planning to go anywhere. Everything was normal, according to big brother. But I highly doubt Joshua left without telling Cam where he was going."

"No sign of him in Cam's apartment? No hint that someone else has been staying there?"

"He doesn't have an apartment of his own. From what I can tell, he couch surfs between a few different friends. So, yes, there are plenty of signs that someone else has been around, because it's not Cam's own place. And there are others who live or crash there, too. It would be impossible to sort out whether Joshua was ever there."

"So he couldn't ask Josh to come live with him. Or even just sleep over."

"I don't think the fact that it wasn't his apartment would stop him. They all seem pretty casual about it. I probably could have stayed there, as long as I promised to look the other way on any drug charges."

"What kind of a mood was he in the last time that Cam talked to him?"

"Fine, according to Cam. Good spirits. Happy with his bonus English assignment. Ready to kick back and relax for a while."

"Uh-huh." In her mind's eye, Erin saw Terry rubbing his chin as he often did when pondering. "And nothing from his school friends?"

Erin had thought that Terry would have been the one to interview Joshua's school friends, but she supposed that since he'd been up most of the night and then would have had a ton of reports to fill out, he probably hadn't been able to get over to the school between the time that school started and he finally clocked out.

"I talked to his loser friends," Stayner agreed.

Erin clenched her teeth at his characterization. Joshua and his friends were not losers. Joshua had been through a lot, that was all.

"Loser friends?" Terry repeated. "Is that what went into your report?"

"No, of course not. But they are. His friends are the lowest class at the school. Nowhere kids. They don't belong to any of the teams or clubs, get rock bottom marks, have no motivation to do anything but go home and game or surf porn on their computers."

"Josh used to be on the sports teams. He got out of them because of the difficult time that he's been having. You have to remember what happened with his dad, and then with Campbell. The kid is lost."

Stayner snorted. "Yeah," he agreed. "They're all lost boys. They're going nowhere and will amount to nothing. Look for them soon begging on a street corner near you."

"And none of them had any idea where Josh might have gone?"

"No idea. I don't know if any of them even noticed that he was missing. It was like, 'Oh, Josh? Yeah, where is he, man?'" Stayner used his best stoner voice. It would have been funny if Erin wasn't so angry at him for his insensitivity.

But he didn't know she was there listening. He thought he was just talking to a fellow cop, and Erin knew that they frequently dealt with the stress of the job with gallows humor and sarcastic or inappropriate comments. He would probably have guarded his tongue if he had known that Erin was there listening. Which was why she hadn't made herself known. She wanted to hear everything he had to say.

"Today was a waste of time," Stayner's tone was annoyed. "The whole day was a write-off. We didn't get any farther ahead on anything." There was a pause in which neither of them spoke. "No one had any motive to kidnap the kid, Piper. He'll show up again when he feels like it."

"You think that he wrote the note," Terry said.

"Him or one of his equally illiterate buddies, yeah."

Erin just about shouted at him despite not wanting them to know she was eavesdropping on the conversation.

Joshua was not illiterate! He had just finished having an article published by the paper. Not the school paper, the Bald Eagle Falls weekly. It might have been small, but it was a real paper and he'd managed to get his article published by them. His marks had fallen not because he wasn't smart enough, but because he'd been through a series of horrible family tragedies and couldn't deal with schoolwork on top of it.

"Well, only time and further investigation will tell. We have to put in the footwork, even if you don't think there was any foul play. We need to do all of the right things, just in case. Don't allow investigative bias to creep in. What would you do if there were signs of violence? A ransom note? What if it was a ten-year-old girl instead of a teenage boy?"

Stayner was silent.

"We'll have a team meeting tomorrow," Terry told him. "We'll go over everything that we've found so far, and we'll talk about what to do next. But think about it. Come up with some ideas and suggestions to bring to the meeting. Show that you can think critically and conduct a thorough investigation."

"Yeah, okay," Stayner agreed, his voice quiet for once instead of blustering. He'd just gotten some good advice from his senior officer, and if he wanted to be respected within the police department, he would follow up on it.

CHAPTER 14

*E*rin took the first tray of flat cookie disks out of the oven and put them on a cooling tray.

"So the cookies need to be folded while they're still warm. Once they cool, they get crispy, and then it is too late to fix any mistakes. This is how you do it."

Her assistant bakers watched closely. Erin hoped that the cookies held together like they were supposed to. She had tested the recipe out already and practiced folding the fortune cookies, but that didn't mean that a batch couldn't go wrong. Too much moisture or not enough, left in the oven a minute or two too long, or something else that she couldn't foresee or control. There were no guarantees.

"The fortune goes inside," Erin placed one of the slips of paper on the flat disk. "Then, you fold the cookie into a half-circle." Erin demonstrated. "And then bring the ends together into the classic fortune-cookie shape. You can rest it on the rim of a glass to cool, or just place it carefully on the cooling rack."

"That's so cool," Bella said. "But I'm a little sad to know the secret of how the fortune gets inside the cookie."

Everybody nodded and laughed, agreeing.

"One of life's mysteries solved," Erin said. "You'll have to move on to how they get the caramel into a Caramilk bar."

She stepped back from the counter. "I'd like to make sure everyone makes two or three, so you get a feel for it." She moved to the next oven and pulled out another tray as the timer chimed. She put it down on another counter across the kitchen from the first. The group split into two. The kitchen was crowded with so many people there. Still, it had seemed like the best idea to show everyone how to make the fortune cookies at the same time, instead of having to demonstrate several times or have everyone showing everyone else, possibly losing something in translation.

She watched as each of the employees tried several fortune cookies. There were some misfolds and some breakage. That was all to be expected. They would just eat the mistakes instead of sending them on to the Chinese restaurant.

After everyone had a go at it, Erin dismissed them. "Great, thanks for coming by for this. I've had Matt print a bunch of fortunes for us, we'll get the rest of the cookies done over the next week, as per the schedule."

Erin had been thinking all day about Terry's advice to Stayner. Imagine that they had proof that Josh had not disappeared voluntarily, and work from there. She put the possibility that Joshua had left of his own accord out of her head and focused on what they knew.

He had come back from Whitewater and written his article. He hadn't been back to Whitewater since then, as far as anyone knew. He had talked to his mother, his friends, and his brother in the days before his disappearance. He hadn't said anything about plans to go away, being stressed out, or anything else that would explain his disappearance.

Had he received any threats? Anything to indicate that he might be in danger? If he had mentioned any threats to his family or friends, she assumed they would have reported it to the police after his disappearance. So he must not have.

How could he disappear in the middle of the night? He'd been there when Mary Lou had gone to bed but wasn't there when she got up. Had he gone somewhere voluntarily, to a party or to see Campbell or a girl, and then something had happened to prevent him from getting home again? Had someone come into his bedroom and taken him away? If so, why wasn't there any sign of a struggle? He could have been drugged or knocked out. He could have been taken at gunpoint or under some other threat. He was a slim teenager, stronger than a ten-year-old girl, but still not man-grown, and not someone who did bodybuilding or martial arts. He had dropped out of all of his sports teams. If someone had threatened him with a weapon or threatened to do something to Mary Lou, he wouldn't have had any choice but to go with them.

If someone had come for him, was it someone he knew? A stranger? Would he have let a stranger into the house?

Was it someone that Joshua connected with Erin and that was why he had written the note?

But if he had been taken from his room under threat, when would he have had the time to leave a note? What kidnapper would have let him do that?

Or had the kidnapper forced him to write that note to throw suspicion onto Erin? As Mary Lou had said, she assumed that Erin's past actions had something to do with Joshua's disappearance. She didn't think that Erin had taken Josh, but she believed it was, in some way, Erin's fault.

"Who would take Joshua?"

Vic looked over at Erin, chewing a bite of sandwich. "What?"

Erin hadn't meant to speak the question aloud. But now that she had, she might as well see what Vic thought.

"Who would take Joshua? If he was taken from his room—or somewhere else in town—who would do that? And why? Mary Lou thinks it was because of me."

"No, she's just worried."

"She said so. She thinks it's because of something that I did."

"Well…" Vic chewed slowly. "I don't know what Joshua would have to do with anything from *your* past. That doesn't make much sense."

Erin nodded. "Right? I mean, I know Josh, but not well. We've talked a few times. But we haven't really had anything to do with each other. So why…?"

Vic wiped a bit of mayonnaise from her lip. "You and Josh. The only time you ever really did anything together was when we were all in the city. Is that what you're talking about?"

Erin thought about it. "You think it's someone who saw us together when we were looking for Brianna? I still don't…" She trailed off, shaking her head. What was the connection? Why would someone kidnap Josh because he and Erin had been in the city together?

"It's not a very long list," Vic said. She licked her finger off and held it up in a 'number one' sign. "There was the girl at the first apartment we went to. The girl with the black eye. The second one, there wasn't anyone there, right? Someone still might have seen us there. Then…" She cleared her throat. "The mob guy. Mickey. But he's in prison, so it wasn't him."

"But there was a girl there, too."

"What reason would any of them have to take Josh?" Vic shook her head. "Nothing I can think of. I mean, he's a white boy living at home; maybe they figured they could get some kind of ransom for him…" "But there hasn't been a ransom demand."

They both thought about that. Someone could have taken him intending to ask for a ransom. But Erin didn't like where that led. That would mean that something had happened to Josh to prevent them from making the demand. She didn't even want to entertain that possibility.

"Maybe one of them liked him," Vic suggested. "They started to see each other quietly, and she eventually talked him into running away with her?"

"Okay, maybe," Erin agreed. She searched in her purse for a piece of paper to write it down. One of the girls they had seen that day. And the note was just to throw Mary Lou off of their trail. So that she thought it was something to do with Erin instead of Joshua running off with a girl. That could be true of any of the girls in town, too. They didn't need to know that Erin and Josh had been in the city together, just that Josh knew her and that Mary Lou had not been happy with Erin.

Mary Lou hadn't exactly kept it a secret.

CHAPTER 15

*W*hen he woke up again, the room was a little lighter. Josh tried to crane his neck around to look all the way around it and, while he couldn't make out what most of the dark shapes around him were, he saw a high window above him with some light leaking in around the edges. Not enough to make the room bright. Just enough to lift a few of the shadows.

He remembered the whispered voice. Someone had been in the room with him the last time he had awoken. That person had blind-folded and gagged him and knocked him out with some drug. The blindfold and gag had been removed again, but his hands and feet were apparently still bound. Josh lay still, trying to learn as much as he could about his environment without moving. It was a large room. He couldn't see all the way around it. It was filled with a lot of shadowy objects, but they didn't seem to be arranged in any particular order, like shelves or furniture. More like a storage room where every-thing had just been shoved in together.

His mouth was so dry he couldn't work up the spit to irrigate it. His tongue felt like it belonged to someone else, clumsy and swollen. There were cracks in the corners of his mouth. His nose also felt dried up, more cracks running from the outside corners of his nostrils down toward his mouth.

There was a noise.

Joshua strained toward it, trying to see if it were a rat or a person or some other random noise from the building itself shifting. He couldn't see well in the dark, but the furtive sound continued and, in a few minutes, he could see the shape moving toward him. Human-sized, not a rat. He didn't dare hope it was someone there to save him. He was grateful for the removal of the gag and didn't want to earn it back by addressing his captor or making any attempt to attract attention.

Eventually, the figure stood over him. He couldn't estimate his captor's height or weight, lying down as he was. His captor wore a dark, shapeless hoodie, and Josh could see a greenish glint of glasses or goggles under the hood. Night vision? A disguise? Just some weird costume or affectation?

It was a struggle to keep from saying anything. Eventually, he heard the hoarse whisper again. It sent a shiver of terror down his spine.

"You're quiet and still this time. That's good. Maybe you're learning."

Joshua's head quirked slightly in a nod, even though he hadn't intended to make any acknowledgment or response. He didn't want the blindfold and gag again.

He wanted to earn his captor's appreciation.

He wanted to live.

"Good," the shadow repeated.

There was a scrape of metal somewhere close. Joshua didn't turn his head to look at it. The figure reached toward him, and Josh turned his head away slightly, worried about being gagged again. Something hard banged against his lips and teeth, drawing an unintentional yelp of pain. Warm fluid flooded over his lip and chin.

"Drink. Open your mouth."

He obediently opened his mouth. Whatever sedative he'd been given was messing with his depth perception. He didn't realize the water flask was right in front of his mouth until it touched his lip again. He tried to purse his lips to drink from it, but his lips were so dry and swollen that he couldn't mold his mouth against the bottle.

The shadowy figure spilled water into his mouth anyway. Joshua choked trying to get it down, but he persisted, and managed to get a few swallows down. The bottle was withdrawn.

"More," Joshua croaked. "Please."

"That's enough for now."

"So dry."

"Well, I don't want to clean you up any more than I have to."

Joshua's face burned. It wasn't his fault that he couldn't tend to his own bodily functions. But it still embarrassed him to think of someone else doing it. He swallowed a few times and tried to speak.

"Who are you? Why am I here?" The words came out in a croak, but his captor could apparently still understand him.

"Some people just can't mind their own business," the whisperer hissed sharply. "Some people just have to keep digging into stuff that doesn't have anything to do with them."

Joshua swallowed. He wanted to protest that he hadn't done anything wrong, that if he'd happened to step over the line and breach someone's privacy by accident, he was sorry. He wouldn't let it happen again. But what could he say when he didn't even know what the problem was?

"Can I… are you ever going to let me go?"

"Haven't really learned your lesson, have you?"

"I… don't know. I'll try to do better."

"A little late for that now."

The hooded figure looked around, light glinting off the goggles. Then, he withdrew again, leaving Josh there to stew and wonder what he had done to deserve such a punishment.

CHAPTER 16

They didn't get anywhere. Not really. Erin made a few notes about who might want to kidnap Joshua or might have been able to entice him away, but she didn't really believe any of them. None of them felt right. The motives were thin and, even if she was right, there was no way they could prove anything. They didn't have any evidence to show to the police to help pinpoint Joshua's location.

She was in a fog as she went through her usual procedures to close the bakery for the day and make sure that everything was set for the next morning.

It was strange how life just kept going on as usual, even after such a tragedy.

She kept making bread and cake and cookies and selling them to people as if nothing had happened.

"I'm meeting Willie at the Chinese restaurant," Vic reminded Erin. "Do you want me to walk home with you first?"

"No, no." Erin waved a hand at her. "I'm perfectly fine walking home."

"I can walk with you, Willie will wait."

"No. Go have dinner. I'm fine."

Vic hesitated for a moment. "If you needed something, you would ask, right? If you want a ride?"

"I'm going to get a car soon," Erin promised, though that wasn't what Vic had asked. "I don't know why it's taken me so long. I'll do it soon."

"You don't need a ride home? We could call Willie."

"No. I need the exercise. Go," Erin insisted.

Vic sighed and shrugged, then did as she was told. Erin chuckled to herself and started to head toward her house. It wasn't like it was a hardship to walk a few blocks from the bakery to the house. Clementine had done it for many years until her health had started to deteriorate. She had only used the yellow Volkswagen for occasional errands. Erin knew she should either get the car fixed up or get rid of it. What good was it doing taking up her garage space?

She needed a car, so she should either start driving the Volkswagen or find something else she could use.

Erin's thoughts were far away. She wasn't paying much attention to anything going on around her. Bald Eagle Falls was a sleepy little place. Despite everything that had happened since Erin had arrived to claim her inheritance, it was still a quiet town. Not the kind of place where you expected to find murder or kidnapping. And certainly not more than once.

"Miss Erin."

Erin looked up to see who was calling her. She saw the figure waving, and her heart skipped a beat. She almost ran to him. Then she realized it wasn't Joshua. His face was too old. It was his brother, Campbell.

They had similar builds and features. Erin often had to look twice before she was sure which of them she was seeing. She took a deep breath to calm herself and then walked toward Campbell, trying to smile.

"Cam, it's good to see you."

He swallowed hard and also managed to dredge up a smile.

"You too, Miss Erin." He hovered there for a moment, trying to think of what to say. "I guess... you heard about Josh."

She put her hand over his, worried. "The last I heard was that he's missing."

Campbell nodded, allaying Erin's fears that something worse had happened.

"Yeah." He sighed. "I wish... I wish I could say that he just decided he'd had enough. Like I did. But Josh isn't that sort. We've always had... different perspectives."

Erin nodded. They walked slowly together, toward Erin's house.

"Have you seen your mother?" she asked him.

"Of course." Campbell nodded firmly. "As soon as I could get here... I did. And stopped by to see her."

"Are you going to stay with her until Josh comes back?"

Campbell chewed on a fingernail. "Uh... I don't know. I didn't really plan on staying."

"She needs someone."

"So you say." He looked up at the sky, avoiding Erin's eyes. "But it seems more like... she's pushing everyone away."

"No, don't think that," Erin protested. "She's had a lot of difficult stuff to get through lately, and not everybody has stood by her..."

"I know. I've been through all that stuff too. I know it's different for Mom, because she's Mom... but people who helped—*You*..."

"I understand why she's upset with me. She felt like I'd put Joshua in danger... or into a bad situation. She already thought that before Joshua disappeared. And then with that note..."

"She knows it's not because of anything you've done."

"Did she tell you that? Because that's not what she said to me."

"Well..." He tilted his head uncomfortably. "No. That's not what she said. But she should trust the people who have stood by her. You helped her when I was in trouble. You were the one who was there."

"And the one who went along with Josh in the city," Erin said, not sure whether Campbell even knew that part. "When... I should have talked him out of it. Or called her. I just... I told them that they shouldn't, but everyone else said it was okay."

"You went with him to the city?" Cam repeated, frowning. "What do you mean?"

"When you were... when you had to be here. And Joshua wanted to help you. He wanted to find Brianna and get the real story. So he could get you off."

Joshua and Mary Lou had apparently not told Campbell anything about it. So many family secrets. Even from each other. Erin took a deep breath, looking up the street toward her house.

"It wasn't a good idea," Erin repeated. "But the others insisted on going, so I went along... to try to keep them out of trouble and keep anything from happening."

Campbell looked down at Erin's compact figure. "How could you keep anything from happening?"

"I thought... I could give them advice and they would listen to me. I was the oldest one, so I thought that maybe they would listen." Erin shook her head. She had been wrong. They hadn't listened when it counted.

"So... what happened?" Cam asked. "You couldn't find Brianna, right? Because she was already..."

Erin nodded. "We, uh... went places that Josh said you'd talked about. A couple of... friends. And then this hotel suite. We met Mikhail."

Cam's face grew pale. "What? Mikhail? Not...?"

Erin shrugged. "Mikhail. Mickey. You... didn't know that? Joshua never said anything?"

"No. He probably knows I woulda beat the crap out of him for something like that. He hasn't got a clue what a guy like Mickey could do to him, or order to be done. He's not someone you play games with!"

"Well, he's off the street now. He can't do anything."

Campbell shook his head. "You really believe that?"

"I know he's in jail."

"But there's no way he's going to stay there for long. And even if he does, he can still order or hire guys on the outside. He's not neutralized just because he's 'off the street.'"

"Well... I don't think any of this is because of him, do you?"

Campbell stared off. "I don't know," he said in a distant voice. "No way to tell. Whoever wrote the note mentioned you. And you met Mikhail. He could have blamed you. Sometimes those guys do.

They just obsess over something. It gets under their skin, and they think that it's your fault, even though it's not."

"He was arrested when he came after me. It wasn't exactly... unconnected."

"Sheesh. Has Beaver talked to him? She's got a good relationship with him. He would tell her, I think."

"He would tell her if he put some kind of order out on Joshua?" Erin couldn't keep the incredulity out of her voice. "He wouldn't do that."

"These mobsters follow a different set of rules. He'd probably be proud of the fact. Be glad that she asked." Campbell had picked up his pace. Erin ran behind him, trying to keep up with his long-legged stride. "Do you know where she is?" Campbell asked. He worked his phone out of his pocket and tapped in a number. "Is she in town? At your house? She hangs out with..." Campbell's anxiety was making him flustered.

"I don't know if she's around. You can try her on the phone."

"She hangs out with..."

"Jeremy," Erin filled in. "Vic's older brother."

Campbell snapped his fingers, nodding. "Yeah. That's right." He shook his head. "I can't imagine her with him. He's so much younger."

"I know." Erin agreed. "But it seems to work."

Vic, Erin knew, was not quite so philosophical about it. She was protective of her brother and didn't like the fact that he was spending so much time with a much-older woman, and a federal agent at that. Erin thought Beaver was good for Jeremy. She seemed to keep him out of trouble. For someone who had previously been working for one of the Tennessee syndicates, that was a pretty big deal.

Campbell tapped his phone with his fingernail for a minute before pressing the wake up button and opening the phone app. "Doesn't she know about Joshua and Mikhail? Why isn't she already on top of this? He could have Josh stashed anywhere. He could be..." Cam broke off and shook his head hard. "If Josh was mixed up with Mikhail, then that should have been the first avenue of investigation!"

"I just didn't think... with him being in jail..." Erin protested.

"Being in jail means nothing," Campbell insisted. "That doesn't mean anything to a guy with connections like Mikhail."

Erin didn't say anything. They continued to walk toward her house. Cam made up his mind and put a call through to Beaver.

Beaver had a naturally loud voice. Erin could hear her over the phone, even though Campbell didn't have her on speakerphone.

"Cam. What's up?"

"I want to see you. Where are you now?"

There was a pause before Beaver responded. "I'm in Bald Eagle Falls. What's up?"

"Can we meet? Maybe at Erin Price's house? I'm not that far away."

"You're already in town?"

"My brother's gone missing, what do you think?"

"I think it took you long enough. Why weren't you here the first night he was gone?"

Campbell's face turned red. He looked over at Erin. She pretended that she wasn't listening in on his call and hadn't heard what Beaver had said.

"I didn't know if Mom would want me around. And I... had things I needed to take care of in the city before I left. I can't just drop everything and go, you know."

"I think that you could have if you had been that worried about your brother."

"Okay... well, maybe the first day I wasn't so worried. I thought maybe he just went out and didn't make it home in time. But... he's not the kind that would just take off and stay away this long."

There was another pause while Beaver considered. "If you want to go to Erin's, I can meet you there. How long until you'll be there?"

"Five minutes."

"I'll be longer than that. But I'll be there within the hour."

"Okay," Campbell said curtly. "I'll see you there."

He tapped the phone to end the call and put it back away. He looked at Erin. "I hope you don't mind, Miss Erin. I don't think meeting her at Mom's would be a good idea."

"No, of course not. I don't mind."

It would allow her to listen in on the conversation. Like with Terry and Stayner, it gave her a way to keep track of the police investigation without being accused of stirring things up herself or asking too many questions.

They walked the rest of the way in silence. It wasn't until they got to the house that Cam appeared to notice the bags that Erin was carrying and offered to help her.

"I'm an idiot. I let you carry everything the whole way by yourself."

"It's fine," Erin said, not passing anything over to him. "It's not that much." She juggled everything, trying to find her keys and to fit them into the lock.

"My mom raised me to be a gentleman. She woulda tore a strip off of me if she saw me treating a lady like that."

He was still holding out his hands to take something from her, but Erin ignored him and opened the door. She hit the digits on the burglar alarm and jerked her head to invite him in.

"Come on. I'll just put these things away. Make yourself at home."

Campbell followed her into the house. "Is Officer Piper at work?" he asked. "Does that mean he's doing better now?"

Erin was surprised to hear that Campbell knew anything about Terry's troubles. "He's just off taking care of some other errands today. He worked too much the night that Mary Lou made the report on Joshua, so he's had to take a few days off." She stepped into the kitchen, trying not to trip over the insistent orange cat underfoot. "But yes, he's starting to feel better."

She hoped that he would be able to get back to one hundred percent, but dreaded that he would not. She didn't tell Campbell that. She wouldn't tell anyone that. And if Terry asked her, she would lie and tell him that he was going to get better and be able to go back to exactly the way he had been before the attack.

CHAPTER 17

*E*rin unloaded day-old bread and cookies into the freezer while she waited for Beaver to show up to talk to Campbell. She decided to keep a few out in case her guests wanted a snack, and arranged them on plates.

Beaver didn't take long to arrive. She didn't wait for Erin to let her in, but knocked briskly on the door and walked in without an invitation. She looked around the front room, then nodded at Erin in the kitchen and Campbell, sitting uncomfortably on the couch.

"Cam." She looked him over. "You're looking pretty good."

Cam rubbed his clean-shaven jaw. "Got cleaned up for Mom," he admitted. "Didn't want to have to listen to her fussing over me too. She's got enough to worry about."

Beaver nodded. She looked at the easy chairs, then back into the kitchen at Erin.

"There's bread and cookies on the table," Erin invited. She went to the fridge to get out butter and condiments.

Beaver made an appreciative noise and motioned for Cam to join her in the kitchen. They both sat down at the kitchen table. Erin slid the butter dish and jam jars onto the table.

"I'm afraid we're all out of Jam Lady jam," she apologized. "And I haven't found a new supplier yet, so you'll have to make do with store-bought."

Cam looked down at his hands, his mouth tightening. Erin realized her faux pas in mentioning the Jam Lady brand. The Jam Lady had, in fact, been Roger Cox. And his incarceration was the reason that there would be no more Jam Lady. Unless someone in his family decided to take it up.

"I'm sorry…"

Cam gave his head a little shake. "He made a good jam."

"Yeah. He did."

"He was a good dad, you know. Before…"

"He seemed like a good guy," Erin said. "I only knew him after the accident, but… I know he was trying to make things work and he loved his family."

"Yeah." Cam's mouth twisted into a grimace. "And we all know where that led."

They were quiet for a minute. Beaver hadn't met Roger, but Erin assumed that Cam had probably told her details of what had happened to his father. And Beaver probably had access to some of his records through her job.

Beaver buttered a slice of bread and slathered it with the grocery store jam. After a few minutes of silence, Cam seemed to have managed to compartmentalize his feelings about his father.

"I want to know about Mickey," he said to Beaver, his tone already accusatory. "Haven't you looked into him with Josh's disappearance? To see if he has something to do with it?"

Beaver took a large bite of bread and chewed slowly. "You think I don't know how to do my job?"

"I want to find Josh. I don't care whether you think it's part of your job or not. Mickey can rot in jail for the rest of his life, but if he had something to do with Josh, I want to know about it."

"What makes you think there was anyone else involved in Josh's disappearance? Other than Josh himself?"

"I know he wouldn't leave my mom like that." Campbell scowled. "He's more responsible than I am. He's the baby of the family, so he's closer to her. And I know he wouldn't leave. We've talked about it."

"He told you he would never leave home?"

"No. We talked about whether he wanted to join me in the city. About getting away from school and life here in Bald Eagle Falls." Campbell's eyes went to Erin. "No offense, but it's smothering. I couldn't deal with living here anymore. And it wasn't much easier for Joshua."

Erin shrugged. She hadn't lived there for that long. She liked Bald Eagle Falls, but she knew that it wasn't for everyone. And she knew there were plenty of negatives. It wasn't all rainbows and roses.

"He could still have changed his mind," Beaver observed.

"He didn't write that note."

"It looks like his handwriting. It's not a big enough sample to be absolutely sure, but it's been sent to the experts for their opinion."

"It might look like his writing, but it's not. Josh didn't talk like that. He wouldn't say that. He wouldn't leave Mom. If he left, he would leave her a long letter, apologizing and explaining everything. That's the kind of guy he is. He wouldn't just leave that little sticky note, accusing Miss Erin…"

Beaver cocked her head like a bird. "What?"

"He likes to write. And he worries about other people's feelings. He wouldn't have scribbled that little note. He would have composed a two or three-page letter. Then I would believe it."

"What did you call Erin?"

Campbell looked confused. He looked over at Erin, not understanding. "Erin?" he echoed.

"Miss Erin," Erin corrected.

"Is that what you always call her?" Beaver asked.

Campbell considered. "I don't know. Most of the time. I think."

Beaver thought about this. "That's considered polite in these parts. You're still a kid, and she's an adult. So even if she's a family friend, you still refer to her as Miss."

Campbell nodded.

Erin watched Beaver, wondering where she was going with this. Beaver half-turned in her seat to look at Erin. "Did Joshua call you Miss Erin too?"

"Yes… I think so. Most of the time."

Beaver turned back to the table and took another bite of her bread. "That's not what the note said."

~

Erin looked at Beaver. She tried to picture the note in her mind—the spiky, messy writing.

"What did it say?"

"It said Erin Price."

"Well... that's still right."

"Calling you Miss Erin suggests that you're closer to him. Not a formal relationship or stranger. More of a family relationship. Not as close as auntie, but..."

Erin nodded. "Yes... that's right. I'm friends with Mary Lou, and even though I didn't know the boys well, I still consider them... close."

Campbell's eyes were intent on Beaver. "So, you believe that Josh didn't write the note?"

"I'm not there yet," Beaver warned. She took a couple more bites of her bread, polishing it off, and leaned her chair back on two legs. "Using Erin Price is quite formal. It suggests a distance between the writer and the subject. And perhaps between the writer and who is being addressed. Is there another Erin? Someone else that would require a last name to differentiate them?"

They both shook their heads. Erin couldn't think of any other Erins in Bald Eagle Falls. Maybe there was a younger child by that name, but not someone else that Joshua would have called Miss Erin. There was no reason for him to call her Erin Price instead of Miss Erin, unless he were angry at her for something. That was still a possibility. Had she made some misstep that had upset him? Not wanting to be interviewed about Beryl's murder?

"Cam... he wasn't mad at me, was he? I thought we were still on pretty good terms."

"Mad at you? For what?" Cam shook his head definitively. "No, he wasn't mad at you for something. He was irritated that Mom was still..." He shrugged, not finishing the sentence.

They were all silent for a few minutes. Erin watched Beaver, waiting to see what conclusion she came to.

"One would think that if he had just left of his own accord, that we might have friends coming forward by now to say that he is fine, even if he didn't want to announce where he is," Beaver said eventually.

Campbell nodded vigorously. "I've tried to talk to some of his friends from school. I get it that if he doesn't want to come forward, they would cover for him and not tell where he was. But they'd probably say to just leave him alone and not look for him. But this... they say they don't know. That he never said he was thinking of leaving. He's not the kind to just disappear for a few days at a time like some kids. It's not the kind of thing Joshua would do."

Beaver sighed. She snagged a couple of cookies and spoke through a mouthful. "It's not my case. I'm not involved in any way. But because it's Joshua... I have an interest in it. I'll talk to the PD about it. Float some ideas."

Campbell looked relieved. "Yes. Thank you."

"Doesn't mean anyone will listen to me. They have their own ideas. But I can at least give them some thoughts."

CHAPTER 18

*T*erry was not on duty, but Beaver stuck around until he arrived home from his errands to talk with him.

Erin was worried he looked tired. She knew she was fussing over him, which he hated, especially in front of a fellow law enforcement officer, but she couldn't help herself. He came into the kitchen while she finished making him a sandwich for supper and spoke in a low voice she hoped Beaver wouldn't overhear from the living room.

"You need to give yourself a chance to recover after that night you were up with Mary Lou," she told him. "If you keep spending all of your days working and running around doing other things, you're not going to be able to get caught up, and…" she trailed off. He knew what would happen. He'd finally been able to kick his migraines, and didn't want to trigger another cluster. She didn't want to suggest that he was weak or frail, but they both knew it was a danger. If he could just take care of himself and make sure that he got enough sleep and didn't work too hard, he might be able to stay in good health and not have to take days off due to migraines or other symptoms.

"I'm tired," he told Erin evenly, "but that's all. Just normal tired after a normal day of kicking around and running a few errands. I'm okay, Erin."

"I just don't want you to get sick…"

"I know. And I can take care of myself. I'm telling you, I'm okay. Relax."

They both looked toward the doorway. Erin couldn't see Beaver from where she was standing. She looked down at the sandwich as she handed it to him.

"Thank you." He took it from her.

"Don't stay up too late with Beaver."

"Beaver is not going to stay long." Terry's voice was firm. "I want to spend time with you, not her. I can talk to her tomorrow if we need more time."

Erin's face got warm. "Oh. Okay."

"I'll see what she needs and send her on her way."

Erin nodded. "Okay. I'll just tidy up in here."

She didn't really have much to do in the kitchen, but wanted to be able to listen in on the conversation. Terry gave her a sidelong look.

"Don't you spend too much time working either. You need a chance to rest just as much as I do."

"I don't have much to do."

He nodded and exited the kitchen. He took his sandwich to the coffee table and sat down on the couch.

"Beaver. What's up?"

"Been talking to Erin and Campbell about Joshua," Beaver said succinctly.

"Not your case."

"No. Not my case. But Campbell is my concern and he was upset about it. He wants me to look into the possibility that Mikhail might have had something to do with Josh's disappearance."

"Mikhail?" Terry's voice was clearly disbelieving. "What would he have to do with someone like Joshua? He's not exactly a high-value target."

"It's always possible that he blamed Joshua and Erin for his arrest, and this was one way of getting back at them."

"You don't think that."

"No," Beaver agreed.

"The police department thinks that Joshua is probably voluntarily missing. If that's the case... there's no point in us investing a lot of resources into it."

"What are your reasons for believing he's voluntary?"

Terry took a moment to reply. Erin tidied a few dishes into the dishwasher, waiting for his explanation.

"He's a high risk after everything his family has been through, especially with Campbell dropping out and taking off like he did. Makes it far more likely that Joshua would be tempted to do exactly the same thing. He's been having problems with school."

"But he's been working on extra credit work to bring his marks up."

"Yeah. But he might have just found that to be too much. Campbell burned out trying to do everything—working and keeping up with his marks at school, sports teams, home, and family responsibilities. It's not a stretch that Joshua hoped to do what Campbell couldn't, but in the end, he decided he just wanted to get out."

"You've interviewed his friends? What do they say?"

"They don't know where he would have gone. But that doesn't mean anything. Just that he didn't tell them what his plans were."

"What else?"

"What else?" Terry's breath whistled out. "There's no indication of break and enter. There's no sign of violence. No ransom note. The note that was left for Mary Lou wasn't looking for ransom and appears to be written in Joshua's own hand. None of that points to abduction."

"Was there anything about the note that struck you as being off?"

Terry cleared his throat. "Well... I did find it a little surprising."

"In what way?"

"The fact that he would mention or try to throw suspicion on Erin. Josh is a decent kid. Not the kind I think would try to cause his mother extra worry. And he was on good terms with Erin. There is no reason I can find for him to want to smear her reputation and make Mary Lou angry at her."

"From what Campbell says, Josh was upset that Mary Lou was angry with Erin."

P.D. WORKMAN

"I wouldn't be surprised. Mary Lou is someone who doesn't usually get riled up... I was a little surprised myself that it has lasted this long."

"Josh didn't discuss that with you?"

"No. But he was by to see Erin more than once. If he agreed with his mother and thought that she was responsible for the police department's investigation of him back in December, why would he visit her? As far as I know, he was expressly forbidden from seeing Erin, but did it anyway."

"So why would he put her back into the crosshairs by implicating her in a note?"

Terry grunted. "Exactly."

"Did it surprise you that he referred to her as Erin Price in the note?"

"No... why?"

"Was that how he usually referred to her? Addressed her?"

"No, but it is her name."

"You don't think it would have been more natural for him to refer to her as Miss Erin or just Erin?"

"I guess so. But if he was trying to make it sound like a third party had written the note, then it would be normal to refer to her as Erin Price. A stranger wouldn't refer to her familiarly."

Beaver readjusted her position. Erin could see her through the doorway. She had put her feet up against the edge of the coffee table. "So, what would your instinct be? Written by Joshua to sound like it was a third party, or written by an actual third party?"

"It is similar to his handwriting."

"Similar doesn't establish that it's the same writer. Even with expert analysis, which you don't have yet. Could it be someone trying to imitate his handwriting, or who just happened to have similar handwriting?"

"Of course," Terry admitted. "In fact, I wondered whether the brothers had similar writing styles."

Beaver made a sucking noise, considering this. She pulled a package of gum out of her pocket and folded several pieces into her mouth at once. She chomped for a few minutes before responding to this.

"What is your scenario if it was Campbell who wrote the note? He came to rescue his brother? To take him out for a drink? And then what happened? It went sideways. Something happened to Josh and Campbell doesn't want anyone to know? Or Josh truly wanted to disappear to where no one could find him?"

"Hmm. I don't really like any of those."

"Then you still think Joshua wrote the note."

"Yes... I think the simplest solution is the most likely."

"And that Campbell didn't have anything to do with it."

"That no one else had anything to do with it. Just one teen who didn't realize what kind of trouble he was going to cause."

"And who still doesn't know what trouble he's caused? Or who is afraid to come forward and straighten it out?"

"Probably doesn't even know. It's not like it's been in the papers or on TV."

Beaver cracked her gum. "I'm going to talk to the sheriff tomorrow. Ask him to consider the possibility that it was a kidnapping."

"Well... that's your right. Do you really think he was kidnapped? Or you're just letting Campbell talk you into it?"

"There are inconsistencies. I don't like them. The more I hear, the less I like them."

"If it was an abduction... we're in trouble. We're already past the first forty-eight hours."

"Yes," Beaver agreed grimly.

"You think that Mikhail's syndicate was involved?"

"It's not the Russians' style, but I think I need to look into it anyway. It's an open loop that needs to be closed."

"Okay. Well... if I'm going to get called in tomorrow, I'd better get to bed in good time tonight." Erin heard Terry get to his feet.

Beaver pulled her feet back from the coffee table, letting each of them fall to the floor with a thump. "A pleasure as always, Officer Piper."

Erin moved to the doorway of the kitchen as they shook hands, and Beaver headed to the door.

"Thank you for the cookies, Miss Erin."

"Any time."

As Beaver walked out of the house, Terry turned back to Erin. "There are cookies?"

Erin laughed. "There are always cookies."

She went to the freezer to get a couple out for him.

CHAPTER 19

*J*oshua was growing accustomed to his imprisonment. He didn't wake up expecting to be free. He remembered from one awakening to the next that he needed to be quiet and still and speak respectfully to his captor.

This time there was a smell. Not the rank smell of the room he was being kept in or his own body. Something that smelled warm and enticing. His stomach, previously fallen into a sort of a dormant state, growled and made itself known.

Food. There was food somewhere close by.

He wasn't able to see where his captor came in from, but could sense him getting closer. Josh pressed his lips together, not wanting to make any extra noise because of the smell, but it was so entrancing, it took all of his willpower not to moan out loud.

The shadows of the figure separated from the surrounding darkness. Joshua's world shifted as the figure sat close to him. He tried to grab something to prevent himself from falling, before realizing that he was still bound and unable to grasp anything, even if he could see it. As the world stabilized, he realized that he must be on a bed, and the dark figure had sat down on the bed, making it sink under his weight.

Joshua remained frozen for a few minutes until he was sure that nothing else was going to move and that he was not going to fall.

"Something for you to eat," the familiar whisper informed him.

Joshua blinked, trying to see through the darkness to see what it was. The figure was making small movements. Joshua heard a spoon scrape across the bottom of a bowl. He started salivating in response, even though he'd thought he didn't have any more spit left in him.

The figure brought a spoon up slowly to Joshua's mouth, perhaps remembering how he'd misjudged distance with the water. Joshua opened his mouth early to make sure that none of the precious food would be wasted.

It was soup. Warm, nourishing chicken soup. Joshua couldn't close his lips properly, they were so cracked and swollen. He slurped, trying to get every last drop without any spilling. The spoon returned to the bowl for another spoonful.

He couldn't believe that he was going to get more than one spoonful. It seemed like an embarrassment of riches. He'd never known that food could taste so good and be so satisfying. Just one spoonful had been enough to change everything.

He ate the next bite, and the next. They kept coming.

He didn't ask for water. He didn't ask his captor any questions about where he was or why he was there, or why his hands had been bound. He didn't know what the shadow shape wanted, other than for Joshua to be quiet and compliant. And it didn't matter.

As long as he got soup.

By the time the spoon was scraping across the bottom of the bowl for every spoonful, his stomach hurt. It felt full to bursting. But he was determined not to say that he was full. He would get every drop he could, no matter how big and bloated his belly got from the soup.

"That's it," the whisperer said.

Joshua swallowed once more, grateful for the way that soup had soothed his raw, dry throat. "Thank you."

"You liked it?"

"Yes, it was wonderful."

"It's an old family recipe."

Joshua breathed in and out a few times. "That's the best kind of recipe."

"Yes, you're right." There was silence for a few moments. "Do you cook?"

Joshua cleared his throat, not sure how much he was going to be able to talk. He hadn't used his voice for several wakenings, though he didn't know what kind of period that covered. It seemed like a long time.

"I cook a little. My mom doesn't always have time and we try to help out." He swallowed. His tongue and his tonsils still felt swollen, hard to speak around. "My dad... he was a good cook."

"What happened to him?"

Joshua wondered if it was a test of his honesty. Everyone in Bald Eagle Falls knew what had happened to Roger. "He's... in a place now. For people with... he has a brain injury. He was... a danger to others."

"That must be hard."

"Yeah. It is. But it's easier than when he was at home, and we had to keep track of him, try to make sure that he didn't wander off. And to... try to keep him calm." Another difficult swallow. "He had... moods."

"He hit you," the figure guessed.

"He... he never hurt us on purpose."

A derisive snort from his captor. "Sure."

"He had a brain injury. It changed things."

His captor covered the empty bowl, obviously preparing to get up and leave.

"Can you... stay for a few more minutes?" Joshua asked.

The reflective surface of the goggles turned toward him. "Why?"

"I just... I miss people. I like having someone here for a bit."

The shadowy figure stayed by him, but didn't continue the conversation. Eventually, Josh's eyes started to close. He tried to keep himself alert, looking for something else to talk about or another way to keep himself awake.

But he was too afraid of how the figure would respond if he started asking questions or did something unexpected. Eventually, he lost the battle against his body and drifted off to sleep.

CHAPTER 20

*E*rin's mind was finally at ease, sure that the police department would now put all of their resources into finding Joshua. Was it just her nature that made her want to fix everything, or was it because her name had been mentioned in the note? Either way, she felt like it was her responsibility to find Josh, or at least to convince the police that he had really been the victim and was not just a runaway.

Maybe it was because when she was a runaway, people had found her and brought her back. Until she was old enough that no one cared to look for her anymore. Right around the time she was Joshua's age. Things had subtly changed at that point. Even though she hadn't yet aged out of foster care, officials were more inclined to shrug their shoulders and say she was old enough to decide where she wanted to be.

Even if she didn't know where she wanted to be, just that she needed to be somewhere else. Somewhere safe.

Terry would find Josh. Or the sheriff or the FBI or one of the other officers would turn up a vital clue that would lead them to Josh. And they would take him home to Mary Lou.

Josh was still wanted.

Erin was more cheerful, mixing her batters and doughs and

preparing the sweet and savory treats for Auntie Clem's loyal customers. She felt generous and benevolent toward them, willing to look past their minor failings. She liked Bald Eagle Falls. She loved Auntie Clem's and her employees and her customers. Things were looking up.

She put a couple of items on sale just for the heck of it. She always carefully planned and advertised her promotions, so the spontaneous sale made Vic raise her eyebrows in surprise.

"Okay… that's nice. That will make people happy."

Erin nodded cheerfully. "I hope so. I'm feeling very philanthropic today."

"Philanthropic. Well, there's a five-dollar word."

Erin just smiled.

If Charley came in, Erin might even give her a free muffin for once.

"We should take some treats over to the police department today."

"Sure. Since you're feeling philanthropic," Vic agreed.

Erin grabbed a box and retreated to the kitchen to fill it with cookies set out on the cooling racks. They were still warm from the oven, but cool enough to be handled without falling apart.

"Do you mind if I run these over?" she asked Vic.

"You're in charge! You can do what you like."

"You don't mind handling things for a few minutes."

"Not at all. Go ahead. Things won't pick up for another hour."

Erin nodded her agreement. She set out toward the town hall to take her gift to the police department. They would need a calorie boost to kick their brains into high gear to solve Joshua's case. She would do everything she could to help them do that.

She was happy and feeling good about herself and the bakery when she returned. There were a few more customers than she had expected, so it was a good thing she had arrived back when she did to help Vic out.

There was a knot of women talking among themselves, not standing in line or checking out the products in the display case. Erin approached them, wondering what the excitement was about.

She saw a familiar neat figure with gray hair. Mary Lou hadn't been in the bakery since Christmas. Erin smiled, pleased. Maybe Mary Lou had heard that the police were now investigating Joshua's disappearance as a possible abduction, and so had forgiven Erin for being mentioned in the note.

Mary Lou had the remains of a fortune cookie in her hand. Erin looked down at it, puzzled. Mary Lou's mouth was a slash of scarlet lipstick across her perfectly white complexion. Not smiling.

No forgiveness, then.

Erin glanced over at Vic, hoping for a clue before she stepped right into something. Vic's mouth was open slightly, but she didn't explain. It took a lot for Vic to be at a loss for words. She always knew the right things to say.

Mary Lou looked Erin in the eye, her own eyes blazing.

"Explain *this*."

Erin looked down at the fortune cookie. She wasn't sure what she was supposed to explain. Mary Lou obviously knew what a fortune cookie was, she didn't need to explain that.

Explain the fact that she was now supplying the Chinese restaurant with gluten-free fortune cookies? Erin didn't know why Mary Lou would care about that. Whether the Chinese restaurant had gluten or gluten-free cookies didn't make any difference to her, did it?

Mary Lou held up the printed fortune from the cookie. It took Erin a minute to focus on the small lettering.

You are never going to find him.

CHAPTER 21

*E*rin gasped in shock. It was a good thing that she had already delivered the cookies to the police department, because she would have dropped anything that she was holding on to the minute she read that fortune and it sank into her brain.

"What? Where did that come from?"

"Where did it come from?" Mary Lou repeated, looking like she had tasted something horrible. "Why don't you explain that to me?"

"I… I don't know." Erin shook her head. "That's not one of ours. That's not one of the fortunes we had printed."

Mary Lou displaced the broken bits of fortune cookie in her hand. "This is one of your cookies. One of your gluten-free fortune cookies."

Erin looked down at it. The texture and color were slightly different from a regular fortune cookie. Not enough that a casual observer would have noticed, but Erin had worked hard on that recipe and had folded dozens of the fortune cookies to be delivered to the Chinese restaurant. If she looked at it really closely, she might be able to tell whether she had folded it or whether one of her employees had.

"Yes," she agreed faintly. "It's one of mine. But that's not one of the fortunes that we put in them."

"Then how do you think it got there?" Mary Lou demanded. "It didn't just crawl in there on its own."

Erin looked for an explanation. Someone had clearly tampered with one of her fortune cookies. How would they do that? Was it possible to remove the fortune that Erin or her staff had inserted and to place another one in its place? It was a possibility, but it wouldn't have been easy. And doing any number of them would have been impossible—one or two, perhaps, but not a dozen.

"Is this... the only one? Where did you get it? Who gave it to you?"

Mary Lou looked surprised at the questions. She pursed her lips to answer, then shook her head. "They're your cookies. You put the fortunes in them. You put a fortune inside this cookie that would get back to me. Saying that I would never find Joshua. I thought you were my friend at one time, Erin. I can't believe you would stoop so low. I can't believe you would want to hurt me like this."

"I didn't. I swear, Mary Lou. I wouldn't do something like that. I don't know what happened, but it wasn't me. I'm just as shocked as you are."

"No, I don't think you could be as shocked as I am. I don't understand why you are doing this. *Did* you have something to do with Josh disappearing? Or are you just taking advantage of what happened to get back at me?"

"No. Get back at you for what? No. I didn't do this."

"Because I accused you of being involved in Joshua's disappearance. You decided to do something that would hurt me. Even worse than him disappearing in the first place. You wanted to rip my heart out."

Tears spilled out of Erin's eyes. "No. No, Mary Lou." She tried to take Mary Lou's hands to reassure her. Somehow, physical contact would communicate to Mary Lou that Erin would never do something like that. "Please, please. No. I wouldn't do anything to hurt you."

Mary Lou jerked back, avoiding her touch. "I'm reporting this to the police. I don't suppose there is anything I can charge you with, but they will have to investigate whether it is actually related to Joshua's disappearance."

Erin nodded. She didn't know what else to say. Who could have replaced the fortune in the fortune cookie? How would they have made sure that Mary Lou got it, and why would they do such a thing?

Whoever had left the note for Mary Lou and had arranged for the fortune to be changed was trying to drive a wedge between Erin and Mary Lou. Looking at Mary Lou's face, Erin doubted they would ever be able to be friends again. Even if they found Joshua. Even if they proved that Erin didn't have anything to do with his abduction or disappearance, she didn't see Mary Lou ever trusting her again.

Everything after that moment was a blur. Erin would never be able to forget how Mary Lou looked as she stood there and accused Erin of changing the fortune and trying to rip her heart out. Until the day she died, it would remain clear in her memory.

Mary Lou thought it was telling that Erin had just been over to the police department. She sneered and insinuated that Erin was trying to ingratiate herself with the police or to influence the direction of their investigation.

It was unfair when Erin had been trying all along to get the police to investigate it as an abduction instead of a runaway. She had been Mary Lou's greatest advocate.

Within the hour, Sheriff Wilmot and Stayner arrived at the bakery looking grim.

"We're going to have to shut down Auntie Clem's to investigate, Miss Price," Stayner informed her.

"But... I didn't have anything to do with this. Not with changing the fortunes in the fortune cookies or with Joshua's disappearance. You know that. I've been trying to get the police to investigate, not the other way around."

"On the surface, it would appear that someone at Auntie Clem's

Bakery might have been complicit in the kidnapping of a minor. Maybe only after the fact, but you know we have to check it out."

"I'll show you my records."

"That's appreciated," the sheriff said. "But we're going to need more than that. We're going to need to complete our own investigation, unimpaired. I suggest that you close for the rest of the afternoon and give us the run of the place. You should be able to reopen again in the morning. If you're going to insist on a warrant, then it's going to be closed for longer while we get the official paperwork."

One afternoon wasn't that bad. And not even all of one afternoon. Erin wanted to fight it to assert her rights as a citizen and business owner, hoping that they wouldn't be able to get a warrant on such thin evidence. But she would be better off cooperating.

Maybe Mary Lou would see that she was doing everything she could to help. The police would know that she hadn't been involved in the substitution of the fortune in Mary Lou's cookie or in Joshua's kidnapping.

And maybe they would find something that would help in the investigation. Something that would point back to the actual criminal in the case.

Stayner and the sheriff waited for her decision. Erin rubbed her temples.

"Okay. Of course. I'll close the bakery. It's just... yes. Vic, we'll start cleaning up." Erin looked at the small group of women gathered in front of the counter. "I'm sorry, ladies, you're going to have to go. If you come back tomorrow..."

She suspected that they weren't going to buy anything anyway. They had been attracted by the drama. Perhaps they had come from the Chinese restaurant when Mary Lou had opened her cookie to see what was going to happen.

Erin herded the women out the door and flipped the sign over to 'closed.' She walked around the counter to join Vic and get started on the closing procedures.

"We would appreciate it if you would just leave everything as it is," Sheriff Wilmot advised. "It would be better if you didn't touch anything."

Erin stood there at a loss. She stared at the sheriff. "But I need to... we need to cash out, and clean up, and get tomorrow's batters prepared so we're ready to start baking in the morning. Some of these batters need to soak for a few hours for the best texture."

"We'll get done as quickly as we can, and maybe you'll be able to come back tonight and finish up. But right now... we want everything left as is."

Erin looked at Vic. Vic nodded encouragingly. "We'd better go, hon."

Erin moved like a zombie, taking off her apron and hanging it up, grabbing her purse, and thinking through what the police were going to do.

"I can show you the order for the fortune cookies... everyone helped make them..."

When had the rogue fortune been inserted in the cookie? At the Chinese restaurant? When the cookies were originally prepared? Erin had merely glanced at the pile of white paper strips she had received back from the printer. Had someone swapped them at the bakery?

"And there are more fortunes here, we didn't use all of them. You can compare..."

"We can find everything. If you'll just make sure the computer is unlocked. And if I could have a look at your purses before you go, ladies?"

Vic turned to face Sheriff Wilmot, her face white. "Certainly not! I have rights."

"Of course you do," Wilmot agreed. "That's why I'm asking for your permission."

Vic and Erin looked at each other. Erin was ready to hand her purse over to Sheriff Wilmot to check. That was the right thing to do, wasn't it? Vic had encouraged Erin to let them search Auntie Clem's Bakery, but now she was going to balk at having her own property searched?

Finally, Vic gave a little nod. Erin handed her purse over to Wilmot as well. Her face was burning with embarrassment. It was a disorganized mess, as it always was, despite any attempts to keep it tidy and well-organized. And of course, it was well-stocked with feminine items that she didn't want the men pawing through. There were personal notes, makeup, used tissues...

Wilmot handed Erin's purse to Stayner, and held his hand out toward Vic. "Miss Webster?"

Vic reluctantly handed her purse over. "There's a handgun in there," she warned. "I have a permit."

Wilmot nodded.

Erin and Vic stood there watching as Stayner and Wilmot methodically searched their purses. Erin felt almost physical pain as she watched Stayner pull each item out and examine it closely. She had thought that he would just take a quick look, seeing if she had anything related to the fortune cookies inside, making sure that she wasn't walking off with any evidence. But he was very thorough. She hated the violation. She folded her arms across her chest and concentrated on breathing. In and out. Slowly and evenly. Beside her, Vic turned away, unable to watch.

Erin was the opposite. She couldn't tear her eyes away. Like watching an assault and being frozen in place, unable to say or do anything.

It couldn't have been more than a couple of minutes, but it seemed like it went on forever. Stayner took one more look into each of her purse pockets to make sure he hadn't missed anything and handed it to her.

"I'll let you repack. So you can put it back the way you want it."

Erin's face burned. She was sure he must be thinking what a slob she was. And just what had he learned about her as he went through her bag? Her whole life was in there. She didn't store everything on the phone or a planner like some people did. Instead, it was all loose notes and papers in an unruly stack in her purse. Hard to break the bad habits she had established.

Erin started to go through the pile, sorting through miscellaneous papers and throwing out what she didn't need anymore. Getting rid of the tissues and random cough drops or hard candies. Making the rest as neat as possible. Maybe she would start using a planner. She wouldn't have to rewrite as many lists that way.

Wilmot had finished going through Vic's purse. He set it down gently and looked at her. "Do I need to verify whether you have a permit?"

Vic's lips tightened and formed a thin line. "In my wallet."

Vic hadn't been watching, but Erin had, and she knew the sheriff had already gone through Vic's wallet. She tried to give Vic a warning look.

Wilmot picked up the wallet and handed it to Vic. Vic impatiently flicked it open and started going through the card file. She stopped after going through it once and tried again, more slowly. Then a third time, separating cards to look in between. She swallowed.

"It's not here. I do have one! I don't know where it could have gone. I'll have to... get them to send me a replacement, I guess."

"If I do a database search, it will show up?"

"Yeah, of course."

Wilmot nodded. He motioned for Vic to pick up her things. "Please leave the handgun at home until you get your new card."

Vic's face was rosy red. She began packing her things back away without answering.

CHAPTER 22

$\mathcal{T}$erry picked them up from the parking lot behind Auntie Clem's. His expression was serious and he didn't initiate a conversation with them on the way back. When they got back to the house, Erin got out of the truck and looked over at Vic. Vic seemed torn whether to go in with Erin or go around the back to her own loft.

"Can we talk?" she asked.

Erin nodded. "Yes. Sure."

They all went into the house. Terry's eyes moved back and forth between Vic and Erin. "Is this a private discussion?"

Erin raised her brows at Vic inquiringly.

"No." Vic sighed and flopped down into an easy chair. "Neither of us has done anything wrong, and if the police department can get that through their thick skulls, all the better."

"Don't attack Terry," Erin warned. "He wasn't there."

Vic chewed on her lip, a stress behavior Erin hadn't seen in her before. Vic was clearly very upset. "Fine," Vic agreed. "As long as he doesn't give us grief and act like we must have been the ones to mess with Mary Lou's fortune cookie."

Erin rolled her eyes and looked at Terry, giving a small shrug of apology. Terry sat down on the couch and patted the seat next to him for Erin to sit down. She took the seat and Orange Blossom immediately jumped up into her lap. He had been yowling around her feet, but she had ignored him.

"Shh..." She petted the cat and snuggled him close. "The grownups are trying to talk."

Terry looked down at Erin and stroked the cat once. "I guess the sheriff made it over to Auntie Clem's."

"Yep."

"Are you okay?"

"I'm fine." Erin looked over at Vic. "We're fine. But... it's embarrassing. Being treated like we're criminals when we didn't do anything. He shut us down right in front of our customers, saying that he was going to get a warrant if we didn't voluntarily let him search Auntie Clem's. And I couldn't supervise or show him anything, just unlock the computer for him and let them do whatever they want."

Vic nodded. "And they searched our handbags! Like we were shoplifters."

"They just needed to be able to say that they didn't miss anything. They made sure that you couldn't walk out of the bakery with any evidence."

"I don't care why. It was... humiliating. So invasive and demeaning! And I have a gun license!"

Terry raised his brows at her angry tone. "Okay."

"I don't know where it could have gone," Vic said in a more thoughtful tone. "It's not like I take it out of my wallet very often. It just stays there unless someone asks for it."

"You don't remember when you had it out last?" Erin asked.

"No. No idea." Vic frowned, trying to remember. "I don't know... when I bought a replacement gun, I guess. After..." Vic glanced over at Terry, swallowing. "You know, after Mickey."

"Maybe you left it at the store? Is that possible?"

"They would have called me, don't you think? If I left it on the counter?"

"I would think so... maybe you dropped it when you thought

you put it back and no one saw. Or... it got put in the garbage with the bag or box the gun came in."

Vic shook her head. "It doesn't make sense. I don't see how I could have lost it. Unless someone has been in my purse. But who would go into my purse?"

Erin couldn't think of anyone who would have had access to it. Other than Erin or one of the other employees when it was placed in Erin's office for safekeeping.

"I don't know."

"I'm so steamed. That's just the cherry on top of everything else."

Erin scratched at a splash of batter on her pants. Despite her apron, she could never seem to get through a day at Auntie Clem's without something getting on her clothes. "I'm more worried about Mary Lou. You can get your card reissued. But I can't take back what happened to her. On top of Joshua being missing... she just doesn't need something like this."

Vic deflated. "Yeah. I'm being miserable for no reason. She's the real victim here. So what if I misplaced my license?"

"How could this have happened?" Terry asked. "Can you walk me through how the cookies were prepared and how Mary Lou got this... strange fortune?"

Erin nodded. "Yeah, I guess... I can't understand what happened. We got the order for gluten-free fortune cookies from the Chinese restaurant. I got the fortunes printed at the Quiki. It was a big cookie order. They keep forever. So... we had everyone working on baking and folding small batches over a few days. You have to fold them while they're still warm, so you can't just do a great big batch and fold them over a few hours or days."

"Who is 'everyone'?"

Erin shrugged. "Everyone. All of the employees. Everyone wanted to try their hand because it's such a unique item. Most people never get the chance to make fortune cookies."

"So it could have been done by any of your employees."

"I guess. But... I can't imagine anyone doing that. Sneaking a different fortune into the bunch. And how would they know... how would they make sure that Mary Lou got the wrong one? Or the right one, I mean."

Terry pursed his lips. "Okay. So what do you think happened?"

"I think… someone must have done it at the restaurant."

"How would they do that?"

"I think… just pull out the fortune that was already in the cookie and then… feed a new one in through the crack into the cookie…"

"Would that have been easy?"

Erin shook her head. "I never tried it. I guess if it was a big enough crack. Or you folded the fortune in half. The fortunes aren't supposed to be folded. But you could."

"So for someone to give Mary Lou that particular cookie, they would have to see her at the restaurant, swap out the fortune, and take that one to her."

"Yeah. And if she was eating with other people… she was at the bakery with other women, I don't know if they were all eating together or if they just… gathered because of the spectacle."

"Then how would anyone make sure that she got that particular cookie?"

Erin nodded.

"Maybe it was someone who was eating with her," Vic suggested. "They took one of the cookies, did a little sleight of hand, and gave her the swapped one."

That sounded a little better to Erin. At least if the fortune had been swapped by a restaurant worker or by someone in Mary Lou's dinner party, that took Erin and her employees off the hook.

"That seems a little complex to be doing at the table," Terry said doubtfully.

"Well then…" Vic stared off into space. "They could have taken a fortune cookie home without eating it, and then replaced the fortune at home. Then go out to lunch with Mary Lou, and pass the swapped fortune cookie to her."

"That's possible," Erin agreed. "Someone could do that."

"Possible," Terry agreed. "You are avoiding the possibility that it could be one of your employees, though. Who had a motive to replace the fortune?"

"It couldn't have been someone at the bakery," Erin insisted. "There would be no way to get the replaced fortune to Mary Lou. Someone had to give it to her at the restaurant."

"What if it wasn't targeted," Vic mused. "What if it's only coincidence that it got to Mary Lou?"

Erin didn't need that kind of help. She glared at Vic, mentally urging her to move to another possibility.

"It had to be targeted to Mary Lou," Terry objected. "It wouldn't mean anything to anyone else."

"Sure it would," Vic argued. "This is Bald Eagles Falls. Everybody knows that Joshua is missing. Anyone who got that fortune would wonder if it was about him and take it to the police."

"That's too big of a coincidence to be believed," Terry objected. "I can write off a small coincidence. But that one fortune was swapped and Mary Lou just happened to get it? I don't believe that."

"She likes Chinese." Vic leaned forward in her seat, trying to explain it away. "She eats at the Chinese restaurant, so she would have a better chance at getting that fortune cookie."

Even Erin couldn't believe that. "The switch can't have been made at Auntie Clem's," she insisted. "It had to be at the restaurant."

CHAPTER 23

*J*oshua wasn't sure how long he had been trying to wake up. He'd been having dreams of waking up. Every time, something bad happened. He couldn't open his eyes. He walked into traffic. He was forced to do something to hurt someone else. He couldn't find the bathroom.

He was pretty sure his brain had been trying to wake him up for some time, but his body wasn't ready to get up.

He shifted back and forth restlessly. He was hot and clammy, sweat standing out on his forehead and temples and running down his back in the occasional cold drip.

He tried to raise his arms enough to wipe his face, and managed to wipe part of his head along his sleeve, mopping up the sweat. But it wasn't long before his face was coated with sweat again.

Eventually, he opened his eyes.

Things weren't much different with his eyes open instead of closed. He still couldn't see anything, just shadows in the darkness.

"Is anyone there?" he asked in a soft voice, reaching out mentally into the darkness, trying to feel someone there. Or not there. He should be able to tell whether the figure was watching him or not. But the air seemed empty and still. How long had he been lying there?

P.D. WORKMAN

He held his wrists in the best lighting he could find and moved his head down to study the bonds.

Just zip ties. Nothing fancy or recognizable about them. They were crusted with blood and his fingers were swollen like sausages. Joshua opened and closed his hands a few times, looking at them. They were numb. He felt like they belonged to someone else. How long had they been tied? Were the zip ties cutting off his circulation? If they were, how long before he would be in danger of losing his hands?

And his feet. Joshua rolled onto his side and pulled his feet up, trying to get a peek at them. But his pant legs were gathered around the bond and it was impossible to see how they were tied or what kind of condition they were in. Like his hands, his feet were numb. And his legs too, for that matter.

He wasn't sure he wanted to live if he were going to lose his hands and his legs. That would be too much.

He looked around him, trying to make sense of the slightly lighter shadows around him. How long had he been in the dark? There was too little light for his eyes to adjust. He would need to be a cat to make out anything around him. Or be wearing night-vision goggles. Maybe when his captor came around for a visit, Joshua could ask to borrow the goggles for a few minutes. Just so he could see what it was like to wear them. Then he would give them back.

He thought he heard a far-off click. Joshua strained to hear anything else. He was lucky that the place he was being held seemed to be free of rats.

Or if they were biting his fingers or toes, he was lucky he couldn't feel them. He studied his hands an inch from his face again. He didn't see any marks that would suggest rats had been anywhere near them. That was a relief. At least if he were found, his family wouldn't have to see anything gruesome.

There was another rustle of sound, and Joshua watched the shadows for any shifts in density.

"Are you there?" he whispered.

His captor didn't answer but, in a minute, stood before him. Joshua didn't say anything, waiting. More food? Water?

"They're never going to find you," the dark figure said.

Joshua's stomach tightened. He had already suspected this. Whoever had taken him away had hidden Joshua too well for anyone to find him. He had no idea whether he was in a warehouse or some other kind of storage unit. No idea whether he was close to home or far away, in the town, the country, or the city. Even if someone from his family had been able to contact him, he wouldn't be able to tell them where to go. Not even a clue, like they often gave on TV. A train going over the railway tracks. Chapel bells. Traffic sounds. He couldn't hear anything outside the room.

"Why did you do this?" Joshua asked.

It wasn't a demand this time. Not something he shouted at the top of his lungs or hurled out as an accusation. He just wanted to know. What was the point of it all? Was it because of something he had done? Some fatal misstep in the past? A girl he hadn't paid attention to or a boy he had beaten in grades or some sport? It wasn't like Josh had even done that well in school. Not lately.

"I needed to put a stop to it," the shadow whispered. "I couldn't think of any other way to stop it."

"Stop what? What did I do?"

"I needed some time. Some space. People were getting too close."

Too close. Josh closed his eyes, thinking. Too close to what? Physically too close to the hooded figure, infringing on his personal space? Town development getting too close to his farm? Or something else?

Too close to what?

"You don't know what it's like," the shadow hissed at him. "You live in a whole different world."

Josh tried to puzzle through this. But the half-clues were not helping him. He didn't want to die without even knowing why.

"I'm not feeling well."

The hooded figure didn't answer for a few minutes.

"Don't feel well how?" he asked after a few minutes.

"I just... I'm so tired and sore. And..." He used his arm to wipe his face again. "I'm hot. I don't know... if it's a fever."

The figure reached out and touched him, but the hands wore

medical gloves, so he didn't know how that would help him figure out whether Joshua really was sick.

The hand touched his forehead, then his cheek. The hand grasped one of Joshua's numb hands and raised them to study the ties and wrists as Joshua had done.

He released Joshua's hand and moved down to his feet, checking them out as well.

"Does everything look okay?" Josh asked. He didn't want to be surprised. If he were seriously ill, he wanted to be prepared.

"Looks fine to me," the shadow told him without emotion.

Did that really mean he was okay? Or did the shadow just not care?

"What do you want? Is there... some way I can get you to let me go?"

"No. There's nothing you could do."

"I want to do something. Isn't there anything?" Josh didn't want to suggest anything specific, but he worried that it was something to do with Campbell. Had Campbell cheated Josh's captor out of money or product? If Joshua could just do something to make up for it, to pay the captor back, he would. He would do almost anything. He didn't care if it were illegal or unethical. People would understand that it was a matter of pleasing his captor or dying. They would understand.

"You've already done enough."

That made it sound like it wasn't Campbell's fault that Joshua was there, but his own. Something that he had done. But what could he have done? He was a kid. And he wasn't involved in anything he shouldn't be. He went to school and tried to get his schoolwork done. He tried to do chores at home and to work part time to contribute to the household income. And when Mary Lou was not going to be home to make dinner, Joshua tried to help out. Too often, he didn't have anything on the table by the time Mary Lou got home. But he tried.

"What did I do?" he begged. "What can I do to make up for it? Isn't there anything I can do to... get out of here?" He swallowed. "I promise I won't turn on you. I won't tell anyone anything I know. I'll help you. And then I'll say I escaped. That I don't know anything. No one will ever know anything."

"It's time for me to go." The figure made a looking-at-his-watch gesture, though Joshua couldn't see anything on his wrist. But maybe there was and his captor could see it with the goggles.

"Is there… did you bring anything to eat?"

The shadow patted pockets in various locations on his body. He had obviously not come prepared to feed Josh. Maybe hoping that Joshua would have fainted with hunger by now.

There was a crinkle in one pocket, and the figure pulled it out. "A cookie," he whispered. "But it's broken up in pieces." He made to put it back in his pocket.

"No. I'll eat it. Please."

His captor considered it for a few moments, then shrugged. He wrestled with the plastic wrapper and managed to get it open. Josh's hands were out of commission, so it was the figure's job to get the pieces of cookie into Josh's mouth.

One at a time, the shadow put little bits of the crispy, bland cookie into Josh's mouth. He didn't have much saliva to moisten it and get it down, but he did his best. He had to do everything he could to get some sustenance into his system.

"That's all." The whisperer crumpled the plastic wrapper and shoved it back into his pocket.

"That soup was so good. Do you think you could bring me some more?"

"No."

Josh tried to swallow the lump in his throat. He had expected a 'maybe' or 'if I can,' not a flat-out no. Didn't his captor think it worthwhile even to string Joshua along? Make him at least think he was going to get fed again?

His eyes stung. He didn't cry. He probably couldn't spare any of his body's moisture for tears. But he was crushed by the denial. The figure intended to let him die. That much was pretty clear.

"Can I… can I write a note to my mom? Or make a recording? Anything?"

"Why would I let you do that?" The whisper was an angry hiss.

"Because... I never got to say goodbye. I'd like to say goodbye."

"People don't get to say goodbye. Lots of people leave or die without ever saying goodbye first. You should know what that is like."

CHAPTER 24

*E*rin stared out at the night. It was late. She should have been asleep already. She would be tired at the bakery the next day if she didn't get the sleep she needed.

But how could she go to sleep when Joshua was still out there somewhere? It had been too long. The longer it took them to track him down, the less likely it would be that they would find him alive and unharmed. She hated to think of him out there, alone and scared.

The police were now intent on finding out who had swapped the fortunes. But it seemed like a mistake to Erin for them to be so concerned about the fortune. It could have been a prank. It could be completely unrelated to Joshua's disappearance. Maybe, as Vic had said, it was never the intention of the fortune-swapper to send the swapped fortune to Mary Lou. If it were just a coincidence, they were wasting their time trying to catch someone who had not even committed a crime.

Erin needed more. There had to be a reason for kidnapping Joshua. It wasn't just random. Not when they had either gone into his house or somehow lured him out in the middle of the night. Someone had gone there intending to take him. And that person had to have a motive.

What?

If they had something against Erin, as implied by the note, why had they taken Josh? Why hadn't they taken Erin herself? Or done something to hurt her—either physically or by hurting someone close to her. Terry or Vic or one of the animals. Joshua was a friend, but they hadn't been that close. She knew him to talk to, but they hadn't shared a lot. Not like with her closest friends. If the kidnapper's motive was to upset Erin or make things difficult for her, there were much more direct ways to do so.

Terry cracked open the door to look at her, then pushed the door open the rest of the way. "What are you still doing up? You're not waiting for me, are you?"

"No… just thinking."

"Do you need anything? You should be getting to sleep so you can get up in the morning."

Erin sighed. "I know. I just can't stop worrying."

"About Joshua?"

"Of course."

"There isn't anything you can do. I know you would like to, but there are only so many avenues to investigate. The police department is looking into them. Beaver and the sheriff are getting the FBI involved as well, in case it was something to do with Mickey, so there will be more manpower on the case. Everyone is doing everything they can. It isn't up to you."

"But I can't *not* be worried about it. Joshua is my friend. My friend's son. And Mary Lou thinks that I had something to do with his disappearance. Or that I'm making it worse. Those fortune cookies… if someone wanted to implicate me in all of this…"

"They couldn't have done much better than to swap the fortunes," Terry finished. He looked at her thoughtfully. "Mary Lou knew that you were supplying the fortune cookies to the Chinese restaurant?"

"I don't know if she knew anything about it. But when she got one, she would have known. There's a note on the menu now that gluten-free fortune cookies are supplied by Auntie Clem's Bakery. And when they bring you the bill in the little tray with the cookies on the tray, there's a little tray liner that says…"

"Compliments of Auntie Clem's Bakery," Terry suggested.

"Something like that, yeah. So… she would have known when she got it that it came from the bakery."

"And then she opens it and sees a message that seems like it was intended just for her."

"Yeah. She was… not very happy."

"No," Terry agreed. "I got that."

Erin was up early as usual the next morning, assuming that the police would be done with the bakery and she would be able to reopen at the regular time. She looked at her phone and found that she had received a text during the night from Sheriff Wilmot.

Have finished with processing the bakery. All yours.

That was considerate of him. Erin didn't have to wonder about whether she would be able to open or not.

But they would have extra cleanup and prep to do since they hadn't been able to run through their usual closing procedure the day before. Erin was going to have to make some adjustments to have the display case filled in the morning and everything ready to go. Less variety than usual. Bigger batches. Maybe some promotional price would attract people's attention and distract them from the fact that the display was plainer than usual. She hadn't had a chance to cash out, so she would have to go with the running totals from the day before and hope that there wouldn't be any large discrepancies. And cleanup. There would be a lot of cleanup, with pans and bowls sitting out for hours with the remnants of batters and doughs drying to them. Ugh.

There was nothing she could do about that.

When Erin got to her kitchen, she was surprised to see that Vic's light was already on. Vic didn't usually get up until some time after Erin, savoring those last few minutes of sleep.

Erin started the kettle and put a couple of slices of bread in the toaster. Before the kettle started whistling, Vic let herself in the back door.

"Morning," she greeted, and smothered a yawn. She was dressed for work, not still in her pajamas as Erin had expected.

"Hi. I'm surprised to see you up so early!"

"I knew you would be worrying," Vic said with a shrug. "You're going to be trying to figure out how to get everything done before opening this morning when we didn't get a chance to close properly last night."

Erin laughed. "Yup. Exactly right."

"So I figured I'd be ready for work as soon as you were, so we can get in a few minutes earlier than usual if we have to."

"You're the best, Vic."

Vic shrugged modestly. "I know."

They both laughed. They moved around each other in the kitchen, used to the routines and anticipating each other's movements. Orange Blossom wound around Erin's legs, seeming like he was trying to trip her up. Even after she fed him, he still wanted attention. Marshmallow was more sedate, watching the morning preparations. K9 hadn't yet put in an appearance. Though he still slept in his crate, Terry usually left it open now. There had been too many close calls. They both wanted K9 to be free in case someone tried to break in.

"How's Nilla?" Erin asked, thinking of the new fluffy white dog that Vic had ended up taking in after Beryl's death.

"Well, you know. Still acting out a little. He hasn't totally destroyed the apartment, but he's not as well-behaved as K9."

"I figured Willie would have him whipped into shape in no time."

"Willie..." Vic's voice was amused, "...is a pushover!"

Erin gasped dramatically. "No! Willie?"

"He spoils Nilla. Feeds him at the table. Tells me not to get after him. Lets him sleep on the bed."

"On the bed?" Erin repeated. She shook her head. "Here I always thought Willie was tough. Disciplined."

"Willie is a puffball. With that dog, anyway."

"Well. I'll have to have a talk with him about how to properly train an animal," Erin said loftily.

Then she yipped as Orange Blossom dug his claws into her leg, trying to get her attention.

"Ouch! Stop that, Blossom. You're supposed to be demonstrating how well-behaved you are."

CHAPTER 25

*E*rin walked into the kitchen, expecting to find it in a complete mess. She knew that the police weren't required to put things to rights after a search, and she knew how much work there normally was to do at the end of the day. Even with a plan in place and arriving earlier than usual, she was still not looking forward to all of the extra work they would have to do.

At first, she thought they must have taken a bunch of her pans and equipment with them as evidence because the counters were clear. She and Vic looked at each other and then started to explore the kitchen to see what was missing. If they had seized her pans, it would make it even harder to reopen in one day. They'd need to go into the city to get all of the replacements she needed.

But a closer inspection revealed that most items were put away in their appropriate slots or drawers. There were a few muffin or loaf pans in the sinks, soaking in water that was now cold, but most of the cleanup they'd been unable to do the evening before had been done.

"Who did this?" Vic demanded, looking around. "Did any of the employees come in last night after they were gone to fix everything up?"

"I don't know." Erin pulled out her phone to look for text

messages or emails that she might have missed. "No one said anything!"

She ducked into her office and looked around. There were no papers scattered around, no drawers left standing open. Even the mug was gone from beside her computer and had apparently been washed and put away.

Erin put in her earbuds as she and Vic started with their morning preparations, so she could place calls with her hands free. She called Sheriff Wilmot's number, planning to leave a voicemail message on his office phone. But it clicked through, and she heard him live on the other end, voice tired and a little clipped.

"Sheriff's."

"Sheriff Wilmot? It's Erin Price."

"Oh, is it that time already?" A pause as he looked at his computer or phone to verify. "I guess it is. I'm just finishing off here and then I'm going to knock off for a few hours. Everything in order there?"

"Yes!" Erin looked around the kitchen, shaking her head. "Did you do all of this? I was so shocked to find everything put away!"

"I helped. Mostly it was Stayner."

"Stayner?" Erin couldn't keep the disbelief out of her voice. She'd always butted heads with Stayner, right from the start. She found him impatient and overbearing. Someone who made assumptions too quickly, was egotistical and didn't have the discernment that he needed to be a really good cop. "He was the one who cleaned up?"

She could see him tearing the place apart, pulling every dish and bowl and mixing spoon out to see if she had anything hidden, but she couldn't see him taking the time to wash all of the dirty bowls and pans and to find their proper places.

"His momma must have raised him right," Wilmot said. "No way he was going to leave your kitchen in a mess."

"Well, please tell him thank you for me. And I'll bake him something nice."

"Will do," the sheriff agreed. "But before you go, Miss Price..."

"Oh." Erin had been about to hang up. She stopped herself. "Yes...?"

"We seized the remainder of the package of fortunes for examination."

"Oh. Well, okay. That's fine." Erin supposed it made sense for him to take some kind of evidence. The fortunes didn't prove anything, except that the fortune Mary Lou had received was not one of the ones Erin had printed. So that was a good thing. It would help convince the police department that Erin hadn't had anything to do with the fortune in Mary Lou's cookie. Even if Mary Lou herself wouldn't believe it.

"What can you tell me about the fortunes you had printed? Where did they come from?"

"We looked for some online. We presented them to the employees, and had everyone vote on them and make suggestions of their own. Eventually, we pared it down to twenty that we liked, and we had the Quiki print them on little slips of paper."

It had been a fun exercise. Erin and Vic had enjoyed going through the suggestions and tallying everything up. In the end, she thought they had ended up with a really good pool of fortunes. They would last for a long time, but when they ran out, they could refresh them, adding some new ones in. People who ate at the Chinese restaurant wouldn't always get the same ones but would see some new fortunes every now and then and stay interested.

"Did you make any changes to the order after you put it in initially?"

Erin frowned to herself as she mixed the batter. Why would she do that? She shook her head. "No. I didn't make any changes. I just gave them the instructions and they let me know when they were ready to be picked up."

"Did you check the order when you picked it up?"

"Yeah."

"How did you check it?"

"Well... I just looked through a few of the fortunes. Made sure that they had printed clearly and weren't cut off."

"How many is a few?"

"A few?"

"You said you checked a few. How many? Two? A dozen? More?"

"I'm not sure. Maybe…three to five. I just pulled a few out, looked at them, and put them back in the bag for later, when we would put them into the cookies."

"And did you check them as you were making the cookies? For quality control?"

"No. I probably looked at a few of them, I don't remember. But not… I wasn't checking each one to make sure that it was perfect." Erin dumped some frozen blueberries into the batter and stirred them gently before starting to scoop batter into cupcake wrappers. "Sheriff… it wasn't really that technical. Everything looked fine. We made the cookies. We delivered them to the restaurant. It wasn't a big thing. I mean, it was a big order, but it wasn't like… it was the moon landing."

"The problem is… Mary Lou's wasn't the only fortune that was… odd."

"Oh." Erin leaned against the counter to steady herself. She pulled her stool closer and sat down. She left the muffins alone for a moment, giving her full attention to the phone. "There were others? Who got them?"

"We opened a number of the cookies at the restaurant and found a few that were strange. Fortunes that could have been referring to Joshua Cox's disappearance. We went through the fortunes remaining in the bag, and a number of them were also… wrong."

CHAPTER 26

*E*rin's head spun "That doesn't make any sense. It had to be someone at the restaurant. No one here would have swapped them."

"Apparently, someone did."

She thought about her employees. Who could have done such a thing? She couldn't think of how anyone would have had the nerve to go into Auntie Clem's and tamper with the fortunes. Had Erin been there while it had happened? How long would something like that take? Had she been out at the front, serving customers while one of her employees excused herself to the kitchen and added the wrong fortunes to the bag Erin had printed?

"No one here would have any reason to do something like that. It must be some kind of mistake."

"We are still investigating."

"I can't understand it. No one here had anything against Joshua." Erin turned and looked at Vic, who was trying to look as though she wasn't listening in on the conversation, and was just putting bread dough into loaf pans as usual. "Vic, no one had any reason to do anything that would hurt Joshua. Or Mary Lou. Right?"

Vic shook her head. "Not that I can think of. But if that's what happened…"

"I don't think that could be what happened. I just can't even picture it. The fortunes were stored in my office. No one went in there."

"Someone could have," Sheriff Wilmot countered, his voice sounding far away. Erin put the phone back up to her ear.

"I would have noticed if someone had been in there."

"Would you? If Miss Victoria had been in there, for example?"

Erin glanced over at Vic. "Well... no."

"And you've never sent an employee in there to get something for you? Or had them stow their valuables in there?"

It was the regular landing pad for purses or backpacks. Out of the kitchen, behind closed doors. Not that it was particularly secure. If people had started to notice things disappearing from their bags, Erin would have locked the door or found a better way to secure them. As it was, everyone just dumped their bags there and pulled the door closed. It kept personal items out of the kitchen. The only people who had access to them were other employees, so it had never been an issue.

"Well... yeah, it's where we put our purses."

"So any employee could have been in there and it wouldn't have seemed out of place."

"At the beginning or end of her shift, yes. But not in the middle of the day."

"An employee would never access her purse in the middle of the day to check her phone or get out... sanitary items?"

"Well..." Of course they would have.

"We don't know what time this substitution took place. I'd like you to think about whether you can narrow the timeframe down. And whether everybody in your shop had access during that time."

"Just the employees."

"Right. I didn't mean the customers. I just want to know if we can eliminate anyone."

Erin sighed unhappily. "Okay. I'll think it over. Thanks."

Erin hung up her phone and looked at Vic. "It couldn't be any of our employees. They've all been just fine... there haven't been any other problems."

"Maybe when they investigate further, they'll find out something that eliminates them. But until then... we're going to have to be more careful."

Erin started making a list in her head of each employee and whether they had a motive to hurt Joshua.

Or Mary Lou.

Or Erin.

Most of the part-time workers at Auntie Clem's Bakery were students. They were fine with just working when they could and not earning a living wage. Most of them were still at home, so their major expenses were covered. They earned what they could to pay for clothes or classes and were happy for the experience. They had stepped up when Erin and Vic had gone on a cruise to Alaska. And when they had judged the cooking contest in Whitewater.

Certainly, none of them had any reason to want to hurt Erin. She paid them. It was because of her that they had been able to find work in Bald Eagle Falls. She and Vic couldn't think of any problem they might have with Joshua, but they didn't know the school politics, so they asked Bella in to pick her brain. Bella was the one who had referred the majority of them in the first place, so she knew them better.

She arrived during the quiet period in the afternoon, when they would be able to talk without being overheard. Bella put on her apron and helped tidy up and put in the afternoon baking so that it wouldn't be obvious that she was only there to talk about the case. And because Bella always helped out. That's what the employees at Auntie Clem's were like. They were like family.

Bella had already heard the basics about the fortune that Mary Lou had found in her fortune cookie, as had everyone else in town. Erin and Vic filled her in on the sheriff's suggestion that the fortunes had not been swapped at the restaurant, but in Erin's office.

Bella shook her head, her big blonde curls bouncing around her face. Her eyes were big and round. "Somebody who worked here? No one would do that!"

"That's what I thought too," Erin agreed. "But... if it was someone who worked here, we need to figure out who it was, or eliminate them, so that the police department doesn't spend all of their time looking into who had access here. That would be a waste and... we don't know how much time Joshua might have."

Bella's blue eyes brimmed with tears. "I can't believe this is happening. I feel so bad for Joshua. I want to find him and bring him home safe. So badly."

"Yeah. We all do. Right now... this is all we can do. Try to help the police out so that they can put their resources into the right places. Not tracking down who at Auntie Clem's could have tampered with those fortunes."

"We don't even know if the fortunes had anything to do with Joshua," Vic pointed out. "It sounds like they're talking about Joshua, but what if they're not? Or what if it is just someone who wants attention, and they're just pretending that it has something to do with Josh? Anybody could have added a few extra fortunes in there, just to see what would happen."

"A prank," Erin said.

"Yes. It could be."

"That's what they said about the note that was left for Mary Lou too. But we know it wasn't a prank. This is serious. We have to assume that the fortunes are serious too. That they are a real clue to... something."

"What did Mary Lou's say?" Bella asked. "I've heard a lot of different stories." She wrinkled her nose. "Some of them pretty nasty."

"It said... that she was never going to find him."

Bella's face was pale. "Man. Talk about cruel. I can't imagine anyone doing that. Especially anyone at Auntie Clem's."

"Everybody has been so good here," Erin said. "I feel guilty in even looking at anyone and asking the question. Is there anyone who... might have had a problem with Joshua at school?"

P.D. WORKMAN

Bella shrugged. "I always liked the Cox boys, Josh especially. Even Campbell was nice to me, though."

"Even Campbell?" Vic repeated.

"Well, he was kind of a jock, you know? Involved in all of the teams? But I never got any grief from him." Bella ducked her head. "He was never one of the ones who would... make fun of me for my weight or anything like that. And Josh wasn't so big on sports, he was more... bookish. More my speed, I guess. We were never that close, but I knew who he was, and he was always nice."

"Maybe he wasn't nice to everyone?" Erin suggested. "Was there anyone he didn't get along with? Or maybe... an ex-girlfriend who might have a beef with him. Anything like that. Maybe a rival. Someone trying to get higher marks than him in school. I know it sounds stupid, but sometimes people do get upset about the littlest things."

Bella pressed her lips together, thinking. She sighed. "We weren't in many classes together. He did good, but I don't remember him competing for top marks."

"And no girlfriend?" Vic prompted.

"No. I don't know if he went out with anyone. There's kind of a core group of kids at the school who date... but Joshua wasn't one of them. Might have taken a girl out for ice cream one day, but... no serious relationships that I know about."

"Someone who wanted to be a girlfriend?" Erin suggested.

"Like a stalker?" Bella asked.

Vic gave Erin a sharp look.

"No. None that I know about," Bella admitted. "I guess I'm not much help here. But Joshua was really pretty quiet. I think he got along good with everyone. I can't think of what anyone would have against him."

"Then maybe he's not the one," Erin said. "Maybe it's Mary Lou." She looked at Vic and Bella, seeking their input.

"Mary Lou." Bella rubbed her face, looking uncomfortable. "I gotta say... I've always been a little bit scared of her."

Erin laughed. "Yeah, I can see that."

"Whenever I talk to her, I feel like she's remembering back when I

130

was four or five and wet my pants at a town picnic. Like she still can't believe that I would have the nerve…"

Vic giggled. Bella glared at her.

"It wasn't supposed to be funny."

"No… but it kind of is. I know exactly the expression you're talking about."

"What does she have on you? I bet you never peed your pants at the picnic."

"Uh… there's the whole transgender thing," Vic pointed out. "I don't suppose you've ever heard her lecture on how being trans is an offense to God."

"Oh, yeah." Bella's face flushed pink. "I didn't even think of that. I'm sorry—I forget sometimes."

Vic grinned. "That suits me just fine. I don't need to be the transgender girl who works at the bakery. I'd rather just be a girl who works at the bakery."

Bella nodded shyly.

"So, Mary Lou," Erin said, trying to bring them back on point. "Do you think it's someone she's hurt or offended? I hate to say it, but I can see her making somebody mad more than Joshua. You don't think that someone is doing this to get back at her, do you?"

"I don't know," Bella said. "I don't think anyone would go from Mary Lou giving her that look to deciding to kidnap Joshua. Especially not anyone at Auntie Clem's."

Erin had to admit that was true. She had seen a lot of things since she had come to Bald Eagle Falls, but as a motive for kidnapping, that sounded pretty weak. Especially someone who had kept Joshua for several days now. Kidnapping was something that needed lots of planning, energy, and follow up. Unless the kidnapper had already gone further than kidnapping and no longer had anyone to look after. Erin didn't want to think about that. Whoever had taken Joshua had to be taking care of him, looking after his daily needs.

"If someone took Joshua… then where is he?" Erin mused. "He would have to be somewhere close by, or someone would notice the kidnapper following a different routine. Right? Everyone knows now about Joshua being missing, and wouldn't someone notice if they were going out of town every day or disappearing for long periods...?"

Vic considered this, nodding. "I guess... but there are lots of places close by that you could keep someone. Old farms, moonshine shacks, caves, mines..."

Erin tried to focus on Bella's face rather than thinking of her own experiences. Bella had been kidnapped and held in a mine, so she knew what that was like, even if it had only been for less than a day. Bella gave a little nod, her expression not changing, but Erin thought she looked a little green.

"Yeah. I guess. Maybe we should ask, though. Whether anyone has gone on vacation or been taking time off work that they normally wouldn't..."

Vic looked in Erin's direction, and she knew that Vic would also be going over their staff list in her head. Was there anyone who had stopped taking shifts recently? Or changed which shifts she was taking. Erin didn't come up with anyone, and Vic must not have either, because she didn't offer anyone.

"I guess we can't exactly ask Mary Lou if she had a problem with anyone in town," Bella said.

"I'm sure the police will have asked her whether she has any enemies. Or whether Joshua does." Erin's chest hurt as she said it. If Mary Lou had given a list of enemies to the police, had Erin headed the list?

CHAPTER 27

*I*t had been a long day. Erin had hoped to get somewhere in her discussion with Vic and Bella. She had hoped that they could identify the kidnapper's motive and point the police department in the right direction, not just to tell them that they were looking in the wrong direction. Erin was sure it could not have been any of her employees, even though the changed fortunes had been found in the bag that she had there. There had to be some other explanation.

As far as they could tell, none of the part-time employees would have any reason to do something to hurt Joshua. And it wasn't for gain since there had been no ransom note. Erin didn't want to believe that something had happened to Joshua to prevent the kidnapper from making a ransom demand.

There was, of course, still Charley. She was Erin's partner in the bakery, and she put in her time too. She had worked several shifts around the right time. It would have been perfectly natural for her to put her purse and other personal items in Erin's office, just like any of the other employees. And if she had been caught going through the fortunes or files or computer in Erin's office, she might be accused of being snoopy, but she had the right to look at any of the financial or electronic records for Auntie Clem's.

But Erin couldn't think of any reason Charley would have for wanting to hurt Joshua or Mary Lou. Or Erin. They were sisters and partners in Auntie Clem's Bakery. It would make no sense for Charley to do anything to jeopardize their relationship. Charley might not get along with Mary Lou. They were both a little prickly and hard to get close to. But Erin hadn't noticed any major issues between the two of them. And Erin couldn't think of whether Charley and Joshua had even met.

She had some fresh, warm cookies that she had made for Stayner. Despite all that she'd had to do that day, she had still held back one tray of cookies and had put it in the oven just before closing so that they would be cooled just enough to transport when she was finished. Willie was picking Vic up, but Erin declined a ride.

"I'm just going to walk over to the police department. I'll give these to Officer Stayner and see whether they've made any progress today."

"We can wait for you," Vic offered.

"No. I don't know how long I'll be. I'll just walk home after."

"Not if it's dark. If it's dark, you call me, okay?"

Erin nodded. It wouldn't be dark for a couple more hours, and she wouldn't be that long. "Sure. Thanks."

"We can drop you at the police department on the way home."

"I'm just going to walk," Erin insisted.

Vic shrugged, giving in. "Guess it won't hurt you to walk a couple of blocks."

Erin waved goodbye and headed out. She was glad for the fresh air and exercise after being at the bakery all day. She didn't get enough exercise, even though she was on her feet all day at the bakery, back and forth between the kitchen and the front counter. It felt good to stretch her legs and feel the sun on her skin.

The police department was tucked away into a suite of offices at the town hall; it didn't have its own building like they did in White-water Junction. Erin had not liked the police station at Whitewater, with its glass walls that made her feel like she was in an aquarium.

Clara Jones was still on reception at the front desk. She would be going home before too long. She gave Erin a measuring look over the top of her rectangular glasses. She pushed back a few strands of reddish, thinning hair. Clara had allowed Erin too many liberties in the office previously and had been reprimanded, so she wasn't about to let Erin just waltz in because she had a box of cookies.

"How may I help you, Miss Price?" she asked crisply.

"I wondered if Officer Stayner is in." Erin displayed the cookie box. "I have something for him."

Clara looked at Erin for a minute before moving. Then she pressed a few keys on her phone and picked up the receiver. "Erin Price here to see you."

Erin took a half-step toward the office. Previously Terry's dedicated office, it was now shared between the two of them. She raised her brows at Clara.

"Just wait here until he's ready for you," Clara said as she firmly placed the receiver back in the cradle.

Erin stayed where she was, looking around the reception area. It wasn't like a doctor's office with inspirational posters or artwork, and magazines to read. There were a couple of hard plastic chairs for visitors, but they were stacked with paper files. Erin didn't want to stare at Clara, but there wasn't really anything else for her to do while she was waiting.

It wasn't long before Stayner came out to see Erin. A young officer, well-built, intimidating when he wanted to be.

"Miss Price. If you'll follow me."

Erin had been expecting to just hand over the cookies and thank him, but she obediently followed him back to the office. He sat at his desk—Terry's desk—and motioned her into the visitor chair.

Erin sat down. She held up the box of cookies. "I brought you some cookies. I wanted to thank you for everything. For the way that you cleaned everything up at Auntie Clem's. That was so considerate of you."

He looked at the box. "I'm sure you know that law enforcement officers can't take anything that might be perceived as a bribe."

"A bribe?" Erin looked down at it. "It's just cookies. I'm not asking you to do something, I'm thanking you for what you've already done."

"You can understand how it looks."

"It's not a bribe. I bring muffins and other treats to the police department all the time."

"But that's to the whole department, and not for one particular thing. This is different."

Erin thought it through. "Well, I can just give it to the police department, then. To everyone. Because you guys are always working so hard."

He nodded. He still didn't take the box from her.

"I'll give it to Clara on the way out."

"Yes, that would be good," Stayner agreed stiffly.

"They're still warm. You should grab one while they're still all melty."

He wiped his mouth. "I will." He allowed a tiny smile, making his face suddenly boyish instead of so stiff. He quickly wiped the expression from his face. Erin put her hands on the arms of her chair to push herself to standing.

"I wanted to talk to you about the fortunes," Stayner said, making a motion for her to stay where she was.

"Oh. I already talked to Sheriff Wilmot about them. He told me that they were substituted at the bakery. I've been talking to Vic, but neither of us can figure out why any employee would do that, or who could have a motive to do something to hurt Joshua or Mary Lou. It just doesn't make any sense."

"Actually..."

Erin's blood turned icy in her veins. She didn't want him to tell her that they had a suspect. They thought one of her employees had cold-bloodedly kidnapped Joshua Cox. She couldn't even wrap her brain around the idea. Who would do anything to hurt Joshua?

Stayner leaned forward slightly. His eyes were intense, drilling into her. "Our investigation has shown that the fortunes were substituted even before they reached the bakery."

"What?" Erin stared at him. "How could that be?"

"Because you changed your order at the printer. You asked them to add some additional fortunes."

"*I* did?" Erin felt the blood drain from her face. She was glad she was already sitting down. "I didn't do that."

"That's what Matt Chatman at the Quiki says. You called in with changes after you had sent in the original order."

"No. I didn't do that. Is he sure it was me?"

Erin knew that he couldn't be sure because it hadn't been her.

Someone had called the Quiki and told them that she wanted different fortunes? She should have checked them when she got the order. She should have checked all of the fortunes, not just a few of them and made sure that they all said what they were supposed to. But that would have been a huge job. How was she to know that they had been changed to something other than what she had ordered?

"He *thought* it was," Stayner admitted. "He said it sounded like you. More or less."

"Well, he's mistaken. It wasn't me. I don't know who would have done that. Aren't there phone records? Can't you look back to see who it was?"

"We will make a request for your phone records and for his. If you could make them available without a warrant, things would go faster."

And time was of the essence in finding Joshua. She didn't know how long he had left.

If he were still okay.

Joshua didn't want to wake up. His mother was shaking his arm hard, but he didn't want to get up for school. He had been up too late, or he had drunk too much. There was no way he would be able to get out of bed and attend to his work.

"Joshua."

"Mmm. No."

"Wake up. Come on, get up!"

"Can't."

The whisper was harsh in his ear. "Wake up now. Or you're not going to be happy with the consequences."

Joshua shifted. It was not his mom. She might warn him about consequences, but that whisper was from somewhere else. Mary Lou would use her voice. She wouldn't care if anyone overheard her. If she had to correct the boys and someone overheard her getting after one of them, it was an embarrassment for them, not for her.

The whisper sent an icicle snaking up his spine. He tried to rub his eyes and open them, but he couldn't move his hands. His eyes were sticky and gritty and didn't want to open. He really needed to sleep more. But the back of his brain told him he was in danger. He needed to wake up and be aware of his surroundings.

Something was wrong.

He rubbed his right eye against his shoulder, and then his left, and blinked hard, trying to clear both of them. But he still couldn't see anything. Just darkness around him, blurry and amorphous. He couldn't identify anything.

"Mom?"

"I'm not your mother."

Josh blinked and tried to moisten his lips, but his mouth was too dry. He looked around for a glass of water, but he couldn't see one. He couldn't see anything.

"What happened?"

"No more questions."

It started to seep back. The long periods spent in the dark, the world looking the same whether he had his eyes open or closed. The dark, whispering figure. The hopelessness of his situation. If someone were going to pay a ransom or find him, they would have done so by now. It had been too long. He and his chances of survival were fading away.

"Do you have food?" he asked finally. It was a question but, hopefully, the shadow wouldn't put it in the same category as questions about what had happened to him or what was going to happen.

The shadow didn't move for a while. Then there was a sigh. "I will get you something. What do you want?"

For a moment, Joshua couldn't speak. He could ask for whatever he wanted? His head filled with all the wonderful foods he missed, his favorite foods as a child, the specials at the restaurants in Bald Eagle

Falls and in the city. Even the little packaged cakes and cookies sold at the convenience store that Mary Lou complained had probably been sitting on the shelf for twenty years.

If he asked for something too difficult, his captor would say no, and maybe he wouldn't get anything. If he just said 'anything,' he might get popcorn or chips, something salty that would make him even more dehydrated than he already was and would burn the raw sores on his lips and mouth.

"That soup," he said in a hoarse voice that sounded too quiet to be his own. "That was really good."

"The soup? You want more soup?"

"Yes."

He didn't know if he dared to ask for water too, or if that would just push his captor over the edge. He couldn't risk it. The soup had a lot of water in it, and that would have to do. He could live with that.

At least, he hoped so.

CHAPTER 28

$\mathcal{E}$rin wondered how long it would take Mary Lou to get word that it was Erin who had, allegedly, made the call to the Quiki to get the fortunes for the cookies changed.

She kind of wished that crimes could be solved as quickly as gossip was spread. But if anyone knew who had taken Joshua, they weren't talking. Not to the police. This time, there was no Peter to innocently spread clues to Erin to allow her to solve the case.

Thinking about Peter, she realized that it had been a few days since she had dropped the baking off for Mrs. Foster and she hadn't heard anything back. Not a thank you from Mrs. Foster. No word that she'd had the baby. Nothing at all.

She'd expected at least a thank you, even if Mrs. Foster still wasn't happy with her. It was the Tennessee way. Erin would have to go by there later to check in and make sure everything was all right. She knew how fast Peter would eat through the baking; it wouldn't hurt to take over another loaf of bread and some of the cheese pretzels he liked.

Terry was at home when she got there, awake and watching through the window for her. He opened the door as she walked up the steps to let her in. She was greeted by an enthusiastic caterwauling and Marshmallow frisking around the house like he'd been into the ginseng. Terry shook his head at the animals. K9 was, as usual, sitting politely beside Terry, though Erin thought that from the way he was watching the other animals, he might have been wishing that he could run and play a little too. Maybe he needed to have a little more off-duty time than he had had recently. With their concerns about intruders, he was on guard even when Erin and Terry were both home.

"You shouldn't have walked alone," Terry admonished, taking her in his arms and kissing her on top of the head.

"It's still light out. There hasn't been any trouble. I do need to walk now and then or my legs will shrivel up and fall off."

Terry rolled his eyes at this. "You say there hasn't been any trouble like we didn't just have a resident disappear. Or have you decided now that Joshua is a runaway after all?"

"No, I haven't," Erin snapped. "You know very well that he's not a runaway. He wouldn't be doing this to Mary Lou. He would have come forward when he realized how upset she was, even if he didn't want to come home."

"How would he know how upset she was?" Terry asked.

"I don't know. His friends would tell him. Campbell would. He'd see the paper or hear his name in the news. Something."

So far, it hadn't been in anything but the local weekly paper, and that hadn't even been a very good article, since the police had still been saying that there was no foul play involved at that point. There were no quotes from Mary Lou or long descriptions about how over-wrought she was. It hadn't made it to the city news, let alone national. Kids disappeared every day. If there was nothing to set Joshua's disappearance apart, it wasn't news.

"Next time, call me and I'll pick you up. Or I can come over and we can walk home together. I don't know why you didn't just have Willie wait for you. He would have."

"I don't feel unsafe walking around Bald Eagle Falls," Erin said. She frowned. Should she? There had been enough trouble since she had moved there. Maybe a reasonable person would be afraid to walk through the town's streets alone. Maybe Erin had faced so many shocks that she no longer knew what was normal and reasonable.

Terry's lips pressed together.

Erin petted Orange Blossom and squeezed him, kissing his head and scratching his chin until he settled down. She reached for Marshmallow to scratch his ears, but he jumped up surprisingly high, switching directions mid-air, and took off, so graceful he made her think of a ballet dancer. Erin laughed at him.

"Well. Everyone else seems to be in fine fettle tonight." She put her purse down and stretched. "Shall we get dinner on?"

"We? Does that mean it's my night?"

Erin shrugged. "I thought we would come up with something together."

Terry seemed to cheer a little at that. Erin was surprised. She didn't think he usually liked to be roped in for the chores, especially in her special domain. Maybe they hadn't been spending enough time together lately. There had been a lot of distractions and outside concerns. And their individual health problems had caused extra stress and friction. They were both feeling somewhat better now; maybe it was time to mend fences.

"What do you feel like?" she asked, walking into the kitchen and considering what was in the cupboards and the fridge. "Soup and sandwiches? Salad? Something more substantial? How hungry are you?"

"Maybe soup, if it's something hearty."

Erin nodded. She opened the big pantry cupboard and looked at the larger cans of soup. There were some chunky soups, some chili, and of course, they could always use one of the lighter soups as a base and add some potatoes, meat, or vegetables to it.

"Mmm... chicken and dumpling?" she suggested.

"Yes!"

She seemed to have hit on a winner the first attempt. Erin smiled and pulled the can off the shelf. "You can get started on that. But if we're going to have chicken and dumplings, we're going to need biscuits."

Terry nodded in agreement. He went to get the can opener while Erin scanned the shelves for the biscuit mix. She turned on the oven and checked the instructions on the side of the box while Terry got out a pot for the soup.

"I can't believe that you use biscuit mix." Terry chuckled.

"I should make gluten-free biscuits from scratch?"

"Of course."

"I've been baking all day. For supper, we get a boxed mix."

"It's fine with me. Just don't let any of your customers see you."

"I think most of them know that I'm not gluten-free at home. And I've never said that I don't use mixes. At the bakery, no. But at home…" She shrugged. "I want to relax at the end of the day."

"We could just defrost some rolls from the freezer. That would be simpler."

"No. For chicken and dumplings, we have to have baking powder biscuits."

Terry was smiling. "Okay, then," he agreed. He dumped the contents of the big can into a pot and set it on the stove. "What else do you want me to do?"

"Maybe some salad," Erin suggested. She knew she needed to watch her weight, and chicken and dumplings with baking powder biscuits weren't exactly low-cal. She'd better be an adult and eat her veggies too.

"Did you hear from the police department about the fortunes?" Erin started to form the biscuits and set them on the pan. "The latest, I mean?" She felt a knot settle in her stomach, taking away the feeling of lightness and well-being that she'd been feeling since they started making dinner together.

Terry looked at her as he ripped up lettuce at the table. "The latest? Was there something today?"

"Yeah. I found out from Stayner when I dropped the cookies off. No one tampered with the fortune cookies at the restaurant or with the bag of fortunes at Auntie Clem's bakery."

"Well, that's good news." He paused, then looked up at her. "What does that leave?"

"They think I called the Quiki and changed the order."

He frowned, brows drawing close together. "They think that you ordered different fortunes than you did?"

"Yeah."

"Why would you do that?"

"I guess I'm an evil genius. Or just evil. Decided Mary Lou wasn't suffering enough and wanted to give the knife an extra twist."

"Maybe if someone didn't know you. No one who knows you would ever think that."

"Thanks. I hope not."

He reached for a tomato and started to dice it. The knife was sharp and his movements were slow. She could tell that he was thinking through all of the implications and figuring out what this new information told them.

"You just got those fortunes. When did you start putting them into the cookies?"

"Just on Wednesday."

"After Josh went missing."

"Right."

"But when did you get the fortunes printed?"

"Saturday. When I—" Erin cut herself off. "Before Joshua disappeared," she realized.

"So you supposedly had fortunes printed before Josh disappeared saying that he would never be found."

Erin put the biscuits in the oven and turned on the element under the soup. She gave it a stir.

"So it wasn't just a spur of the moment thing," she said quietly. "It was planned ahead. Taking Josh, putting new fortunes into the cookies. Implicating me. It was all thought out ahead of time. There wasn't anything spontaneous or off-the-cuff about it."

"No. Couldn't have been."

"But why? Why would anyone do this?"

"The typical motive for kidnapping, if not for the kidnapper's own... recreation... is greed or coercion... but the kidnapper hasn't asked for anything."

"Revenge?" Erin asked, the knot in her stomach tightening even more. How was she even going to eat her chicken and dumplings? "It isn't like the kidnapper hasn't communicated at all. He hasn't asked for anything, but... he left the note for Mary Lou, pointing the finger at me. And he arranged for the fortunes to be printed saying that we would never find Joshua. That's more like... he's trying to get back at Mary Lou or me... turn us against each other, make us feel worse."

Terry sighed. "I need to talk to the sheriff."

"Wait until after dinner?"

Terry nodded. "Yes. Of course. There's plenty of time after dinner to discuss it."

"I was really happy at first, realizing that the fortunes weren't tampered with by someone at the bakery. But... all of this just makes me feel worse. I'm still glad it wasn't someone that works for me. But it's personal. I just don't know which of us it is aimed against."

CHAPTER 29

*E*rin had arranged to take the day off at Auntie Clem's so she could get some other things done. She stopped in anyway at the quiet part of the morning, arriving through the front door like a customer and checking to make sure everything was going smoothly.

"No problems," Bella offered cheerfully, "other than the occasional misshapen loaf. Business has been brisk today."

Probably because of the rumors about Erin being involved with Joshua's disappearance. The findings about the fortunes being printed wrong probably just ramped up speculation more. Business always improved at Auntie Clem's when a major crime was committed. She could almost count on it as a marketing technique if things ever slowed down too much. Commit a crime, or start gossip about a crime being committed, and everybody would start coming around to find out the details.

"What can we get for you today?" Gwen asked cheekily. "There's a sale on banana bread."

Erin smiled. "I want to grab a few things for the Fosters, actually." She indicated the various baked goods that she thought she should take, and Vic put them into a box, which would be easier for her to take to the door than multiple bags, which might end up crushing the goodies.

"Thank you. Give me a call if anything comes up," Erin advised.

They agreed, but Erin wasn't expecting there to be any trouble. It wasn't like Mary Lou would be coming in with another fortune cookie.

But that made Erin think about the Chinese restaurant. They still had a large supply of cookies, and there was no way to know how many of them contained fortunes designed to upset people. They would have to completely redo the order. Get new fortunes printed, mix up new batches of dough, and start baking and folding all over again. It had been a big job the first time. It would go faster the second time, but she still wasn't looking forward to it. They would all be thinking about Joshua and whether he were going to be okay.

With every day that passed, it became less and less likely that they would find him well and safe.

But miracles happened. There had been that girl in Utah. And there had been other cases. Sometimes girls escaped after years of being held prisoner in basements or back yards.

Girls, Erin realized, not boys. It was never boys.

"Are you okay, Erin?" Bella asked.

"Oh. Yes, I'm fine. I was just thinking…" Erin didn't finish her thought, but Bella could apparently read it in her face and voice anyway.

"Yes," she said soberly. "I'm worried too."

When Erin arrived at the Fosters' house, Peter and his sisters were playing in the yard. They were noisy, and Peter directed and bossed the girls mercilessly, taking his role as big brother very seriously.

When he saw Erin pull to the curb in front of the house, he ran over. "Miss Erin!"

"Hi, Peter. How are you?"

"Good!" He looked at the box as she picked it up to take to the door. "When do I get to come to Auntie Clem's Bakery again?"

"I don't know, sweetie. You'll have to ask your mother."

"Dad says it's nice that you're bringing food to the house so he or Mom don't have to go out to get it."

"I hope it helps. I know your mom probably isn't having a very easy time getting around these days."

"She has to rest a lot," Peter agreed. "That means she has to lay down and we're supposed to be quiet and not disturb her." He rolled his eyes and looked around at the little girls. "They are not very good at being quiet," he informed her. "It's best if we come outside."

"Yes, better to be where you can make some noise," Erin agreed. It would be difficult for them to all be inside, playing or looking for something to do that wouldn't make any noise. She remembered being in homes where one of the parents worked on shift, and how hard it was not to raise her voice or do anything that might involve banging or other noises for hours on end. It had been so easy to forget and get involved in something either by herself or with foster siblings that would end up getting out of hand. Then the foster mom would be thundering in, shouting at them to be quiet. Erin could remember that feeling of horror when she would suddenly realize what she had done and have to face the fury of an angry parent.

At least Mrs. Foster wouldn't be that way. She had always seemed like a very nice woman, patient even when Peter was in his argumentative 'lawyer mode.'

At least, Erin hoped she was as patient when she was out of the public eye.

"Is she on bed rest?" Erin asked Peter.

He looked at her, scrunching up his brows, uncertain. "She's resting."

"Is she sick? Did the doctor tell her she has to stay in bed or it will hurt the baby?"

Peter shook his head. "I don't know."

"Would you take these things into the house? Or should I ring the doorbell?"

"I'll take them in. Do you want to watch the girls for a minute…? I'm not supposed to leave them alone."

"I'll watch them," Erin agreed. She smiled at the little girls and chatted with them while Peter took the box into the house.

Peter was back again a few minutes later and, by the working of his jaw, she guessed he had helped himself to a cookie as payment for his labor.

"Is there anything your mom needs? Does she need me to pick something up or need people to help with meals…?"

"Nnno…" Peter was hesitant with his answer. "She doesn't want people doing things for her."

"It's hard to accept help sometimes. Would you tell her that if she needs anything, she should give me a call? She knows how to reach me at the bakery and, if I'm not there, my employees can give her my cell number or shoot me a text. Okay?"

Peter nodded. "Okay."

"Are you looking forward to the new baby coming?"

"Yeah. She says maybe this one will be a boy. I'd like it if she had another boy."

"That would be nice, wouldn't it? But he won't be big enough to play with you for quite a while."

"I know." Peter looked at the girls he was watching over, and toddler Traci in particular. "But I could still share boy things with him. Like trucks and Spiderman stuff that I've outgrown."

"Yes, that's right. That would be nice."

"How is your kitty?" Peter asked. "Is he okay now?"

Orange Blossom had recovered from his poisoning and didn't seem to have suffered any long-term effects. Peter had mentioned it more than once.

"Yes, he's okay now," Erin told him. "Back to yowling at me, demanding his dinner."

Peter giggled. "Is he really noisy?"

"Yes. Just ask my neighbors. They can hear him all the time."

"People complain about dogs barking."

"Yes. But not usually about cats meowing, unless they're outside cats that are… really noisy. Not inside cats!"

"I'm glad he's okay."

Erin nodded. "You don't know who made him sick, do you?" she asked tentatively. She knew that she shouldn't be. Mrs. Foster had made it clear that she didn't want Erin involving Peter in any of her

149

investigations, even if he offered something. She should just say goodbye to Peter and continue on with her other errands.

"I don't know…" Peter trailed off. "Maybe one of the guys that was being the Grinch."

"One of the boys involved in the burglaries?"

He nodded.

"But you don't know for sure. You don't know who it would have been."

"No. I don't talk to the big boys."

"And no one at school ever said who it was."

Peter shrugged. "They say lots of different things. You can't tell which ones are true, though."

"So is there someone… that you think might have been involved in making Orange Blossom sick?"

"No. I just think… it must have been one of them because they're the ones who wanted you to stop. So if you were taking care of your cat, maybe you wouldn't keep looking for them." He shrugged. "But I don't know who it was."

Erin suppressed a shudder. She hated to think of someone getting into her house or getting some contaminated food into her house that Orange Blossom had eaten. She had a burglar alarm, and a policeman and K9 unit living with her. It should not have been easy to poison her cat.

She remembered the man who had walked up to her at one of the fundraising activities. A Santa beard and suit had obscured his identity, so she still didn't know who it had been. Someone she would have allowed into her home? Was he a friend, an acquaintance, or a complete stranger? Could *he* have anything to do with Joshua's disappearance?

She couldn't imagine that anyone she knew would have had anything to do with kidnapping Josh. Still, she would have said the same about the burglaries. Was it one of the boys she had served after-school snacks to at the bakery? A teacher or administrator at the school? Someone from out of town? She wasn't even sure he had been an adult. Some of the kids at the school were as tall as adults and had deep voices. There was no way to know who had been lurking behind that beard.

The motive for the burglaries had been obvious—greed. But the motive behind Joshua's disappearance and the swap of the fortunes was not anything to do with money. Not that she could tell. The kidnapping and notes seemed to be aimed to hurt.

That didn't eliminate those who had been accused or arrested in connection with the burglaries, though. They might very well have wanted to hurt Erin.

"Peter," Karen whined as she rode closer to him on her tricycle. "You're not supposed to talk to strangers."

"Miss Erin isn't a stranger," Peter said. But he shrugged at Erin. "I need to watch them."

"Of course. I'll see you later, okay?"

He looked as if he would say something else, then nodded. "Sometime," he sighed.

CHAPTER 30

*M*att, the owner of the Quiki Print outlet down the street from Auntie Clem's Bakery, didn't look happy when he saw her approaching.

"Miss Price," the words burst out of him in a rush. "I am so sorry about all of this. I didn't tell the police that it was you that changed the order. I told them that I thought it was you when you called—when I got the call—but I don't know you well enough to know for sure yes or no. I told them I don't really know you, just from you coming in the day you put in the order. I never thought when you called after to say that you wanted some other fortunes added, that it might not be you. You see?"

He wiped his mouth with the back of his hand, his eyes round and worried.

"It's fine, Matt. I don't know what happened or who it was that called, but it isn't your fault. You thought it was me, and you did what you thought I wanted done."

"Yes." He nodded vigorously. "I would never have done something like that on purpose. If I wasn't sure that it was you when you called, I would have called back or emailed you to verify. It just never occurred to me."

"I understand."

"And the police…" He looked sick at the thought of her being tangled up in the police investigation. Apparently, he didn't know how many other times she had gotten cross-threaded with an investigation. "I did not mean for them to think that it was you, just that it sounded like it could have been you and I never thought to ask."

"Yes. Matt. It's okay."

"They are pulling my phone logs, to try to figure out who it was that called. I know about the time you called—that the call came in —so they should be able to figure it out, right?"

"Right. That will help. Because that call didn't come from my phone." Erin stopped for a moment and considered whether she had lain her phone down where someone else might have picked it up and used it for a minute to make a call to the Quiki. But she couldn't think of any time that day it would have been out of her sight or off of her person.

Matt nodded, looking only slightly reassured.

"Was there anything about the person who called in?" Erin asked. "Anything that might tell us who it was? Like… if they had an accent, or a cold, or their voice was different than mine in some other way?"

"I'm sure the police will believe that it was not you," Matt rushed to reassure her.

"I know. But I'd still like to know who it was. We need to find out who is doing this, not just to convince the police that it wasn't me."

"Oh." Matt thought about it. "Well… no, I can't think of anything special about the voice. It was just for a minute, you know —very short conversation. I didn't notice… that it was any different than yours." He considered it further. "Maybe… maybe the accent was different, I don't know."

He was clearly not a native English speaker, so Erin wasn't sure how good he would be at identifying different American accents.

"Different how?"

"I don't know," Matt muttered. He bit his lip and rolled his eyes to the ceiling, trying to come up with something. "You sound like… you didn't grow up here. The Bald Eagles Falls families, they all sound the same. More or less."

Erin nodded. "A Tennessee accent. And I pretty much lost mine, because I was raised up north."

"Yes. But some people, it comes and goes. It depends who they are talking to and what they are saying. If they are talking to me, less accent. If they are talking to an old friend from high school here, very strong."

"So you didn't think anything of it when I called back and talked with more of a Tennessee accent."

"Yes. I thought it was you, still."

Erin thought about that. Someone around her age and timbre. But who had grown up in Bald Eagle Falls or the surrounding area. Unfortunately, there were a lot of people who fell into that group.

"Was there anything else? Any background noise? Where did you think I was calling from?"

Matt scratched his nose. "I thought… you were maybe in your garage or in a storage unit. I just thought you had ideas of more things to add to the fortunes you asked for. And you were busy with something else, so you called instead of coming in or emailing me."

"Right."

"I am so sorry that my mistake caused anybody pain."

"I know. Me too. I'm sorry that this ended up being such a mess. I just wanted people who can't eat gluten to be able to have fortune cookies. To put some fun sayings in them so that people would enjoy them."

"What can I do? Do you think the police will be able to find who did this? Is there anything else I can do?"

"Well…" Erin shrugged. "The reason I came in here was to see if you could reprint the fortunes for me. Just the original ones this time. Because we have to remake a whole bunch more cookies."

Matt's face lit up. "That is a wonderful thing to do. Very good. And this time, free of charge. I will replace them at my cost."

"You don't need to do that. You're still putting time and materials into it."

"But I should have gotten verification the first time. I should have gotten it right. So this time, I will get it right."

Erin protested once more but, in the end, she let him do the reprint at his own cost. She had to cover her costs to replace the cookies, and that was not insignificant when she had to eat the cost of both of the ingredients and her employees' time to bake and fold the replacement cookies. The Chinese restaurant was going to get their cookies. Erin would make sure that they were right this time.

CHAPTER 31

"*A* woman," Erin mused as she went through her tai chi forms. "I don't know why I assumed it would be a man."

Vic was sitting on the steps up to her loft apartment. "What?"

"Oh. Just being a crazy lady and talking to myself."

"Yeah; what about?"

"The person who called in the change order to the Quiki was a woman. Someone pretending to be me. So the kidnapper is a woman. Or the kidnapper has an accomplice who is a woman. I don't know why…" She paused as she worked through a form that made her turn her back on Vic. "But I always assumed that it was a man."

"It's probably two people," Vic said. "Sometimes it's couples that do this kind of thing. Working together. The woman is emotionally abused or thinks that she has to."

"Or in some cases, she's the leader," Erin said. She remembered a couple of cases. It wasn't necessarily the men who were always the planners.

"Well, but *usually*," Vic reiterated.

"I don't know. Maybe. I pictured a man, anyway. I know Joshua isn't big, but I thought it would take a man to kidnap him. Someone big enough and strong enough."

Vic nodded.

"Not that women aren't strong," Erin said. "Or can't be big. But..."

"You assume," Vic agreed. "I thought a man too. I don't know why, after what happened with Theresa. And not just her, but some of the others we've run into since Aunt Angela died. We've both had firsthand knowledge of women committing violent crimes."

Erin paused in her tai chi, thinking about that. She turned her head and looked at Vic. "It couldn't be Theresa, right?"

They had never captured Crazy Theresa. Erin kept waiting for the news that someone had been able to track her down, or that she had been pulled over for a traffic stop. Somehow, someone had to find her and arrest her. She couldn't keep running for the rest of her life.

"No. She wouldn't come back here, it would be too dangerous."

"But she's crazy. Would she care?"

"She doesn't want to get caught. And why would she do it? Take Joshua? There's no reason to."

"Just because she's crazy." Erin shrugged.

"She still doesn't do things without a motive."

"But it doesn't have to be one that we would understand."

"Maybe she... thinks that I like Joshua. I don't know. You know she gets ideas into her head, and that she might do something that didn't make any sense to us, if it meant that she could hurt one of us or... get one of us close to her. I don't know the reason."

"She likes you." Erin pondered. "So is there any way that taking Joshua would get her closer to you?"

"He's not a rival. She wouldn't know that he was any kind of friend. The only time I've done anything with Joshua is when we went into the city looking for Campbell, and Theresa wasn't around for that. She wouldn't know that me and Josh even knew each other."

"She hates me. And Willie. Because she thinks that we've alienated you from her."

Vic turned her hands palms-up. *So?*

Erin couldn't connect it up. Kidnapping or hurting Joshua would hurt Erin, but only indirectly. And Theresa would have to know that she cared about Joshua or Mary Lou.

"And you don't think she would randomly take Josh and try to make us feel bad with the notes," Erin suggested.

"This wasn't random," Vic reminded her. "She planned this out. She knew about the fortune cookies, and she knew about you and Joshua being friends. Or you and Mary Lou."

"So it has to be someone in Bald Eagle Falls. Nobody outside of town would know about either of those things."

"Well…" Vic wobbled her hand back and forth in a 'maybe' gesture.

"Who else would know?"

"I don't know. Not specifically. But word spreads. Maybe this wasn't anything that anyone was gossiping about, so it didn't go very far. Still, people do leave town, talk to friends out of town, post stuff on social media, all that. You posted on the Auntie Clem's social media accounts about the gluten-free fortune cookies, didn't you?"

Erin's heart sank. "Yes."

"So anyone who follows you or liked those posts, they could have seen that. Or if someone shared it, one of their friends might have seen it."

"I always ask the employees if they would share stuff around when appropriate," Erin sighed. "If they think something is interesting or worth sharing."

Vic nodded. "It's sound business."

"But I didn't post about Joshua," Erin said. "I never posted about him."

"We need to go right back to the beginning."

Erin closed her eyes as she started to go through the final forms of her tai chi. "Let me just think for a few minutes. Finish this up."

Vic fell silent and let Erin finish without any further discussion. When she was done, Erin sat in the grass. It wasn't the most comfortable place to sit, but the weather was warm enough that it wasn't *that* uncomfortable.

"Back to the beginning how?" she prompted.

"We need to go over anybody who had a motive to kidnap Josh, to hurt you or Mary Lou, or to drive the two of you further apart."

Erin wanted to say that the list was pretty short. But, in fact, it wasn't nearly as short as she would like it to be. She had been involved with investigations that had hurt the organized crime clans around Bald Eagle Falls who had tried to establish business there. And the Russian mob. Anyone in those organizations could have something against her. But having fortunes printed? That didn't sound like something a mobster would do.

Then there were the people she had put in prison since arriving in Bald Eagle Falls. None of them could have done anything to Joshua directly, but there were other ways to reach out and influence people from prison. Someone could have been hired to do the job. Or it had been a favor. Or someone had just thought that it would make the person in prison—or still in jail awaiting their trial—grateful, and that was enough. It wasn't a short list. How had she accumulated so many enemies in the short time she had lived in Bald Eagle Falls?

"Are you thinking about the parents?" Vic asked.

Erin hadn't been, but she didn't need to ask who Vic was talking about. Of course it could have been the parent of someone arrested for the Grinch burglaries. That had been Erin's doing as well. Dozens of families had been affected. And most of them probably knew of Erin's friendship with Mary Lou and with Joshua.

"Oh, boy."

Vic nodded slowly. "That was very recent and people are still sore about it. I mean, things will go back to normal eventually, but it's going to take a while."

"I just keep thinking about Mrs. Foster and Mary Lou. If they could both be so angry with me because the police had to *talk* to their sons... not that they were arrested or even suspected... then how much madder are the parents of the kids who were arrested?"

"They shouldn't be." Vic asserted stubbornly. "If their kids got arrested, that's not your fault. They shouldn't have been involved in the burglaries to begin with!"

"I know... but that's not the way they feel. As far as they're concerned... it's almost like I'm the one who coerced them into a life of crime."

"Stupid. If they were my kids, I wouldn't be protecting them and giving them excuses for breaking the law and hurting other people."

Erin shrugged. "You can never tell what you would do in someone else's situation."

"I know I wouldn't condone my family members breaking the law."

Erin looked at her for a minute. Vic's brows grew closer together. "What?"

"I was just thinking about Jeremy. And about the rest of your family being involved with the Jackson clan."

Vic's face flushed. "I wasn't talking about that."

"I know. But is it that different?"

"I don't know what Jeremy might or might not have done. If he was mixed up in something when he first came here... well, I don't know exactly what it was. And I don't want to know. He's clean now, right? He's an honest, law-abiding citizen here in Bald Eagle Falls. He's left whatever clan stuff behind."

"As far as you know."

"Yes."

"And if he's still involved in some illegal activity? Would you go to the police if you suspected something?"

"I don't know. I guess I would... probably talk to him first, find out what was going on. See if there was a way to get him back on the right track..."

Erin nodded. "And the rest of your family? What have your dad and other brothers been involved in?"

"I don't know, and I don't—"

"And you don't want to know," Erin finished. "You mean, kind of like those families whose kids were involved in the burglaries? You want them to stop, but not to have to go to prison for it."

"The school kids aren't going to get sent to prison."

"Some of them will. The ones who were old enough. Or violent enough."

Vic stared off into space. "I can see them being upset about what happened and wanting to get back at you somehow."

"Yeah. But by kidnapping Joshua? Why wouldn't they do something to hurt or scare me directly? Joshua wasn't the one who got them arrested."

CHAPTER 32

*I*t seemed like a long time had passed. Joshua didn't know how long he had been asleep or passed out. He didn't like being awake. It was tedious and painful, and he ended up lying there for hours just waiting for something to happen. It was better if he could escape to unconsciousness as quickly as possible. He didn't have to worry about the pain and the fever. He didn't have to worry about the long periods of boredom.

"Joshua. I brought food."

Even before his captor said the magic words, Joshua's senses were coming alive, telling him that there was food in the area. Making him start to salivate like a wild animal. *Food, food, food!*

Josh sat up as well as he could and blinked his eyes, rubbing them on his shoulders, trying to wake up as quickly as possible.

The shadowy figure sat again on the edge of the bed and worked the lid off of a plastic container. As soon as the seal was broken, Joshua's stomach hurt with the smell of the chicken soup. He wanted and needed it so badly.

"Thank you," he breathed. "That smells wonderful. Thank you so much."

He tried to wipe the unsightly drool away from his mouth. But despite how dehydrated he was, the saliva continued to gush.

The shadowy figure pulled out a spoon and dipped it into the warm, fragrant broth. He brought it up to Joshua's lips. Joshua greedily slurped it. He had a hundred things he wanted to tell his captor at once. How wonderful it was, how he never needed to eat anything else, if he would just keep bringing the chicken soup. How it tasted like what his grandmother used to make with homemade noodles in it. Josh was transported back to her kitchen, always full of delightful simmering soups, baking bread, jams and preserves and pickles.

But he didn't say anything to start with, slurping the soup off of the spoon as quickly as it could be lifted to his mouth.

Eventually, the spoon started to slow. Joshua could hear it scraping the bottom of the bowl. His captor scraped up as much of the remaining liquid as he could and offered it to Joshua.

"It's so good," Joshua said. "Just like my baba used to make."

"It's not your baba's recipe," the figure hissed.

"No. I didn't mean that. I just mean... it reminds me. It's so good. It makes me think of all of those days helping her when I was little. We would go there in the fall. Mom would make Campbell and me help get all of the garden produce put up for the winter. We were good at it. And Dad too. He was always good at cooking."

"But now it's just you. You're the only one who is left of your family."

Joshua bit his scabby, dry lip. He wanted to protest that his dad and Campbell were not dead, they just weren't at home anymore. Joshua wasn't the only one left. He wasn't even the only one left in the house. His mom was there too. He had always loved her, wanted to tell her all of his successes and to hear her praise. He knew that she didn't give praise like some of the other moms did, always telling their kids that they were so smart and talented at everything. No one was talented at everything. Joshua knew that when his mother said he had done a good job of something, he really had. She didn't make stuff up or gush. The slightest word of approval from her meant that he'd done a stellar job.

"Soon, you won't have to be here anymore."

Josh cocked his head and blinked his eyes. Because he was being let go? Or because he was going to die? He was glad that his captivity was coming to an end, no matter which way it was.

He just hoped that his mom would be okay.

CHAPTER 33

The ladies' tea had been a quiet and somber affair. Usually, there was lots of visiting and laughter. The women enjoyed getting together on their day of rest to just sit and relax and have a cup of tea together and talk. They shared what had happened during the week, any gossip that hadn't yet been shared and rehashed, and expectations for the coming week. A nice way to end the week.

But with Joshua still missing, and people now believing that he really might have been kidnapped rather than just running away, people didn't want to smile or laugh too much. Mary Lou wasn't there, and they talked about her in hushed tones. All of the disasters that had befallen her family in recent years. She really didn't deserve to have something else like that.

Charley was assisting Erin. The ladies' tea was a bit early for her, but she made it when she was needed. Vic was, Erin assumed, in the city to run errands, maybe to attend the LGBT-friendly church there, or maybe she had gone to do some spelunking, or visit a mine with Willie. She hadn't said what her exact plans were, but that was generally how she spent Sundays off.

Most of the women had started to wrap it up and say their goodbyes. A couple had left already. Erin collected teacups as they were finished, wiping down the tables as she went.

The bells on the door jingled. Erin looked up to see if someone had forgotten a purse or if Terry had come to help her with clean-up. He sometimes did if he wanted to go somewhere together.

She was surprised to see Mary Lou in the doorway. The low buzz of goodbyes between the ladies who remained in the bakery ceased. Everyone was quiet, looking at Mary Lou.

She nodded and smoothed non-existent wrinkles in her pantsuit self-consciously. She forced a smile and a few hellos.

"Yes, nice to see you..." she murmured to no one in particular. She was looking toward Erin. Not directly at her, eyes kept low, but it was clear that it was Erin she was there to see.

"Hi, Mary Lou," Erin greeted warmly. "It's good to see you."

She waited for the other ladies to vacate the bakery, but they hung around as if they wanted to see what was going to happen next.

"That's it for the day," Charley said loudly. "We need to close up shop. See you on Monday. Sale on blueberry muffins." She made motions to shoo everyone out.

The women renewed their goodbyes and reluctantly left Auntie Clem's.

"Old vultures," Charley muttered as she shut the door behind them and flipped the sign over to 'closed.'

"Thanks," Erin told her.

"Yeah, no trouble. You just need to speak up. Don't be so worried about offending people."

"I have to think about that," Erin protested. "If I want to keep people's business, I need to stay in their good books."

"Not as much as you think you do," Charley said firmly. "You're the only bakery in town. If they don't want to pick up mushy bread at the grocery store or drive into the city, you're the only game in town. So stop acting like people will stop coming if you tell them it's closing time."

Erin shrugged, knowing that Charley was probably right. Erin was too much of a people-pleaser. She had grown up trying to keep her various foster parents happy, trying to read every tiny change of expression and to understand all of the unwritten rules. It hadn't always been easy to make friends at new schools and to fit in with families or cliques that had been formed years before. Charley hadn't had to worry about stuff like that. She didn't understand how precarious relationships could be.

"I'll wash up in back, you can take care of things out here," Charley offered. She grabbed the last of the teacups and trays and took them into the kitchen.

Erin turned to Mary Lou. She wanted to hug her and ask how she was doing, but Mary Lou had always been cool. Even when they were getting along, Erin wouldn't have dared hug her without a clear invitation.

"Hi."

Mary Lou looked around. She'd been in Auntie Clem's many times before. There wasn't exactly anything to comment on. "The tea went well?"

"Pretty quiet today." Erin didn't say that people were worried about Joshua and Mary Lou. She would know that without Erin having to twist the knife.

"I see. And you are doing well? Where is Victoria today?"

"In the city, I think. She goes to church there."

"When she goes to church."

"She goes pretty regularly." Erin didn't want Mary Lou judging Vic to be less of a Christian because she didn't get to church every single week like most of the Baptist ladies. Mary Lou's opinion of Vic was already low enough.

"Does she."

Mary Lou again looked like she was searching for something to talk about. What was Erin supposed to do? Ask her about Joshua? Ask her why she had come? There was no clear path for the conversation to follow.

Erin looked away from Mary Lou, out the front window of the bakery. It was a beautiful day. Clear blue sky. Before long, Terry would probably be coming to pick her up.

"I owe you an apology," Mary Lou said finally. She was a plainspoken woman and she didn't try to weasel out of it. "I shouldn't have blown up at you over the fortune cookie. It wasn't anything to do with you."

Erin shrugged. "Well, they were my cookies. You knew that."

"But you weren't the one who put it in there. I should have gotten more information before assuming that it was your fault."

Erin looked at her curiously, wondering what it was that had made Mary Lou change her mind. "I would never do anything to hurt you. And something like that… it was cruel."

"And I should have known that isn't the kind of person you are. I jumped to conclusions without thinking about what kind of a person you are or whether my conclusion was reasonable. I was hurt and I just lashed out." Mary Lou gave herself no quarter. "That was the wrong thing to do. I know better."

"You're going through a terrible time. It's understandable."

"That does not excuse it."

"Then… I accept your apology." Erin looked at Mary Lou directly. "How are you managing?"

Mary Lou shook her head. "Not well."

"The police are investigating who it was that had my order for the fortunes changed. Maybe that will lead somewhere."

"Officer Stayner told me that. But… it probably won't lead anywhere. Who knows if it was even the same person, or if it was just someone who wanted to… hurt me."

"The order was changed before Joshua disappeared."

Mary Lou's eyes widened. "What?"

"So it had to be the same person, or an accessory."

The older woman nodded slowly.

"Have they told you anything else?" Erin asked. "About their progress, I mean. Whether they have found anything. Actual evidence."

"They won't say very much to me. I don't know whether it is because parents are always suspects in their children's abductions or just because they are playing things close to the vest."

"You're not a suspect."

Mary Lou leveled a stare at her. "Of course I am. How many parents have tried to cover up violence they have done to their children by saying they were abducted?"

"But Josh isn't a two-year-old. If you had done something to him, he would have fought back." But even as Erin said it, she knew it wasn't necessarily true. There were plenty of reasons for teens to stay quiet when they were being abused. Domestic violence victims learned to keep quiet—even adults. There were women and men killed by their partners every day. The police department couldn't overlook those statistics just because they knew the spouse or parent. However reasonable and nice people seemed in public, you never knew what happened behind closed doors.

"Do you have any idea who it was?" Erin asked.

"I wish I did. I'm afraid that I'm not the easiest person to get along with. I'm sure I have offended many people over the years."

"But people who would kidnap your child? That's a pretty severe consequence."

"I suppose it is. But I don't know who it was. I can't think of anybody in my life, in Bald Eagle Falls, who would do such a thing."

Despite her feelings about the gossip and the secrets in Bald Eagle Falls, Erin had to agree. That level of violence seemed extreme. Yes, they had seen more than their fair share of crime since Erin had arrived in Bald Eagle Falls, but that had mostly been related to the Plaints and to organized crime. And those had been cleaned up. There wasn't any reason to suspect that they were still operating in Bald Eagle Falls.

Except that a boy had been kidnapped.

"I wish we could just rewind," Erin said with a sigh. "I wish we could just go back in time and stop this from happening."

"I would do things differently," Mary Lou asserted. "I would keep a better eye on him. I would pay more attention to what he was doing for school, and that he wasn't getting into any trouble. I thought that after he was questioned by the police about the burglaries, when he was released, that he would be safe. But what if one of the kids who were involved thought that he had informed on them?"

"And they did this… to get back at him?" Erin thought about that. "Or to keep him from being able to testify in court?"

"They must have, don't you think?" Mary Lou asked. "People knew that he had been questioned by the police. When they started to make arrests, they thought that he had something to do with it."

"Right. I guess that's possible."

"What else?" Mary Lou demanded. "What else could I have done?"

"I'm not sure there's anything else you could have done. You can't protect someone twenty-four hours a day. Even if you had been awake and someone came into the house, how would you stop them from taking Joshua?"

Mary Lou looked at Erin, frowning.

"What?" Erin asked, disconcerted.

"You really don't think that I had anything to do with it."

"No. Why would I?"

"Because I'm the most likely suspect. Especially with the notes pointing in other directions. Why would anyone want to implicate you? The only person who would want to implicate you would be someone who wanted attention distracted from themselves. And that would be me. Family members. Spouses and parents," Mary Lou said bitterly.

"I don't know why someone would want to misdirect attention to me. I assumed... that was for your benefit. Someone wanted you to think it was me. That I had... done something that had caused harm to Joshua."

"Why?"

Erin sat on one of the chairs that had been vacated by the ladies from First Baptist and motioned Mary Lou to take another. After a hesitation, Mary Lou sat down.

"If that first note hadn't had my name on it, then who would you have suspected?"

"I have no idea. Just like I have no idea now. Maybe the parents of the other kids. Maybe... someone that Campbell was in trouble with."

"But you wouldn't have suspected me of having anything to do with it."

"No. You're not the first person I would have suspected of kidnapping Joshua."

"I didn't know anything about it." Even though Mary Lou said that she didn't suspect Erin, she wanted to be clear that she hadn't known about it or had anything to do with whoever had decided to take Joshua.

"No," Mary Lou agreed. She closed her eyes and massaged the worried creases in between them. "Nothing to do with it. It was a diversion."

Erin nodded. She tried to imagine what Mary Lou's day would have looked like without that note on the paper.

CHAPTER 34

"*D*id you ever read Joshua's article?"

Mary Lou gave her head a little shake. "Maybe sometime... but I couldn't bear to now. It would just be too hard."

"Did the police look at it?"

"I'm sure they must have. They wanted to know everything Joshua was doing. Where he had been, how he was doing at school. I told them about him going to Whitewater Junction to do interviews, all of that."

"I never read the article either."

"I'm sure you still could. The newspaper will still have copies of it. And the library will have kept an archive copy."

Erin nodded. There wasn't any way for someone to get rid of all of the copies of Joshua's article. But the note had distracted Mary Lou from reading it. And Erin too.

"We should read it. In case there's something in there... the kidnapper didn't want you to read."

Mary Lou shook her head. "I don't know if I can."

"Well, I will." Erin pulled her phone out. "Do they post it online?"

"No, they are old school."

"How late is the paper open?"

Mary Lou looked at her watch. "Everything will be closed now."

"Somebody must have it."

"Everybody has it. You must get it at your house. They deliver to everyone."

Erin couldn't remember seeing it. "Maybe. In the recycling pile, or maybe Vic picked it up."

Mary Lou nodded. "I don't want… to get my hopes up. So I'm going to let you go home and look at it. I won't expect to hear anything from you. Okay?"

"Okay." Erin touched Mary Lou's arm. "Take care, okay?"

Mary Lou sighed. She didn't answer. Erin really hoped that things didn't take a turn for the worse. She couldn't imagine how Mary Lou would get through it if they did.

"Is Campbell still in town?"

"Yes. He's at home. I don't know how long he's going to stay."

Hopefully, until things were resolved.

Erin really hoped that they wouldn't end badly.

Mary Lou left. Erin went to the kitchen to help Charley finish up. Charley raised an eyebrow. "So? How did it go?"

"Okay. She's not mad at me anymore. She doesn't suspect me."

Charley rolled her eyes. "She never should have in the first place. I can't think of anyone less likely to have kidnapped the kid. Really? You?"

"I don't think that she thought I kidnapped him… Maybe that something I did caused him to be kidnapped, and that I wanted to hurt her and get back at her by putting the bad fortunes in the cookies. I don't know. It's all emotion, not logic."

"Yeah. You're right there. It doesn't make any sense that you would have something to do with his disappearance."

"Thanks for cleaning up back here." Erin took a look around, and everything seemed to be more or less in place. "I guess that means it's time to go home."

"Is Terry picking you up?"

"I think I might walk." Erin hadn't heard anything from Terry. But when she said she would walk, she suddenly remembered how upset he'd been about her doing that after visiting the police department. Maybe not a good idea. She hesitated.

"You want a ride?" Charley asked.

"Yeah. Maybe that would be a good idea. If it's not an inconvenience."

"How could it be an inconvenience for me to drive you a few blocks?"

Which Erin took to mean that she didn't mind doing it. They grabbed their purses and went out the back door to Charley's car, taking care to lock the bakery securely. No point in inviting people to mess around in there while she was gone. She'd discovered enough bodies already.

Erin had a sudden flashback to Mr. Inglethorpe, lying in the middle of the floor of Auntie Clem's kitchen, a pool of red pie filling around him.

"Whoa!" Charley grabbed Erin's arm and steadied her. "Are you okay?"

Erin blinked, trying to clear the images from her brain. "Yeah." She breathed hard. "Sorry, just moved too fast, I guess."

Charley walked Erin to the car and opened the door for her, supervising to make sure that Erin got in without any further difficulty.

"You don't need to cover up for me," Charley said flatly when she slid into the driver's seat and put her key in the ignition.

"Cover up?"

"That you're having flashbacks."

"Oh." Erin was a little flustered. "Was it that obvious?"

"I've known for a long time."

"Well… it's not really a secret. But I don't like to talk about it."

"Sure. Understandable. I'm just saying, you don't have to pretend for me. Personally, I don't think you need to pretend for anyone else, either. It shouldn't be a secret. People should be able to talk about what's bothering them, about mental health and trauma and all that stuff."

Erin nodded, the movement very small. Charley might not have even seen it. "What about you? Do you... have that?"

"Flashbacks to when Bobby died?"

Erin didn't say anything. Both of them were quiet almost all the way to Erin's house.

"Yeah. Of course I do. It was a terrible thing. I try not to let it bother me, but sometimes... well, you can't control it, can you? And sometimes it controls you."

"Yeah. Sometimes."

"It's easier for me, I think," Charley said. "I'm the irresponsible sister, so it's okay if I blow off some community event or stay up until the sun rises before going to sleep, or have a bit too much to drink now and then. People just say..." Charley made a careless motion. "That's Charley. What do you expect?"

Erin knew that she herself had written off many of Charley's behaviors as just Charley being irresponsible. Was she being unfair? Was it not Charley being irresponsible, but Charley trying to handle her own PTSD symptoms?

"I didn't know."

"I wouldn't expect you to. Like I said, it's easier for me. People don't pay that much attention to my outrageous behavior because they expect it. I can handle it however I want."

"You could get therapy."

"Like you do?"

Like Erin didn't. She'd had enough therapy in the past that she just didn't want to have to deal with it again. Therapists wanted to know all of her secrets and history, wanted to know all of the intimate details of her life, and then just had generalized recommendations for relaxation exercises or pills that didn't work.

Erin cleared her throat and opened her door. "Thanks for the ride."

"No problem. Have a good rest of your day."

Erin slid out of the car.

"When are you going to get that Volkswagen fixed?" Charley asked.

"What?" Erin bent down to look down into the car at Charley.

"The yellow Volkswagen in your garage. If you're keeping it, you might as well drive it. Why don't you get it fixed up and drive it?"

"It was my Aunt Clementine's."

"Yeah…?"

Erin knew that the car was now hers, and there was no reason she couldn't take it out, get it tuned up, and drive it. Why was she holding on to it? It was like people who saved the good china or silver for a special occasion that never came instead of using them every day. What was she waiting for?

"I don't know," she admitted.

Charley grinned. "See you later, Sis."

Erin shut her door, and Charley squealed the tires as she sped away.

Terry was sitting on the couch watching TV. He blinked at Erin, and she wondered if he had fallen asleep. Orange Blossom was snoozing on the couch beside him and, while he looked up at Erin, he looked pretty dopey and just put his head back down to go back to sleep.

Blossom knew that Terry was the owner of the bothersome dog, so he usually wouldn't cuddle with Terry. But he was clearly comfortable where he was and didn't intend to move.

There wasn't anything wrong with Terry occasionally falling asleep in front of the TV. She just didn't want him regressing to the point where all he could do was sit in front of the TV and fall asleep during the day. When he'd been suffering from migraines and other problems following his injury, he hadn't been able to do anything else. It wasn't by choice.

"Hey. Did I wake you up?"

Terry shook his head. "No. No, I was just…"

"Closing your eyes for a minute?"

He cleared his throat. "Uh… exactly. Is it that time already?" He looked at the clock on the wall. "I didn't realize it was so late. Did you walk or did you have someone drop you off?"

"Charley."

"Oh." He gave a laugh. "I should have recognized her driving style."

Erin shook her head. "She's so bad. I tell her to behave, but it doesn't seem to help."

"No, the ones like her, it's worse if you tell them how to behave. They always have to do the opposite of what you say."

Erin recognized her own rebellious feelings in his statement. She was pretty good about not letting that little rebellious gut-reaction dictate her actions as a grown-up. As a child, she hadn't been quite so good at it.

And sometimes, just sometimes, she still did things just because someone told her not to.

"I don't think she's the worst driver in town, though," Erin said.

"No? She has to be pretty close, if you're talking about wanton recklessness." He stopped and reconsidered his statement. "Well... except for Beaver."

"Yeah. Did you know she has a glove box full of tickets?"

"Who do you think gave her most of those tickets?" he countered.

Erin laughed.

"And don't ask me why I keep issuing them," Terry said in a tone of disgust. "Considering that she never pays them. She just gets someone to have them wiped off the record."

"She is a federal agent."

"But she shouldn't be able to do that. She should have to take responsibility for her... creative driving."

Erin chuckled. "Yeah. Good luck with that. I think she'd just laugh at the idea."

Terry nodded his agreement.

"Do you know if we have a copy of the paper?" Erin asked, changing the subject.

"What paper? Oh, the weekly?" Terry looked at the coffee table in front of him, stacked with a number of flyers and other papers. He pulled out a copy of the Bald Eagle Falls weekly. "Here." He held it out to her.

Erin took the paper and looked down at it, frowning. "Oh... not this week's, last week's. The one with Joshua's article...?"

"Mmm. I might have taken it in to work with me."

Erin kept her mouth shut, trying to restrain a sharp question as to why he would have done that. It was her paper, not his. He could have picked up the one that was delivered to his house and taken it in. But of course, it was a lot less complicated just to grab Erin's.

"Did you, or didn't you?"

"I don't know." He closed his eyes to think about it, but shook his head, unsure of the answer. "Why?"

It shouldn't be that hard for him to remember whether he had taken it in to work or not. But he still forgot things more easily. Things he should have been able to remember.

"I want to read Josh's article."

Terry's eyes narrowed. "What are you investigating now?"

"Nothing. I just want to read his article. I didn't, because it came out the same day as he disappeared, and I was more worried about helping find him."

Terry continued to look at her, not believing it. Or maybe remembering that the day Joshua had disappeared, she had pretended to know nothing about it.

Erin ground her teeth. A bad habit and one that she shouldn't let creep back in. She forced herself to yawn and licked her lips. "I need a drink. You want something?"

"It must be late enough for a beer, if you're home."

Erin nodded her agreement and got him a beer and herself a glass of water. Terry popped the top on his can.

"You just want to read Joshua's article. Not because you're conducting your own investigation of his disappearance."

"What's wrong with that? He was pretty proud of the article. I should at least read it."

Erin went back through the kitchen to the back door, where the paper recycling bin was stored. She skimmed off the top couple of layers of flyers and miscellaneous lists, looking for the weekly. But it didn't seem to be there. She dug farther and found the previous week's. So Terry must have taken the issue with Joshua's article in to work.

"Can you go to your house and get me your copy?"

"Erin…"

"I want to read it. If you don't want to go out, just give me your keys and I'll go."

Terry didn't move to do so. He hadn't given her a key to his house. There was no reason she needed her own key, because he had taken to staying with her almost all the time.

Erin shook her head and walked out the door.

CHAPTER 35

Terry didn't chase after her, calling for her to stop, like she half-expected him to do. He didn't get up and offer her his key or to go get the paper at his house. He didn't follow her outside at all.

Erin went to Mrs. Peach's door and rang the doorbell. It took a few minutes for Mrs. Peach to get to the door. She was an older lady and moved slowly, but she still took a daily constitutional around the neighborhood. Erin just had to be patient and wait for her.

"Oh, hello, dear," Mrs. Peach greeted. She looked around Erin as if expecting someone else to be with her. Terry or Orange Blossom, maybe. Or Vic.

"Hi, Mrs. Peach. I was wondering if you could do me a favor. Do you have the weekly paper from last week? The one that had Joshua Cox's article on the front page."

"Oh, yes. I have that around here somewhere."

"Could I borrow it? I'll give it right back, I don't need to keep it, I just want to be able to read it."

"So sad about that boy, isn't it? I wonder what on earth happened to him."

Erin nodded. Her eyes burned and she wasn't sure if she could say anything, with the lump in her throat.

"I'll just see if I can find that," Mrs. Peach said, giving Erin's arm a comforting pat.

Erin wondered if Mrs. Peach knew that she and Josh were friends, or just recognized that she was a little teary-eyed over the comment.

She had to wait for a while as Mrs. Peach walked through her house, probably to the back door where she kept her own paper recycling. Then searched through it for the paper and walked back across the house again to the front door. Erin wondered if she should have offered to go around to the back door so Mrs. Peach didn't have to make the trek all the way back and forth.

"There you are," Mrs. Peach offered, holding it out to Erin. "That one?"

Erin looked down at the front of the paper, half expecting it to be the wrong edition yet again. But it wasn't. Josh's article was right there on top, the lead story.

Of course, Bald Eagle Falls didn't get much real news, and the lead story had been about the cook-off in the next town over. Not anything earth-shattering.

"Thanks so much, Mrs. Peach. Do you want it back?"

"No, you can keep it, dear. Or put it into your paper recycling. Don't throw it in the garbage. It should be recycled, you know."

"Yes," Erin agreed. "I'll do that. Thanks."

Mrs. Peach nodded and closed the door.

Erin walked back into the house. Terry was still sitting on the couch, and pretended to be occupied with the TV. If he didn't want to discuss it, that was fine with Erin. She walked past him into the kitchen and picked her glass of water up. She sipped it as she sat down at the table by herself and spread the paper out, looking for what was wrong.

Josh's assignment had been to write about the cook-off, but of course, he had focused on the murder that had taken place before the kick-off event. Beryl Batcombe. She had been one of the judges, like Erin. They had arrested Clayton for it. Beryl had stolen his family recipes and passed them off as her own family recipes. The plagiarism had incensed Clayton and he had started stalking Beryl and her part-time boyfriend, Chef Kirschoff. Eventually, he had killed Beryl and had also tried to kill Chef Kirschoff.

Josh didn't know all of the details, but he'd gotten everything he could from Erin and the other witnesses, and had put most of it together, filling in the cracks with guesses and speculation that were pretty close to being on target.

He was a good investigative reporter. Better than Erin had expected him to be. Especially considering that he was still a teenager.

Erin read the entire article and then sat looking at the paper, her eyes unfocused. So what had he discovered that someone didn't want Mary Lou to read? The kidnapper had cut Joshua's article out of Mary Lou's paper and had left the sticky note about Erin there in its place.

What had Joshua discovered that the police didn't already know? They had Clayton in custody. He had been charged with the murder and would go to trial.

Was Clayton involved in the kidnapping? Had he hired someone or imposed on one of his friends to make Joshua disappear? Or was there someone else involved?

She studied the article again.

Who had he interviewed?

Erin. Each of the winners—six of them.

Not Clayton, because Josh was a juvenile and couldn't get into the jail to see him without permission. And of course, Mary Lou would deny him permission.

He had a few quotes from Chef Kirschoff as well.

For a moment, Erin just let sadness wash over her. She had counted Chef Kirschoff as a friend. She had enjoyed working with him and talking about recipes with him. But he had turned out to be amoral. Cheating on his wife with Beryl Batcombe, giving her the judgeship even though he knew she had stolen the recipes she had published as her own family recipes.

The guy probably cheated on his taxes too.

Joshua had focused mostly on Beryl Batcombe's murder, because it was, as he had said, the most interesting part of the contest. Who would really be more interested in the coke and ice cream treats than in the woman found dead in a freezer?

Erin already knew all of the details. Beryl had been gassed with carbon dioxide and dragged into the freezer, most likely hoping that everyone would believe she had died in there. But they hadn't. It had been evident to the medical examiner that she had been moved.

Joshua had been good. He'd asked Erin about how she had felt, what it had been like to find Beryl, and so on. And he'd apparently asked other people involved in the contest about their feelings as well. The responses were emotional and resonant. They pulled the reader in.

She tried to picture each of the winners. She had looked at their pictures on the display boards at the hotel when she and Vic had gone back to Whitewater to look for Joshua. All of the happy faces, people excited about placing top in their class. And about winning the large cash prizes. Who wouldn't be happy about that?

We look forward to hearing more from Joshua Cox.

It was just a little note at the end of the article. Joshua's name and photo were at the top of the article, and his name was included again at the end, indicating that he would be writing again.

Erin frowned.

She picked up her phone and dialed Mary Lou.

"Erin?" Mary Lou sounded frightened. Surely she didn't think that Erin had discovered evidence that something worse than being kidnapped had happened to Joshua? Not that fast. If Erin had found out something serious, it would have been the police calling Mary Lou, not Erin.

Or maybe she was just afraid of what Erin was going to tell her about Joshua's article. Maybe that she had to read it. Or that Erin knew what it was that had inspired the kidnapping.

Or that she didn't.

"It's okay," Erin said. She didn't want Mary Lou to think that it was all over. Not either way. "I just wanted to know... was Joshua going to write more for the paper?"

Mary Lou didn't respond at first. Erin pictured her patting her hair thoughtfully, trying to get herself into the right frame of mind, considering Erin's question.

"He enjoyed writing that article," she said slowly. "He was fascinated with the process of interviewing people and developing the story. And his teacher was hoping that some extra assignments would boost his marks. So... yes, I know he planned to do more than just the one article. But I don't think there were any particular arrangements."

"The news article said they were looking forward to more from him. You don't know if he had started on something else?"

"No."

"Do you have his notepad?"

"What notepad?"

"The one he was using to write notes about the interviews. He had one when he came to talk to me in Whitewater."

"I just assumed he made notes on his phone. You know how kids these days are. Everything goes on the phone."

Erin shook her head, remembering clearly. "No. He was using a real notepad. Pen and paper. Like a reporter."

"What did it look like?"

Erin tried to remember the details. "It was just a little pocket memo pad, you know, they fit in a shirt pocket, spiral-bound on top. It was a dark color cover, but I don't think it was black. Maybe dark green."

"I'll look in his room."

Erin wasn't sure whether Mary Lou would hang up, call her back, or go and check while Erin was still on the line, so she waited. She could hear Mary Lou moving around, and pictured her climbing the stairs at her house to Joshua's room. Erin vividly remembered Josh mounting the stairs to go and prepare the guest bedroom for Brianna after Campbell had been arrested. She assumed that's where all of the bedrooms were. She could be completely wrong. He might have a man cave in the basement.

She wondered whether Mary Lou had to walk past his empty room every day. But if their bedrooms were close to each other, then Mary Lou would have heard something the night that Joshua was taken, wouldn't she? Unless he had gone willingly. Erin still didn't know what had happened, how the kidnapper had managed to get Joshua out of the house. It wasn't necessarily with brute force. Especially not if it was a woman. A woman would have to be pretty athletic to overcome him and remove him by force, especially without waking Mary Lou.

Mary Lou laid the phone down and began opening and closing drawers, dragging them open, shuffling the contents, and banging them shut again. Erin imagined Joshua's drawers as being filled with a combination of stuff from school, electronics, and some old books and toys from when he was younger. The old Joshua and the new Joshua, trying to make sense of his life and what he was going to be.

She couldn't hear Mary Lou anymore, and wondered where she was looking. Under the mattress? In his school backpack? Through the clothes hanging in his closet or scattered on the floor?

Mary Lou returned to the phone, sounding out of breath. "I've got it. Memo pad with a dark green cover. Don't schools do anything to teach kids penmanship these days? I remember when I went to school, we had to practice our printing and writing every day..."

"I'll come over," Erin said.

Mary Lou didn't respond immediately. "I'm going to call the police," she said. "This is their job, not yours. They can look through it and see if there is anything that might relate to his... disappearance."

"I might be able to figure it out," Erin said. "I've read through his newspaper article, and I remember when he interviewed me. I know more of the background for Beryl's murder and the contest. I'll spot something a lot faster than the police."

She was aware that she was venturing into dangerous waters. How many times had she been told to stay out of an investigation? But she wasn't going to stop now. She was the only one who had thought of the notepad. Who knew how much else she would be able to spot that the police wouldn't have any idea of? The murder had taken place in another town and been investigated by another police force. The Bald Eagle Falls police department wouldn't even know where to start.

"I am calling the police," Mary Lou repeated firmly. "I don't know how long it will take them to get here. So if you want to see it before they get here…"

"I'll be right over," Erin promised.

She folded the newspaper and jammed it into her purse. She paused in the living room, looking at Terry.

"Can I borrow the truck?"

He looked at her, frowning. "Where are you going?"

"To talk to Mary Lou."

"Have the two of you made up?" He sounded surprised.

"Yes," Erin said, impatient. "Just today. And I want to go over to her house to have a visit, now that we're on speaking terms again. So can I borrow the truck?"

"First you're reading Joshua's article and now you're going over to his house."

"Yes."

"What did you find out?"

Erin chewed on her lip. "He might have planned to write other articles. I want to look through his notes."

"That's not your job."

"I want to help. What is it going to hurt to look through his papers and see if he has any notes for other articles he wanted to write?"

"You know how it has turned out in the past, these harmless investigations of yours."

"I'm not doing anything dangerous." Erin turned toward the door. "I'll walk, I guess. I'll see you later."

She didn't need the truck. Mary Lou's house was just 'over the way.' Hopefully, the police wouldn't be in a rush to see what Mary Lou had found and Erin could still get there first. It was a Sunday afternoon. The sheriff wouldn't want to be rushing over to Mary Lou's to look at new evidence that probably wouldn't lead anywhere. Stayner wouldn't want to. Terry was home, off duty. Tom was also off.

"Erin!"

Erin turned her head back toward the door when Terry called her. He was standing on the threshold. "Here."

He tossed her the truck keys. Erin wasn't expecting him to throw them. She batted them out of the air and then had to step onto the lawn and fish them out of the flower border.

"Sorry," Terry said with a chuckle.

"Thank you."

Erin climbed up into the truck and started the engine. She waved at Terry and pulled out, careful to start off smoothly and not make the tires squeal. She was in a hurry, but there was no point in aggravating things further.

CHAPTER 36

*E*rin knocked on the door at Mary Lou's and waited impatiently. She knew that local custom said she could just knock and enter, but she wasn't comfortable with that. Especially not with Mary Lou.

Eventually, the door opened. Mary Lou didn't greet her, just pulled the door open and motioned Erin in. She had the memo pad in her hand. They sat down in the living room. Erin leaned eagerly toward her.

"Can I have a look? Maybe we should be wearing gloves."

"It's not something that whoever took him touched. If it contains something incriminating, they would have taken it with them. If they knew about it. They obviously didn't know anything, or it wouldn't have still been in his room."

Erin swallowed. She had a big lump in her stomach. Would there be anything in the notebook? Chances were, it would just be short notes of his interviews with the various people he had talked to about the contest and Beryl's death. Nothing new and nothing incriminating. Nothing that would point them in the direction of the kidnapper.

"Have you looked at it? Is there anything...?"

"I don't know. You read his article?"

"Yes."

"Hopefully... you'll recognize if something is out of place... something that someone wouldn't have wanted him to know or to follow up on."

Mary Lou handed the notepad over to Erin.

Erin held it in her hand, looking down at it and remembering the moment that Joshua had taken it out of his pocket, looking all professional and proud of himself. Not just a kid doing some boring work for extra credit. Writing was something that he was really interested in. While it may have started out as an assignment to write about a somewhat boring cook-off contest, there was a murder involved. He was excited to dig into the details and to figure out what had happened.

Erin wished she had spent a little more time with him. She didn't think she had said much that had been helpful to him. And then... it was right about that time that Charley and Chef Kirschoff had nearly been blown up with a CO2 canister. Erin had been right in the thick of things as she tried to get to Charley to find out what had happened and if she was okay.

Erin focused on the memo pad and turned the cover. There were a few random facts about the competition and questions to ask in the interviews. Then some more excited notes about Beryl Batcombe's death and questions like "Murder?" and "What was it like to find her?" that Joshua had, in fact, asked her those questions. She had told him as little as possible and sent him off to talk to the police or the contest organizers.

Would it have made a difference if she had spent more time with him? If she had listened to what he had to say as well as what he had asked?

Had he known something that had led to the kidnapping?

~

Joshua's penmanship wasn't *that* bad. Still, Erin did have to spend some time deciphering a number of the entries and wasn't even sure then if she had interpreted them correctly.

Erin was aware that she was under the microscope. Mary Lou watched her every move and change in expression, trying to analyze whether she was finding anything that would help them solve the case and recover Joshua safely. She hated the pressure and the scrutiny, but what was she going to do? Tell Mary Lou to quit looking at her? Say that she had to go somewhere private to read the notebook?

Instead, she did her best to ignore Mary Lou's stare and just to focus on what was in the book.

The notes got shorter and more excited as Josh proceeded through the interviews, and culminated with the day that the carbonated beverages had been judged and Clayton had blown up about Chef Kirschoff and Beryl Batcombe being corrupt. The day they had caught Beryl's killer.

Then the notes started to run dry. Facts and figures about the contest. Listings of expenses and how much it had cost to run. The hundreds of thousands of dollars of prize money that had been awarded.

Erin kept going. There were a few more notes about the winners of the prizes. Short bio notes and questions he had asked them. And then… nothing more. A few blank pages remaining at the end of the book.

Erin stared at the blank page. "Did he… were there any more notebooks?"

Mary Lou shook her head. "A few from when he was a kid, you know the little cartoon ones you put in birthday loot bags. That one," Mary Lou nodded toward Erin's hands, "came from a package of six." She easily anticipated Erin's next question. "That was the only one taken out of the package. The other five are still there."

Maybe he had switched to using his phone, like Mary Lou had expected. Maybe he found that he wasn't an old-style newspaper reporter, but one who was more comfortable in using modern technology than an old analog system that couldn't even be searched by keyword.

"What about his phone? Did he put anything on it? Was it… missing? Did he have it with him?"

"The police have his phone. It was still here." Mary Lou swallowed. She would know as well as anyone how important a phone was to a teenager. It was his lifeline, his entire world. He wouldn't have voluntarily gone anywhere without it. He wouldn't have left it behind on purpose.

"And there wasn't anything on it about the contest? More interview notes?"

Mary Lou wrapped her arms around herself as if she were cold. "I have no idea. I don't know what they found on it. They don't call me and tell me all of the developments. But I don't get the idea that… they thought it was very important. I don't even know if there is anyone in the department who is qualified to search a phone properly."

"I wouldn't expect it takes a lot of skill."

"There's more to it than just opening each app," Mary Lou countered. "How much stuff is stored in the cloud? What's on his camera roll? How many programs did he use where the information disappears after a few minutes or days? Kids use some pretty sophisticated methods to hide stuff."

Erin thought about the police department. Stayner was young enough that he would know some of the tricks. But the rest of them?

The sheriff was still using a *flip phone*. He claimed it got better reception than any of the newfangled smartphones. Maybe he was right. It was important, as remote as they were, to have coverage that was as reliable as possible.

Erin started going through the notebook a second time. She had to find something of importance before the police came and took it away. If she didn't find anything, what were the chances that they ever would? She was the one who had been in the contest, who knew all of the players.

Mary Lou gazed at Erin with sad eyes. She could tell that Erin wasn't getting anywhere. It had ended up being a dead end, just like every other avenue that had been investigated.

"The contest was already investigated," Erin said. "With Beryl's murder, the police already did background checks on everyone who was involved. They would have checked to make sure that everything was kosher, right? When Clayton accused Beryl and Chef Kirschoff of being corrupt, they would have looked into everything."

Mary Lou made a face. "It isn't like on TV," she pointed out. "You don't get an answer in half an hour. It can take years to root out corruption. All kinds of federal agents looking into every possibility."

Erin shook her head. Would it really take as long as all of that? They already knew that Beryl had plagiarized the recipes in her book and that Chef Kirschoff hadn't been honest about everything he was handling. So they would have known if there were other problems. They already knew who to look at.

"And that's if they got anyone other than the local police department to look into it," Mary Lou continued with the bad news. "Do you really think that the FBI would get involved in a backwoods Tennessee cooking contest?"

Erin held her arms over her stomach. "But there was a murder. They must have taken it seriously."

CHAPTER 37

*M*ary Lou shrugged helplessly. "I don't know. You would have to talk to the police department in Whitewater Junction and see if they would tell you anything. But I suspect you already know that they aren't going to tell you anything at all. They're not required to tell you about their investigation and what they have found yet, and whether they involved any federal departments."

Erin nodded. Of course they wouldn't tell her anything. She could barely get anything out of the Bald Eagle Falls police, which her boyfriend was a part of. Although she had always suspected that it would have been easier to get information out of the members of the police force other than Terry. He always tried to be extra careful not to tell her anything unless it were already public knowledge.

She had to start at the beginning. Erin paged through the notebook again. If she knew nothing about the cook-off, what information would she have found the most interesting? What would be the best parts to write additional newspaper articles on? Any follow-up news was being published after the contest was ended, so all of the hype was gone.

He could publish the results of the science fair that had been held in coordination with the contest. Or the hot dog eating contest. But those were not really exciting, other than for the people who had won.

He could do a follow-up story on what people were going to spend their prize winnings on, or where the next contest was going to be held. He could do profiles of the winners, or the sponsors, of any of the organizers who had been involved in getting it set up in the first place.

But Joshua didn't have notes on any of those topics. Other than some basic bios. A follow up on the contest winners would be interesting to people. Where the recipes they used had come from, whether they were traditional family recipes or of the winner's own creation. What had drawn them to enter the contest. What they did in their 'normal' life. Maybe a couple of profiles a week. Or the three winners of the beverage contest one week and the three winners of the ice cream contest the next. That would have a nice symmetry.

Erin stared down at the facts and figures in the notebook, her vision blurring.

"Erin?"

Erin closed her eyes, thinking.

"What is it?" Mary Lou asked, her tone more urgent.

"I'm not sure… I don't know where it takes us or if it helps us to find him…"

"What?"

Erin opened her eyes and looked at the page she had open. "He's written down all of the information on the prize monies and the costs of the contest. The sponsors and what they all contributed, stuff like that."

"Yes," Mary Lou nodded. "A reporter would need to know the basics when starting a story."

"Yes… but we knew the prize monies back at the beginning before people entered the contest. That was what attracted so many people. The chance to win a quarter of a million dollars."

"Right."

"Then why isn't that information at the beginning of the notepad?"

Mary Lou cocked her head to the side. "Does that matter? He needs it to write the story, whether it's at the beginning or the end."

"He wrote it after Clayton was arrested."

"I don't understand what your point is."

"All of that stuff was well-established by that point. And with everything that had happened, there was speculation that a lot of the local sponsors were going to lose money. The hotel, the restaurant that got blown up, there were all kinds of losses."

Mary Lou got up and walked across to the kitchen. She turned on an element on the stove and put the tea kettle over it.

"Why is that important?"

"I don't think he was writing an article on how much money was being offered for the prizes."

"No. You're right. It would be a bit late for that. And he must have included that information in his first article. It wasn't published until after the winners were announced, but he must have written how much each one was awarded."

"Yeah. He did," Erin agreed, remembering the little table showing that very information.

"Then what is it you think he was writing about?"

"Did the police say that they were going to send someone today?"

"Yes… but I don't know when. I didn't encourage them to come immediately, because I knew you wanted to look at it before they got here."

"I think… do you think it's possible that Chef Kirschoff's reason for running the contest didn't even have anything to do with food?"

"Well… of course. It could have been the money rather than the food. But he was giving money away, so it wasn't greed, was it?"

"The sponsors must have provided some of that. Otherwise, why were there sponsors?" Erin mused. She watched Mary Lou watch the kettle.

"But the prizes were announced before they recruited any sponsors. So the prize money must have come from Kirschoff. Or he already had it from somewhere."

"He comes here, he offers these great prizes, he says it's all about culture and Tennessee and giving the local communities a well-deserved boost. But he's never even been here before."

"He must have been, to be involved with Beryl," Mary Lou pointed out.

"But he said he'd never been..." Erin trailed off. Of course he had lied to her about it. To avoid any suspicion. He said it was his first time ever in Tennessee. Why would anyone think anything different? Why would anyone suspect him of being involved with one of the judges, who he had apparently never met before? "It wasn't about the food. It wasn't about Tennessee and giving our economy a boost and bringing our communities together. That was all just cover."

"But cover for what?"

The kettle started to whistle.

~

"It's time to get up, Joshua."

Josh didn't want to move. He was too tired to get out of bed. He didn't know why anyone was waking him up in the middle of the night. He kept his eyes closed and tried to drift back off to sleep. It wasn't hard. He didn't seem to have any energy at all anymore, and the best thing for him to do was just to close his eyes and turn off his brain.

He didn't want to think. He didn't want to escape. He just wanted peace.

The hooded figure was there. Hood and goggles. That was over-doing it a little, wasn't it? He had nearly figured out who she was.

At first, he hadn't known. The figure dressed in shapeless clothes, hood, and goggles was sexless. It could have been anyone. And that had been the point, hadn't it? To be anonymous. To keep her identity from Joshua.

But he'd gradually pieced together that his captor wasn't a man. She didn't smell like a man, for one thing. Not that she was wearing a bunch of perfume, but he caught hints of her shampoo and deodorant when she leaned over him, and he knew they weren't men's products.

It was hard to judge her height when he was lying on the bed. But he knew that when she sat on the edge of the bed to feed him that she was shorter than he was. He wasn't huge, but mostly women were shorter than he was and men were taller. Campbell said that he'd shoot up the rest of the way one day and be as tall as any of the other boys in his grade.

The whisper that was intended to hide her sex also masked her accent, but she seemed local. The speech patterns all sounded Tennessean. Her food tasted like his grandma's food. No hints of different origins. No unusual spices or textures. All exactly like his grandma had made in her kitchen those autumns that he and Campbell had gone to help her with her canning and preserving. They didn't come out of a can. She wasn't lying when she said it was one of her grandma's recipes.

And he knew. He knew that taking him had not been chance. He hadn't been held for ransom. She hadn't wanted to harm him. But she had not planned to keep him alive, either. She hadn't brought him regular meals or been concerned about his health. He'd been dehydrated since that first day, and she confirmed that she was intentionally withholding water.

It wouldn't be long. That's what she had said.

He didn't know why she wanted to get him up now, but he didn't see the point. It wouldn't be anything good.

CHAPTER 38

*E*rin was hoping that she would be able to relax and they could work everything out once the sheriff got there. But when he showed up, he had Terry and K9 with him, which did not help Erin to relax at all. She had just told Terry that she was not going to be investigating Joshua's disappearance. Then they had arrived to find out that she had been reading through the notebook and trying to come up with a theory on the case.

He raised his eyebrows at her and didn't say anything to censure her. But he also didn't sit beside her on the couch. He sat on one of the easy chairs a few feet away. K9 lay down obediently beside Terry's feet as he was trained to do, but he pointed his nose at Erin and whined, clearly confused by the situation.

Welcome to the club, K9.

It just didn't seem like anything could be easy for her.

Mary Lou explained about the notepad, how Erin had known that Joshua had used it when he was conducting his newspaper interviews and had taken note of the fact that the paper said he was going to be contributing further stories. So, one thing had led to another, and there Erin was, full of theories that she hoped to run by the police department. Like she was the detective and they were not the first line of investigation.

Terry paid careful attention to Mary Lou and did not look at Erin, even when it was her turn to talk. Erin turned the notebook over to Sheriff Wilmot, open to the page that began with the listing of the prize monies.

"He was investigating the financial affairs of the contest *after* it was finished," Erin pointed out.

Wilmot looked down at it. "Maybe. Or maybe he kept reference materials in the back and interview questions and notes in the front."

Erin frowned, thinking about that.

"It's an old technique," Wilmot said. "Maybe not something that someone your age would have thought of…"

"But Joshua is younger than I am."

"Yes."

"Where would he learn that?"

"Maybe from a seasoned reporter. Someone mentoring him about how to handle the interviews and writing the article. Why would he use a notepad instead of something electronic? Because he was learning from someone old-school."

Erin cleared her throat and looked down.

Was that all it was? He was keeping reference material in the back of the book?

She didn't believe it.

"I don't think that's why," she said, though all she had was a gut feeling and not proof. "I think… he was investigating the contest itself."

"For what?"

"For something financial. Like… money laundering."

Wilmot considered this. He looked at Terry, who didn't have anything to say about it.

"Why do you think that?"

"I wondered a few times myself, when Chef Kirschoff first came here and said that he was going to run this contest. I wondered why he would choose to do it here, when he said he'd never even been in Tennessee before. If he was going to run a contest like that, why wouldn't he do it in a bigger metropolis?"

"But that's an argument against trying to launder money here. It would make more sense for him to do it somewhere there were a lot of similar contests running and a bigger population, so it wasn't as obvious, wouldn't it?"

"It depends. It was a big deal for us, and everybody knew it was going on, but there aren't many federal agents out here who would ask questions. And all of those 'know your client' rules that banks have for money laundering, they would know exactly who Chef Kirschoff was, and that the money being transferred around was for the contest, right? They wouldn't need to ask for a bunch of details, because they already know, it's all for the contest. They know who Kirschoff is, they know the sponsors and the prize winners, so it's all established."

"I suppose. So what exactly would make you think there is anything like money laundering going on? It all appeared to be aboveboard."

"He didn't have sponsors before he came here. So, where was the money coming from?"

"Maybe he was just confident in his ability to raise money," Terry contributed.

"A million dollars? The prize money itself was three-quarters. Then, you add in all of the expenses, advertising, honorariums for the judges, salaries for employees, and all of that. He knew that he could come into backwater Tennessee and raise a million dollars in a depressed economy?"

"But he did, didn't he?" Sheriff Wilmot turned a couple of pages in the notebook, where Joshua had written down the amounts being contributed by the various sponsors. "He was able to get the money, the venues, cover all expenses..."

Erin nodded. "I'm no expert," she said. "I'm not even great at math. But right from the beginning, it didn't make sense to me. Especially on such a tight timeline. Why rush in and do this contest with only a few weeks' lead-up? Somewhere he said he'd never been before?"

"But he clearly had been here before," Terry said. "Considering he was having some sort of affair with Beryl Batcombe. We don't know how long he was planning the contest and what contacts or sponsors he already had in place when he got here. It seemed like it all fell into place pretty quickly."

Erin nodded.

"Yeah. And there was the part about holding it in the winter. If you're using dry ice, why not hold it at Halloween when you can tie into a spooky theme? Or if you're making ice cream and cold beverages, then why not hold it in the summer when it's hot and people will appreciate it more? Why hold something like that in the winter?"

"Well, we'll look into it," Wilmot said. "I'll review the notebook and maybe we'll get the feds in to see if there was money laundering. But if there was… those investigations can take a long time and I'm not sure it gets us any closer to… figuring out what happened to Joshua."

"If he was investigating money laundering, then he was kidnapped to stop him from figuring it out," Erin pointed out.

"And that makes it… who? Kirschoff himself? Someone in his employ?"

"It could have been Kirschoff, I suppose." Erin thought it over. "But I thought he was out of town by then. He could have come back, or assigned someone else to do it, but pretty much all of the organizers were gone the day after the contest concluded. And… there was a woman involved. We know that."

"How do you know that?" Terry demanded.

Erin looked over at him. "Because whoever called in to the Quiki to change the order impersonated me successfully. I suppose some men can do a convincing woman's voice, but the more obvious solution is that it was a woman."

"Oh." Terry looked taken aback. Obviously, he thought she had been digging more deeply than that, finding things that the police hadn't and not letting them know. "So… a woman. It could have been a girlfriend."

"No." Erin shook her head. "He was dating Charley."

"That doesn't mean that he wasn't dating someone else, from what

I understand of the man's morals. And," Terry gave Erin an uncertain sideways look. "You know Charley's history. Would you be able to say with one hundred percent certainty that she wasn't involved? Even if it was only the phone call?"

Erin knew that Charley's history with organized crime was a problem. She could never say that Charley wouldn't be involved with something like a kidnapping. She had turned out to be innocent of Bobby Dixon's murder, but she had still been a soldier in the Dixon clan, until she and they found out that she had Jackson blood. Erin couldn't be one hundred percent sure. She was pretty sure, but not that sure.

"She's your sister," Mary Lou contributed. "Her voice is similar to yours. More Tennessee, but…"

"She wouldn't do something like that," Erin insisted. But her face was warm and she knew that it was only her feeling, not proof of any kind.

"Kirschoff could have been seeing someone else," Wilmot reminded. "Or it could have been an employee. Or someone else who benefited from the money laundering scheme."

"Who benefits?" Erin asked. "I mean, besides Chef Kirschoff, who wouldn't want it to be discovered?"

"Anyone involved in the money laundering."

"The promoters," Terry contributed. "It sullies their reputation to find out they were involved in something like that, even if it was innocently."

"You and Miss Victoria as judges," Mary Lou said.

The thought made Erin sick. If she didn't know what was going on, how could she be thrown in with everyone else? But she knew it was true. If it turned out that the contest was just one big money laundering scheme, it would reflect badly on everyone involved. And everyone knew that she and Vic had been involved, that Auntie Clem's Bakery had gotten as much positive publicity out of it as they could, under Charley's direction. If the contest was tainted, so were they all.

"The winners of the contest," Terry said. "What is going to

happen to their prize winnings? Do they lose it? Does it get tied up for ten years while the feds investigate?"

"I have no idea," Wilmot said, shaking his head. "I've never been involved in an investigation like that."

"They participated in good faith," Erin protested, "they didn't know what was going on." She would feel terrible if Bella got bad publicity and lost her winnings. She had been counting on putting her money toward college. She didn't know the other winners very well, but she felt bad for them too.

"Maybe I'm just imagining things. Maybe there's good reason for all of this…"

Sheriff Wilmot raised his brows. "It's not for us to decide whether it's true or not, just to follow the breadcrumbs. No one is going to even know that you suggested it, unless you spread it around town."

"Well…" Erin's face got warm. "Sometimes things *do* leak from the police department."

Wilmot and Terry looked at each other, and the sheriff nodded, conceding the fact. "Sometimes, they do."

"But this isn't about who would suffer if money laundering was exposed," Mary Lou said flatly. "This is about finding my son."

Erin needed to hear that. "Yes. It's about Joshua," she agreed. And she knew Bella would give up all of her money if she knew that it meant Josh could be returned home safely. Bella was just that kind of person. She cared for others. And Josh, even though he wasn't a close friend, was still someone she cared about.

"We'll need to dig down," Wilmot told Terry. "Background on the winners. Anyone that Joshua mentioned having an interview with either in the article in the paper or in that notebook. They are all suspects—" He glanced aside at Erin. "Especially the women. They are the first priority."

"Can you find him?" Mary Lou asked, looking at Wilmot, her eyes as intense as spotlights. "Is this going to find him, or is it just going to… make someone take action if they haven't already?" She looked at her watch. "Or has it been too long to even have hope anymore?"

"We have to have hope," Erin encouraged. "Don't give up."

"But I need to know. I need to know whether to expect to find him again." She stared at the sheriff. "Please."

His mouth thinned and formed a straight line across. "I don't know, ma'am." He gave a little headshake. "At this point… it doesn't look good."

CHAPTER 39

Sheriff Wilmot and Terry got up. They had work to do. It was late in the day, and maybe it was already too late for Joshua, but they had to try what they could.

"Erin, I'll drop you at home," Terry said, reaching a hand toward her to help her up.

Erin stayed where she was. "If you don't need the truck, just leave it here and I'll get home in a bit. If you need it, go ahead. I can walk."

"I don't want you walking by yourself."

"I'll be fine."

"You don't know what kind of people may target you. If people know that you're looking into this... look what happened to Joshua. I don't want you getting snatched or hurt."

"Do you need the truck?"

Terry sighed and looked at the sheriff. "Can I hitch a ride with you?"

"Of course."

"Okay." Terry nodded at Erin. "I'll leave it with you. But still don't leave it too late, please. And maybe... let me know when you're leaving here and have Vic and Willie watching for you to get home."

"Are you really that worried?"

Terry's brows drew down. "Of course I am."

She again felt herself blushing. She stood up and kissed him goodbye. "I won't stay too long. And you take care of yourself. You can't pull an all-nighter like you used to. I don't want your head getting worse again…"

He nodded. He was probably embarrassed at her saying so in front of the sheriff and Mary Lou. Men wanted to look strong and invulnerable. Especially a police officer like Terry. So much of his self-worth was tied up in being the protector. Not someone who could fall prey to illness or injury. She shrugged an apology and sat back down, letting him go without any more fuss.

She and Mary Lou watched the two men leave. Mary Lou turned back to Erin, eyes narrow. "Was there something else…?"

Erin pulled the folded newspaper out of her purse. "I have the article here. I don't know if it will help, but…" She unfolded it, spreading it across her knees. "Okay. It has the names of the winners in both categories. I guess we start there."

"Who were they?" Mary Lou leaned forward.

Even though Erin didn't know all of them, Mary Lou had lived her whole life in Bald Eagle Falls. She would know not only the people, but their families and their histories. Sheriff Wilmot and Terry could conduct their background checks, but they wouldn't know the mountain's history like she did.

"Okay. Here we go. The first prize in beverages was Eugene Bath. He's the one who made that carbonated mint tea. It was actually really good."

Mary Lou just looked at her.

"Right. And then Bella Prost."

Mary Lou closed her eyes, thinking about Bella.

"I really don't think it could be her," Erin said. "I work with her, and… she's just not that kind of person. She liked Joshua. She wouldn't have done anything to hurt him, even if it did mean losing her prize and people thinking that she participated in something underhanded. She just wouldn't."

"I make it a policy not to assume that children will follow the examples of their parents and make the same good choices—or bad ones—that their parents would make." She met Erin's eyes. "I think you're right about Bella. I don't think the girl has a mean bone in her body."

Erin nodded, relieved. "She said that Campbell and Joshua never bullied her like some of the other kids at school. She thought they were both really nice boys. I've never heard her say anything against them, and I just don't think she would do anything to hurt Joshua."

"Who else?"

"Louisa David. She's the one who got third place after Clayton was disqualified. She made this really good mango fizz. Like a mango lassi, but fizzy…"

Mary Lou nodded.

Erin wasn't sure why she kept babbling. What did Mary Lou care about what kind of drink Louisa had won third prize for? Or even what Bella had said about Campbell and Joshua? Those things didn't matter.

"Louisa is a young woman, like you," Mary Lou said after some consideration. "Her voice would have the same timbre. Again, more of Tennessee in her accent. But that's true of pretty much anyone around here."

"Matt at the Quiki said that she probably did have more of a Tennessee accent than me. So that's okay. Do you know anything else about her?"

"Her people have been around here for a long time. I've never heard much about Louisa. Graduated school, got married, had a few kids. But nothing… exceptional. Not someone who I think had a lot of ambition."

Erin remembered Charley babbling about Beryl's ambition while she had a concussion. Beryl had wanted to be something. She wanted to be famous for her recipe book, for her cooking, she wanted to start up her own restaurant. She had used all of her influence to get the opportunities that she wanted. Louisa sounded about as far from Beryl as she could be. Erin couldn't picture a woman her age with young children making the trek from Whitewater to Bald Eagle Falls in the middle of the night to kidnap a young man. And then what? Where would she stash him? How would she look after him in between all of her other commitments? Or would she?

She could always have an accomplice. Her husband, probably. He could have been the one to kidnap Joshua, and was holding him in a cabin in the woods somewhere that no one knew about.

But it didn't feel right.

"So that's all of the soft drink winners. Then it's the ice cream winners."

Mary Lou fiddled with her teacup, empty or cold by now. She waited for Erin to continue. She must have heard who the winners were at the time, but a thing like having her son abducted could certainly have erased that knowledge from her memory.

"Doc Edmunds won first place."

"I remember hearing that," Mary Lou said, the corner of her mouth lifting in just a hint of a smile. "I imagine he'll be using his money to rebuild the veterinary office. He'll probably add on a full-service animal shelter."

"Probably," Erin agreed. "And if we're only looking at women, we can probably skip over him."

"He has a nurse-receptionist there. And he has a daughter, though she moved away a long time ago. I can't imagine she would come back here to kidnap Joshua because she wants the prize money. She'd have to get rid of her father before she would inherit it."

"Do you think we should look into Sarah, the receptionist?"

Mary Lou rubbed her eyes. How much sleep had she gotten over the past week? Probably not very much.

"No, not yet. She's too many steps removed. Maybe she has a burning desire to work at a fancier vet office or to open an animal shelter, but I doubt it."

Erin went on to the next name on the list. "The last two are both women. Deidre Robinson and Hannah Clark."

Mary Lou sighed. "Does that mean it has to be one of those two, or that we're on the wrong trail? Do we really think that one of the prizewinners took Joshua? Because she didn't want to lose her money?"

"I don't know. But if it was related to the contest, if they really were laundering money, then these are the names we have to work with. I don't know all of the people who worked with Chef

Kirschoff or for the sponsors. I met a few people in Whitewater…"
Erin let her mind do a quick review of the people who had worked
on the contest. "There was a woman who acted as a tour guide,
telling us about Whitewater and its storied history… but I don't
think she was even from there, I think she was someone with Chef
Kirschoff. She wouldn't have known where to find Joshua. She
would have had to come back here from… wherever they went to
next."

"I haven't noticed anyone strange around town. Any outsiders, I
mean," Mary Lou said. "It's all been very quiet since the contest
ended. Like everyone was taking a breath."

"I knew a few of the people at the hotel. And the other judge that
they brought in, Lara Gross."

"Lara Gross."

Erin waited to see what Mary Lou thought of her. Mary Lou
shook her head. She wasn't going to magically come up with the
answer.

"Deidre Robinson. Hannah Clark. Lara Gross. Is it one of them?"

Mary Lou covered her face with both hands. She rubbed her face
briskly and palmed her eyes and sat there for a minute with them
covered.

"Do you know them?" Erin asked.

"Deidre Robinson. Is that the mother or the daughter?"

Erin looked down at the newspaper. They hadn't included
pictures of everyone. There had been too much else of interest. Beryl's
death, the explosion at the restaurant, Clayton's arrest. Who wanted
to see the faces of the prizewinners? But Erin had seen them at the
hotel when she and Vic had gone back. There had been posters with
pictures of all of the prizewinners. If Erin could just access them in
her memory.

"I think… oh, it's hard to be sure. I think that Deidre was an
older woman. Grandma type. White hair."

"The mother, then. She wouldn't be able to sound like you on the
phone."

"No. Probably not. I should check, though…" Erin pulled out
her phone and did a web search to find the pictures of the prizewin-

ners. There had to be promotional pictures of them online. The first couple of searches that she tried didn't bring up any results.

"What is it?" Mary Lou asked.

"I can't get anything..."

"No service? It can be spotty out here."

"No, I mean... my searches aren't producing any results. I'm looking for the contest results, but searching the name of the contest doesn't bring anything up."

Mary Lou shrugged. "That's not surprising, is it?"

"Well... yes, it is. All of the publicity that they did, and none of that got posted online? No summary of events or promotional flyers for the contest?"

"It was all done locally. Not on the internet. People in these parts, they're a close community. Posters go up at the library and town hall. Or in people's shop windows. In the weekly newspaper or the penny saver. We don't go looking for that kind of thing online." She gave a little laugh. "Not us old folks, anyway."

"I knew the newspaper wasn't online, but nothing? They didn't put anything online? I didn't even know that was possible." Erin switched over to one of her social networks and did a search there. People must have posted pictures and tweeted and shared the results on social media. At least the young people, even if the older ones weren't into social media.

But the results were sparse, and she didn't find any pictures of Deidre Robinson. Erin switched over and searched for Hannah Clark. More results for her. Social media profiles. Some pictures of her with a bowl of the ice cream she had made, smiling sunnily at the camera. Erin searched for Lara Gross. She had professional headshots on her company website, her work history on LinkedIn, and all of the other things that Erin would have expected.

"I guess Deidre just doesn't have any social media," she said.

Mary Lou nodded, not surprised.

And Erin shouldn't have been surprised either. There were plenty of white-haired grandma types who didn't have social media accounts. They hadn't grown up on computers. Many had never learned to do anything on the internet but read their mail, if that. Maybe just texts on their phones. If they had smartphones and not an old flip phone like the sheriff.

But no social media? No one else had posted pictures of her on their accounts either? No one in her family had written about granny winning a big cash prize in the cooking contest?

No one?

CHAPTER 40

"*T*his doesn't feel right," Erin said. "You said that she has a daughter?"

"Yes… oh, you're taxing my memory if you expect me to be able to remember that. She would have been my age. But we didn't go to school together."

"And she was in Whitewater, so she wouldn't be in your school yearbook."

"No."

Then Mary Lou raised her hand in a 'wait' gesture. Her brows drew together.

"Yes."

"Yes?"

Mary Lou got up. She spun in a slow circle. "Where did I put those? I don't know if I ever even unpacked them after we moved here."

She hadn't always lived there. Erin had forgotten that the house was just a rental. Mary Lou and her family had lost everything in the financial disaster involving Angela Plaint. Including their house. It was really remarkable that Mary Lou hadn't held a bigger grudge against Angela.

"I think… in the attic," Mary Lou decided. She started toward the stairs.

"Do you need help?" Erin asked, standing, unsure what to do.

"No, no. There are actually stairs. No messing about with ladders."

Erin sat back down. She watched Mary Lou go up the first flight of the stairs and then she disappeared down the hall.

Erin held her breath. Were they going in the right direction? It could be completely wrong. It could be someone who worked for one of the big sponsors. Some of them were huge corporations with thousands of employees. How would they ever find a needle in a haystack like that?

She waited. She had figured it would only take Mary Lou a minute to go up to the attic and find the books she was looking for. But they were packed away. And there were probably a number of other boxes that had never been unpacked either. And maybe none of them labeled clearly.

Erin shifted her position, anxious. She wanted to be there, digging through the boxes, finding the books. Like when Erin had been looking for Clementine's journal, back when she had first come to Bald Eagle Falls.

But Clementine's journal hadn't been in any of the storage boxes. It had been in the hands of Davis and Joelle. They had stolen it from Erin and used it for their own purposes.

What if someone had stolen the yearbooks? Maybe that's what it had all been about. Not about kidnapping Joshua, but about getting into the attic to find the yearbooks.

But who would know that they were there, other than Mary Lou? How would anyone know that she hadn't just thrown them out? Not everyone kept their high school yearbooks. The teenage years were a horrible time. Plenty of people didn't want to remember anything about that time. Erin had never had a yearbook, and she wasn't sure she would have wanted one. What good would it have been for her?

She could hear boxes being moved around up in the attic. So Mary Lou was still at it. She hadn't passed out in the hot, dusty attic.

Erin forced herself to look down at her phone and to work

through a few more searches. The time would go faster if she kept herself busy. Before she knew it, Mary Lou would be back down with the yearbooks for the years that she and Deidre's daughter had been in high school.

She almost succeeded in distracting herself from Mary Lou's search.

But not quite.

It was eerie how nothing was showing up on her searches for the contest or for any mentions or pictures of Deidre Robinson.

"Here we go," Mary Lou announced, appearing at the top of the stairs. She held a small stack of hardcover books in her hands. She rejoined Erin, and they sat side-by-side on the couch so that they could look at the books together.

"So I was thinking, we didn't go to the same schools, so there wouldn't be any pictures of her in my yearbook. But I forgot about sports. Our school teams played against each other more than once. And she was on the basketball team."

"Great! Good thinking."

Mary Lou picked up one of the books and started to flip through it. She started at the back, which appeared to be the standard place to put pictures of the various winning teams. Her eyes searched for the girl that she remembered. Or nearly remembered.

"Ah-hah. Here she is." Mary Lou put her face close to the page, taking in the small black and white picture. "Rosalie. Deidre's daughter is Rosalie."

"Rosalie," Erin repeated. "Rosalie Robinson?"

"She probably went by her married name. It was… Brandon." Mary Lou pointed at one of the boys' teams. "She married Marcus Brandon, her high school sweetheart. Of course, they didn't stay together, but she kept his name. Probably the only thing she ever got from him."

"Okay. Rosalie Brandon." Erin tapped it quickly into her phone. There would be hits for Rosalie Brandon. She still wasn't young enough to have a huge social media presence, but it would be more than her white-haired mother. "Let's have a look…"

Erin trailed off. Again, the results were sparse. There were other

Rosalie Brandons, of course, but no Rosalie Brandon in Whitewater Junction, or one of the other small towns nearby.

"Why aren't they on here?"

"Not everyone is," Mary Lou said. "The only reason I have an account on any social media is so that my sons can share things with me or message me. But I figure… by the time they have kids, at least I'll know where to find the baby pictures." She laughed weakly.

The laugh quickly turned to a sober expression. She was clearly reconsidering whether either of the boys would ever have children for her to spoil and coo over their baby pictures. Campbell wasn't exactly pursuing the path toward being a responsible father. And Joshua…

Erin tapped in a couple more searches. She tapped one of the results. "There's an obituary." She skimmed through it quickly, checking the names of the mother and ex-husband. "Did you know she had died?"

Mary Lou shook her head. "It's been so long. I didn't remember that, but I'm not surprised. It isn't like we were ever friends or kept in touch. It just would have been one of those cases where you say, 'Oh, I remember her, she was on the Whitewater girls' basketball team the year we won the championship.'"

Erin nodded. "So this is a dead end." Clearly, their kidnapper was not Rosalie Brandon, returned from the grave. That would be a whole other genre of mystery.

"I suppose it is. I thought for a minute that we were on to something. Like maybe somebody had intentionally erased information from the internet. You always hear that once something is uploaded to the internet, it can never be deleted, but that always seemed a little far-fetched to me."

Erin continued to look at the obituary, her eyes unfocused. She blinked a couple of times. She was getting tired, and she knew that Mary Lou was tired too. They both needed to sleep. Maybe she would have a dream that would tell her where to look next. Her subconscious brain could work on the problem while she was sleeping. And then in the morning… they could figure it out. They could find Joshua.

The words in the obituary cleared when she blinked. Erin looked at it again. "Rosalie had a daughter?"

"Oh, did she?" Mary Lou was politely uninterested.

"Kim Brandon." Erin tried one last time, tapping the name into her browser search box.

Nothing.

Kim Brandon had to be the right age. If Rosalie and Mary Lou had gone to school together, then Kim Brandon had to be somewhere between Erin's age and Joshua's. If Rosalie had married her high school sweetheart, then the baby had probably followed quickly. She had taken the Brandon name, so she wasn't likely a child of a later marriage or relationship.

"She has to be here. She has to have a social media account. Something. Who wouldn't have some kind of internet presence?"

But looking harder didn't help. Erin couldn't find anything on the woman. It was, as Mary Lou had said, like she had deleted herself from the internet. She had closed all of her social media accounts. Had every reference to herself that she could find deleted from the record.

And not only that, but had any pictures of her grandma deleted as well. She had wiped out every reference to Deidre Robinson that she could find. Made people take down any pictures they had posted of her receiving her check and showing off her maple ripple ice cream. Kim had probably made up some sad story about her grandma. How she was being stalked online after winning the contest, so they had to take everything down for her protection.

And why? Why had it been so important to take down any online information about Deidre and her granddaughter?

CHAPTER 41

*B*ecause Kim had a plan. She had a plan to stop Joshua from finding out about the money laundering. Erin didn't know how Kim had figured out about any financial issues to begin with. Maybe, like Erin, she wondered about the rush to run the contest, the large sums of cash, and the unlikelihood of ·picking Whitewater Junction, Tennessee for the location of a contest that was supposed to garner attention from sponsors and media.

Maybe she was an accountant or some kind of agent or auditor herself. It was impossible to know, since every trace seemed to have been removed from the internet. Maybe she was a computer genius.

But Kim had discovered financial improprieties in the contest and she didn't want her grandmother's name sullied. Or didn't want her to lose the prize money. If Kim were the only grandchild, then she would be in line to inherit that money. Maybe grandma was sick, or Kim planned on helping her along, or she just wanted the money to be there when she eventually died.

"It's Kim," she told Mary Lou with certainty. "Got to be."

Mary Lou looked at her, unblinking. They were moving things forward, but she didn't seem to be happy or excited to have discovered this news.

"Maybe she is," Mary Lou said. "But where does that get us?"

Erin considered what to do next. They clearly couldn't just go to Whitewater and knock on Kim Brandon's door. That wouldn't help them to find Joshua. Terry would probably throttle her.

"Call the guys, I guess. Let Terry and the sheriff know what we found and let them follow up. I met Deputy Coleman over in Whitewater, he seems like he knows what he's doing. They can call him and have him look into it…"

Mary Lou nodded. But her eyes were empty. There was no guarantee that the police would find any reason to interview Kim Brandon. And if Kim didn't feel like talking to the police, she didn't have to. And they still wouldn't know where to find Joshua.

Terry and Sheriff Wilmot agreed that there was good reason to look more closely at Kim Brandon, but it didn't feel like progress. They would run background, check to see if she had any previous charges or convictions, and talk to Deputy Coleman to see what he thought of her. But they still had to check out the other suspects as well. They couldn't just trust Erin's and Mary Lou's instincts on Bella or any other contestants. They would prioritize the women over the men, but only because the person who had called the Quiki with the changed fortunes was a woman. Or passed as a woman on the phone.

"Maybe we should go back to Whitewater," Erin suggested. "I know it's getting late, but…"

"I'm not going to sleep tonight," Mary Lou said.

"No. We could just look around. Talk to Detective Coleman and answer any questions he might have. It's better to go to him than to make him come to us, or interview us over the phone. He'll want to see us face to face."

"Of course," Mary Lou agreed.

"Yeah. Do you mind if I drive?" Erin didn't want to tell Mary Lou that she looked terrible. Erin was afraid that she wouldn't be able to drive to Whitewater safely. Mary Lou might not be able to fall asleep, but that didn't mean she was alert enough to drive.

Mary Lou nodded. "That's fine. You know the way."

It wasn't hard. There were paved highway and road signs all the way.

Erin shifted to rise. "Do you need to do anything before we go?"

"I should tell Campbell where I'm going."

Mary Lou didn't pick up her phone as Erin expected, but got up and walked toward the back of the house.

Campbell was home, but he hadn't bothered to come out when the police were there to talk to his mother about Joshua? She was surprised that he hadn't at least been there to offer emotional support. But Campbell's experience with the Bald Eagle Falls police had not been positive. Maybe he was afraid he would distract them from the real issue. Or that they would accuse him of having been involved.

Mary Lou came back a moment later, Campbell slouching along behind her. His head was bowed. He looked up at Erin through his lashes, looking remarkably vulnerable and childlike for a young man that she knew had been experimenting with the wild life.

"Do you mind if I come along, Miss Erin?"

Erin considered. Of course she didn't mind him going along, but she needed to make sure that he wasn't going to cause trouble. He couldn't be jumping in to do anything rash. If she said he couldn't come along, he would probably just follow along in his car without permission anyway.

"Yes, you can come. But if you have any weapons, you leave them at home. Same with anything else you might have that you wouldn't want the police to find on you."

"No one is going to search me."

"Those are my conditions."

Campbell looked at his mother, blushing around the neck. "Fine," he said. "I just need to get something from my room."

He went up the stairs, hands in pockets, still hunched over.

Mary Lou looked at Erin. "Thank you."

Erin wasn't sure whether she was saying thank you for allowing Campbell to go with them, or thank you for ensuring that he didn't have any contraband with him. She nodded.

Campbell was back in a couple of minutes, and the three of them went out to the truck.

Erin was barely out onto the highway when her phone started buzzing with a call. She tapped on the Bluetooth button and saw Terry's number come up on the screen.

"Hi." Maybe he had something more to ask or something to report back on Kim. Erin didn't expect them to get anything that fast, but maybe Kim had a record. Maybe she'd done this kind of thing before or made threats that they hadn't known about.

"Where are you going?"

Erin glanced over at Mary Lou, then looked back at the road. "Uh, we're just heading out of town."

"We?"

"Mary Lou and I wanted to..." Erin trailed off, hoping that something would occur to her. Mary Lou would jump in with an explanation, or Terry would interrupt to discuss whatever he had called her about.

"You wanted to what? Where are you going?"

Erin cleared her throat. "We wanted to check something..."

"In Whitewater Junction?"

"Uh, yes."

"We already have Coleman and his team in Whitewater. If we need something checked out, they can do it."

"I know. And I'm sure they'll do a great job. But we just hoped... I don't know... if Deputy Coleman wants to talk to us about what we found out and about stuff that happened at the contest, I can answer his questions. We'll be right on hand. And if he finds out that she has... a storage locker or something that they check tonight... then we'll be close... if he finds anything."

"You need to stay in Bald Eagle Falls."

"We'll be back. By the time you're done..."

"I'm probably going to be on most of the night. Erin, it's getting dark, it's late, you're not going to be able to find anything or talk to anyone tonight. Leave it until morning."

Mary Lou spoke up. "Joshua may not make it until morning, Officer Piper."

"You're not going to find him tonight. You don't know what kind of condition he is in or what kind of situation you could walk into.

Trust the process. Going into Whitewater tonight and messing around… you're not going to find anything. You're not going to move the case forward. I'm sorry, Mrs. Cox, but you need to come back. This is dangerous."

"We'll check in with this Deputy Coleman. Surely it's not dangerous to talk to him."

"No, I didn't say that. But I don't think for a minute that the two of you—"

"We will be fine. You're not going to talk me out of it, Officer Piper, so you may as well not even try."

"It's my truck," Terry protested, his voice rising.

"You said I could use it," Erin argued. "It isn't like I'm stealing it."

"I did not say that you could take it out of town and go looking for kidnappers."

"I'll bring it back tonight, just like I said. You did give me permission."

"Not to go out of town."

Erin was watching the road signs, her foot down on the gas, figuring that once she got far enough away from Bald Eagle Falls, she could say that she was close enough to Whitewater that there was no point in turning back. She might as well go on to their destination. She knew it was a bad argument, but it would have to do.

"How did you know I was leaving town?" she asked, thinking about her phone. A lot of couples had apps to share their locations. She had never installed one, but was it possible that Terry had put one on her phone without her realizing it? Or that he had hacked her location some other way?

"GPS tracker in the truck," Terry informed her.

"Oh." Erin eased her foot off of the gas. He could see how fast she was going and where she was on the highway. There wasn't any point in trying to fudge where she was and say she was closer to Whitewater. Though Whitewater was not far, and she would be reaching the halfway point before too long.

"My truck is valuable to me. If anyone takes off with it, I want to be able to track it down."

"Yeah, right. That makes sense," Erin agreed.

"I wasn't planning to use it to track you," Terry said. "But you're important to me too. Come on, Erin. You know this is a bad idea. Don't make me come to Whitewater to get you."

"You've got work to do there. Do the stuff that the sheriff asked you to."

Terry made a growling noise. Then he sighed. Erin knew when she heard it that he wasn't going to follow her. He wasn't going to try to physically coerce her into returning to Bald Eagle Falls. He'd hoped that just telling her to return would be enough.

And normally, it would. She wasn't an unreasonable person. But Joshua was missing and they didn't know how long he had left.

She couldn't look at Mary Lou's fading hope and do nothing. They had a clue. They had a path to follow.

They had to follow it and see where it led.

CHAPTER 42

$\mathcal{E}$rin felt guilty as they pulled into Whitewater. Night was falling quickly. She knew that Terry didn't think it was safe or a good idea for them to be there. But she couldn't sit at home with Mary Lou and do nothing.

"Do you want to have a look around first? Before it gets completely dark?"

"We won't have long."

"No," Erin agreed. She took Mary Lou's response as a 'yes,' and started to work her way through the main streets of Whitewater. A lot of the residents actually lived outside of the town limits in the surrounding farms and acreages. There would be no way to find Kim without directions if she lived outside of town.

But they weren't going to search for Kim. They would leave that for the police. They were just going to take a look around, get the lay of the land, see if anything jumped out at them, and then they would go to the police station and talk to Coleman. If he hadn't already called it a night and gone home for dinner or bed.

Even though it was getting dark, Erin recognized most of the streets. She had walked them while she was getting ready for the contest and while it was on. She had gone back and looked through the streets with Vic, hoping to somehow just find

Joshua. As if he had just run away and they might find him walking down the street or sitting on the library steps smoking a cigarette.

But what more were they going to find this time? They weren't even looking for someone who might be out walking around, but for someone who was locked up, behind closed doors.

But Erin felt strongly that they were doing the right thing. Mary Lou and Campbell did not object, so maybe they had the same feeling. That they were close. If they just drove by the place Joshua was imprisoned, they might feel it. They would find him.

They all watched out the windows, studying every building they went by. Some of them, Erin automatically discounted. Stores and businesses that were open to the public. Joshua couldn't be hidden somewhere close to people, where he might make a noise and draw attention. It would have to be an outbuilding. A storage unit. A garage or shed of some kind.

And those were not in short supply.

"Do you think he's here?" Campbell asked his mother.

Her face was a stony mask. She sat in the passenger seat and didn't turn around to look at Campbell, who was sitting with his knees turned to the side because the seats were so close together.

"If it was Kim Brandon who took him... then he must be here somewhere."

"You don't think that she kept him somewhere closer to Bald Eagle Falls? Or out in the woods?"

"Maybe."

"But she couldn't do anything that would draw people's attention," Erin said. "If she suddenly started disappearing for an hour or two every day, people would notice. They would wonder what she was doing, where she was going all of a sudden."

Assuming she was taking care of Joshua. That wasn't guaranteed. It had been so long, what were the chances that she had kept him alive? Why would she? She wanted him to be gone permanently, didn't she?

They drove by a low brick building. Erin had to strain her eyes to see the sign out front, which had one dim spotlight shining on it.

Two other spotlights had burned out and not been replaced. It was the Whitewater Junction General Hospital.

"I didn't know they had their own hospital here. When Charley and Chef Kirschoff were hurt, they were taken into the city."

Mary Lou nodded her head. "These little rural hospitals, they aren't good for much more than broken arms or the stomach flu. If you are very ill, or there's an accident, they don't have the kind of trauma care that a city hospital has."

Of course not. It wouldn't make sense for a little hospital to have the personnel or expertise to man a trauma center. Erin drove slowly past it.

"It looks more like an old folks' home or hospice than a hospital."

Erin had worked in hospice care. She'd been in a few places like that. Rooms that tried to imitate the home environment as much as possible, to be comfortable for the patients despite IV stands and other necessary hospital equipment. Quiet places, where the lights were kept dim, the music quiet and comforting, and any PA announcements were kept to a minimum. There was no Code Blue in places like that. No reason to resuscitate patients who slipped gently into the dark.

"Yes," Mary Lou agreed. "They probably have some hospice care here. Or a dementia ward. Places where you just… house people until they're ready to go."

Erin pulled to a stop.

CHAPTER 43

*C*ampbell and Mary Lou looked at her.

"What is it?" Campbell asked.

Erin looked at the little hospital, frowning and thinking. "So Deidre won the cooking competition. And we figure Kim is probably her sole heir."

"Right," Mary Lou agreed.

"And Kim has kidnapped Joshua to keep the whole corruption thing quiet. So that no one can find out about it and take away Deidre's money or smear her reputation, whichever it is."

Campbell was listening attentively. He hadn't heard the whole theory before. He just knew that they were going to Whitewater to look for Joshua and talk to the police about a suspect.

"How long?" Erin asked.

"How long what?" Mary Lou asked in confusion.

"How long was she planning to hold Joshua? Or how long did she figure she was going to have to protect Deidre or wait until she could get the money?"

"Kidnapping someone and planning to hold them for more than a few days is crazy," Campbell contributed. "You can't look after all of someone's needs for that long; it takes you away from everything else. And if they get sick... and you have to worry about if they are going to figure out how to escape, or someone is going to cotton on to what you're doing. The longer you hold someone, the more dangerous it is."

"But she had this whole plan. She must have been planning to hold on to Joshua, because she didn't... do something permanent in Bald Eagle Falls. If she wanted him permanently out of the picture, she could have done that. Nobody would have connected it to Whitewater. However she got into the house or got him out of it, she could have gotten rid of him permanently. If that was what she had wanted. Then she wouldn't have to worry about taking care of him. Or about him escaping or giving her away somehow."

"Then... you don't think she planned to hold Joshua for this long?" Mary Lou asked.

"No. She had it all planned out. We know it wasn't a spur-of-the-moment thing, because she called in the change order to the Quiki before she took him. She had a plan, and she followed through on it. Only... he should have been released by now. Two days, three, you don't plan to kidnap and hold someone for any longer than that, right?"

Cam's words echoed in her ears.

The longer you hold someone, the more dangerous it is.

Campbell looked at the hospital. "So why are we stopped here? You don't think Joshua's in there, do you? That she's a nurse, or that she would bring him here if he got sick? Kidnappers don't do that. If something happened to him... she would just run."

"Without her money?" Erin shook her head. "We thought it wasn't about money, because she didn't ask for a ransom. But she's waiting for the money. She thinks that Deidre is going to die and she's going to inherit."

"You don't get money the day after someone dies," Mary Lou said dryly.

"No. And if you've been through a death in the family like that, you know that. But does Kim know that? Or maybe she's gotten Deidre to put everything in their joint names, so that they don't have to probate. So as soon as Deidre dies, it is automatically Kim's. She can cash out and run, and send us a message about where to find Joshua."

If she was smart enough to figure out that the contest had been laundering money, then she was smart enough to know how to get around waiting for weeks or months while Grandma's estate was probated.

"And you think her grandma is in there?" Campbell finally made the connection. He looked at the lights still on in the hospital. "And Kim is just waiting for her to die?"

"Or maybe trying to help her along," Erin agreed. It happened. People did things to speed up the inheritance process.

"But there wasn't anything wrong with Deidre," Mary Lou dismissed. "If she was dying, then how would she make the ice cream that won one of the prizes?"

"It only took a day. She wouldn't have needed a lot of energy for that. Or maybe she didn't get sick until after she won the prize money. After Kim decided that she wanted it."

They traipsed into the hospital. Erin was sure that visiting hours were probably over. But she had a few tricks up her sleeve. She had worked in hospice before.

She approached the main reception desk and spoke very quietly to the nurse situated there. "We're here to see Deidre Robinson. Is she..." Erin raised her eyebrows and hesitated awkwardly.

The nurse recognized the signals. Rather than objecting that she couldn't give them any information, she tapped the name into her computer and glanced over the records. "Deidre is still with us," she relayed back in a whisper.

"I'm sorry we're so late. We just got the call yesterday that she might not make it... we've been driving for seventeen hours..."

The nurse nodded understandingly. She picked up a slip of paper and a pen and wrote the unit and room number. "You just go down that hallway," she explained. "Take a right and go all the way to the end. There's another desk for the unit nurse there. She'll show you to Deidre's room."

"Thank you so much."

Erin turned to Mary Lou and Campbell and whispered to them. "We got here in time. It isn't too late."

They all hoped that it wasn't too late for Joshua too.

Erin led the way down the corridor. When they reached the Palliative Care unit, the lighting was dim, as Erin had pictured it. There was an air of quiet expectation about the place. A portal between life and death. Erin didn't usually believe in an afterlife. But when she was in a place like that, when she watched a soul transition from life, that was when she really wondered if there was a place for the person's consciousness to go afterward.

Erin flashed the slip of paper with the room number on it at the unit nurse. "We're here to see Deidre. Do we just go in? Is it okay?"

Neither nurse had even bothered to ask if they were related. Anyone who came to say goodbye to a dying patient was family.

"Just over there." The nurse in a pink smock smiled and pointed. "Third door down. She's sleeping comfortably right now."

This time it was Mary Lou who took the lead. Erin and Campbell followed.

CHAPTER 44

$\mathcal{E}$rin could vaguely remember the white-haired woman smiling on the contest poster. She had seemed bright and vibrant. Matronly, friendly, the kind of person that would have made the perfect grandma in a commercial or family movie.

That woman was gone.

Deidre's hair had yellowed and thinned, as had her face. Her wrinkled cheeks were sunken in, and there was no evidence of the warm pink blush she had worn the day of the contest. Her eyes were closed, the sockets around them appearing bruised. No machines were beeping loudly or monitoring her vital signs. Her breathing was shallow and somewhat labored. Stopping and starting again in an irregular rhythm, so that Erin didn't know when to expect the next breath, if at all.

Mary Lou sat down in the chair right next to the bed. She took Deidre's hand and squeezed gently. "Deidre? Mrs. Robinson?"

Deidre stirred. Erin was surprised. She had thought that Deidre was too far gone, that she was in the last sleep of her life and they wouldn't be able to rouse her again. She had seen that state enough times.

"Deidre? It's Mary Lou Hensley, Mrs. Robinson. Do you remember me?"

Deidre's head moved back and forth and her breathing seemed to grow louder and more strained. Erin bit her lip, worrying that waking Deidre now was going to be too much of a shock to her system and they would only hurry her demise.

"Deidre." Mary Lou gave the older woman's hand a little shake. She patted Deidre's cheek. Not slapping it, just patting it, hopefully enough to arouse her one more time. "Deidre, I need your help. Please."

Finally, Deidre's eyes cracked open. Her irises were dark, it seemed like her eyes were very distant. Erin didn't know if she could see Mary Lou.

"Who is there?" she asked unsteadily.

"My name is Mary Lou. I went to school at the same time as your daughter Rosalie. Except I went to Bald Eagle Falls. We played Whitewater in the girls' basketball playoffs. Do you remember that?"

"We won," Deidre recalled, her mind much sharper than Erin had expected. "Rosalie was on the team that year. She got twelve points in that game."

Mary Lou laughed. "Yes. She did. Well, I wasn't on the Bald Eagle Falls team, but I was watching. I remember Rosalie."

Deidre licked her lips. Her mouth stayed partway open and Erin knew it was dry. She was dehydrated. They hadn't put her on an IV— no lifesaving measures. There was a cup on the side table. Warm water that had probably been sitting there the whole day. Erin reached around Mary Lou to pick it up and gently put the straw to Deidre's mouth. "Do you want water?"

Deidre sucked. Just a little sip of water. Not enough. Deidre nodded her thanks. Erin went into the tiny bathroom and found a washcloth. She got it wet and squeezed it out, then returned to the bed. She sponged Deidre's dry lips gently. Deidre smacked them together a few times.

"Where is Rosalie?" she asked.

"Rosalie isn't here," Mary Lou told her. "Has Kim been in to see you?"

"Oh, yes." A little nod. "Kim has been here. She's a good girl, Kimmy."

"I'm glad she's been visiting you. Does she take care of you?"

"Yes. Yes, Kimmy is a good girl."

"Does she give you your medications?" Erin guessed. "Or bring you food?"

"Sometimes she brings me soup. Like the chicken soup I used to make her when she was a little girl." Deidre's mouth moved, remembering it. "She's a good cook, but she doesn't get the soup quite right. Not quite right."

Erin wondered what Kimmy was putting in the soup.

"Is she coming back today?"

Deidre's head moved as she looked around the room. Trying to orient herself as to date and time, probably. Or looking to see if Kim were already there.

"No, it's late," she said finally. "She must have gone home to sleep."

"Where?" Mary Lou leaned closer. "Did she go back to the farm?"

"No…" Deidre's voice was soft. Not uncertain, exactly, but trying to remember the details. "We left the farm a few years ago. We needed to be in town. Here."

"What street? Do you know the address? We should go and see her."

"She'll be back in the morning."

"But we should see her tonight. Can you tell me where she is?"

Deidre closed her eyes and snored slightly. Talking required too much energy. She had done well to even wake up and remember those details in the first place. Very well.

She was holding on better than Kim had expected her to.

They went back out to the unit nurse's desk. Erin put down the piece of paper with the unit and room number, and snagged a pen from the nurse's pen cup.

"I'm so glad we got here in time. We should go see Kimmy, see how she's holding up. I wrote down the address when she called me, but everything has been so crazy in the rush to get here." Erin opened her purse and pulled out a stack of notes written on various types of paper. Her purse was always a mess. "It's in here somewhere, but…" she paused, blinking rapidly, leafing through the notes. "I just can't find it. Maybe I threw it out. I honestly don't even know how we made it here…"

The nurse took the pen and paper and handed her a tissue from the box strategically placed on her desk. "There, dear, let me just write it down."

"Thank you. I think right now I would forget my head if it wasn't screwed on tight."

"It's a very difficult time for family members. Don't be so hard on yourself."

"Is she okay?" Erin looked back toward the hospital room where Deidre was once more sleeping peacefully. "She didn't look like she was in a lot of pain."

"No, that's all managed. We don't let them suffer. Our goal here is to make them as comfortable as possible until the end. It's very important for our families."

Erin nodded. She remembered what it was like. Once an elderly person reached a certain point, it was more important to give them painkillers than to extend their lives.

The nurse slid the paper back to Erin. "There you are, now. Bless you for coming to see her. I'm sure she knew you were there, even if she didn't wake up."

Erin didn't tell her that Deidre had woken up, and even talked to them.

"Thank you for taking such good care of her. Nurses are guardian angels without the wings."

The nurse smiled appreciatively. "You take care now. I'll see you tomorrow."

CHAPTER 45

They went back out to the truck and got in. Mary Lou looked at Erin.

"Guardian angels without the wings?"

Erin hesitated. "Do guardian angels not have wings? Did I mess that up?"

Mary Lou chuckled. "Just don't expect to hear something like that from an atheist."

Erin shrugged. She could feel herself blushing and was glad that it was now fully dark so that Mary Lou couldn't see it. "People still like to get compliments. As long as it makes her feel good, I don't see the harm."

"I just wouldn't expect you to use that form of compliment."

Erin glanced back at the hospital. "I've worked in end of life care before. People say lots of religious things, even if they don't believe it. It's kind of expected. I guess being there just brought it back."

Mary Lou nodded and didn't say anything else about it. "So... are we going to Kim's house?"

Erin looked at her and glanced back at Campbell. "It wouldn't hurt to drive by there, would it? Just get the lay of the land? I know Terry wouldn't want us to talk to her, but we can look, can't we?"

Erin remembered visiting Theresa; she, Vic, and Willie going out there to see if she could answer some questions and find out if she had seen Terry and Detective Jack Ward. That had been a mistake.

It had been terrifying and led to their being held at gunpoint and Erin being injured, but they wouldn't have found Terry or been able to save Jack if they hadn't done it. So in the end, that had been more important than what they'd had to go through. She couldn't imagine what life would be like if Terry had disappeared and never been found. Or if they did find his body later.

So she knew she could be wrong about checking out Kim's home. They might be walking right into the barrel of another gun held by another crazy person. But they had to do what they could to find Joshua. Kim may have initially intended to release him once Deidre died and she could claim her inheritance and run, but it was taking much longer than expected. It was dangerous to try to hide someone for long.

Mary Lou and Campbell both agreed that it was perfectly reasonable to go over just to make sure everything looked fine. They wouldn't go in and question Kim. But there wasn't any harm in just driving by.

"Should we call that deputy?" Mary Lou asked.

"We can go over to the police station after. I know where it is. Then we can tell him face-to-face what we've been able to sort out. He'll be much more likely to act if we talk to him directly, right?"

"We may as well wait until we have some more evidence," Campbell agreed. "If we can find anything else. If not... well, he already knows everything we know or have guessed. We don't have anything new to tell him yet."

"Except about Deidre being at death's door," Mary Lou said dryly.

"Except for that," Cam agreed.

Erin decided that they were all on the same page. She tapped the address into the GPS navigator and waited for the highlight line to appear on the map. The town seemed very small when reduced to gridlines on the LCD screen.

After waiting what seemed an excessively long time with so few streets to choose from, the short line appeared, directing them a few blocks away. It was quiet enough that Erin could flip a U-turn in front of the hospital, and they were soon at Kim's house. Erin removed her key from the ignition and took her foot off the brake pedal so the truck's lights would shut off. They all sat there in the dark, staring at the house.

It was a little, old house. Not as big as Clementine's house, where Erin lived. A dollhouse, a real estate agent might call it. She would be surprised if there was more than one bedroom. It was on a fair-sized lot, land being cheap in a small town. Erin could see the shapes of dark trees around it.

"Is there a shed?" Erin asked, "Any garage or outbuildings?"

"I see the roof of a garage," Campbell offered. Erin could see little in the dark. "Let's just… walk around and see."

Even though Erin had told Campbell not to bring anything illegal along with him, he still managed to open the garage door. Erin had already tested the doorknob and found it locked just a moment before. He was obviously pretty quick with the lock picks. It would have taken her several minutes of fiddling to encourage it to open. Erin pretended not to notice. Mary Lou said nothing. Campbell entered first, his tennis shoes silent as he moved in. After a glance around, he took out his phone and thumbed it on, using just the screen's glow to light up the space in front of him.

As with most garages, there was all manner of parts and equipment around the perimeter of the inside, one car instead of two, and very little clear space for walking. It was pretty obvious from the start that Joshua was not being held captive in the garage. But Campbell didn't retreat. He circled the car, looking in the windows and shining his phone screen inside. He used his t-shirt like a hot pad to open the driver's door without getting his fingerprints on it, then pressed the trunk release button inside.

Erin was nervous about looking in the trunk. She didn't think they were going to find anything horrible and gruesome in it, but…

Mary Lou hung back, and Erin and Campbell advanced to have a peek inside. There was no smell of decomposition as they approached, but Erin still took a deep breath before looking into it to brace herself.

Let it be empty.

They looked in at the same time. There was no body in the trunk. Erin breathed back out. Campbell lowered his phone for a better look. When he still couldn't see very well into the shadowy depths, he turned it around and turned on the flashlight LED.

He ran it over the items in the trunk, moving things carefully without touching any surfaces that might take a print. There was some clothing, not recognizable as Joshua's. As Campbell shifted stuff around, Erin saw a large roll of silvery duct tape and an opened plastic pocket of large zip ties. She felt acid rising in her throat and looked away, swallowing. It took her a moment to get her composure back, and she looked again. Campbell disentangled a headband from a dark hoodie, and Erin saw that it was a pair of hefty-looking goggles like would be used to play a VR game. She looked at Campbell, frowning.

"Night vision," Campbell whispered.

Night vision? So that someone could walk through the woods without a flashlight? Hunting? What innocent reason could Kim have for needing night vision goggles, duct tape, and zip ties? Erin tried to puzzle through it, and settled on hunting, though everything in her screamed that it was not. There was no innocent explanation. Kim had to be the kidnapper.

She wished that she had been able to find something about Kim online. What she looked like, so they would recognize her when they saw her. Whether she was big or small. How old she was. If she could have physically overcome Joshua or whether she had an accomplice.

They could be in the house now, Kim, Joshua, and a big, menacing man.

"We have to call the police," Erin told Campbell.

He ignored her, carefully moving the clothing and the items he had looked at to the side to see what was underneath. Erin tried to memorize the positions everything had been in when they opened the trunk. He was messing with everything, and they didn't want Kim to know it when she next came out to the car.

There was a tote bag that was black on the outside with brightly colored stripes on the lining. Campbell opened it up and shone his phone light inside. Some pretty print fabric like pajamas. Some bottles clinking around the bottom. Things for Kim to take to Deidre at the hospital? Clothes that were familiar and comfy and some drinks to tempt her appetite? Campbell teased the clothing out and unfolded one pajama top.

Erin's stomach again took a nosedive. This time, it was Campbell who looked at her for an explanation. Erin pressed one hand to her stomach and the knuckles of one hand to her teeth.

"It's a nurse's smock," Erin told him. She looked across the car at Mary Lou, worried. What if one of the nurses they had seen had been Kim and now knew they were on to her? Erin fought the impulse to pull out her phone and look the woman up on Facebook to see what she looked like, reminding herself firmly that Kim didn't have a Facebook account and there was no point in looking to see if one had somehow magically appeared.

"This stuff wouldn't still be here," Campbell said. "The first thing she would do if she thought we were on to her is get rid of everything incriminating. She wasn't at the hospital. She was at home, watching TV or in bed."

But they hadn't seen the flicker of a TV inside the house, and none of the windows showed lights on inside. For most of the town, it was still too early for bed. Except for bakers who had to be up before dawn.

And maybe Kim, being a nurse, had to go to bed early for a morning shift. Erin tried to slow her breathing and calm herself down. Kim didn't know about them. She didn't know that they were snooping through her trunk. They were perfectly safe.

Campbell had moved on. He roughly refolded the smock and put it in the pile with the rest. He looked at the soft drink bottles that were clinking around in the bottom of the bag.

But of course, they were not soft drink bottles any more than the nursing smocks were pajamas. They were medication bottles. Not the orange plastic prescription bottles like Erin got at the pharmacy, but glass vials of clear liquids to be injected with a needle.

Campbell didn't let her see them long enough to know whether they were something she might have been giving her grandmother, or something used to incapacitate Joshua during the kidnapping. And maybe to keep him sedated since then.

"But where is she keeping him?" Erin asked. She looked into the trunk for some other clue. She didn't think it could be too far away; she wouldn't want people to notice her absence for long periods of time. She was careful.

Unfortunately, there was no map in the trunk with an X marking the spot where Joshua was being held.

"In the house?" Campbell motioned in the direction of Kim's house. Or her grandmother's house. Whoever's it happened to be.

"No... I don't think so. Why would she need the night vision goggles? She could just turn on the light."

"Then he would see her."

"Keep him blindfolded."

Campbell nodded, conceding the point.

Erin racked her mind for anything that the items in the trunk might suggest. The hospital, but of course Kim wouldn't be able to hold him at the hospital. How? In a closet? The morgue? Masquerading as a coma patient? That didn't make any sense or require the use of the goggles.

There were no other clues in the trunk. So forget the trunk.

Erin walked around the car, using her own phone as a flashlight this time. Mud in the treads of the tires? Some kind of leaves or pine needles that would magically lead them to the exact place in the woods Kim had been visiting?

On TV, the detective always found the necessary clues. They were always right there, and the detective had everything needed to examine them and to come to a conclusion of the place where the abductee was being kept.

In real life, lots of missing person cases were never solved. Some abductees were discovered years later. Sometimes, not even their remains came to light. It was too easy to hide someone, especially with all of the caves and wilderness areas near Whitewater.

Still, Erin kept walking around the car, looking for some clue that they had missed. It was muddy, but she was not an analyst who could tell where the mud had come from. It looked like Kim had been off of paved roads at some point, but how long ago? How far away? She walked past Mary Lou without discovering anything else that would show them where Kim had been.

When she got around to the driver's door, Erin slid into the seat.

"Don't touch anything," Campbell warned.

"I know. I'm not," Erin agreed, holding her hands up in front of her. Though she had put her hands down on the seat when she had climbed inside. She wiggled around in the seat to try to smear or obscure any handprint she might have left on it. She looked at the sun visors. No maps. No park membership stickers on the windows or hanging from the rearview mirror. No gas receipts in the center console.

She used her thumbnail to press the release for the glovebox. It was neat and tidy. Owner's manual. Invoices and receipts for car repairs in a plastic pouch. Sunglasses. She pressed it closed again with her knuckle.

Campbell walked to the door and looked down at her. "Anything?"

Erin sat there, looking around the interior of the car. She double-checked the back seat. Fabric bags for shopping. She closed her eyes, thinking.

They needed to call the police. Like Terry had said, it was too dangerous for them to be investigating it themselves. They needed to let Detective Coleman know what they had been able to find so far. He could get a search warrant. He could get Kim's phone, and maybe that would tell them where she had been.

Terry.

Where she had been.

Erin's eyes sought out the small LCD screen mounted above the radio.

CHAPTER 46

*E*rin ran her finger around the outside, looking for the power button. She pressed and held it in. The LCD screen flashed to life, the brand name splash screen appearing.

"The GPS?" Campbell asked.

"The GPS."

Mary Lou came closer.

"What?"

"What are the chances that she's going to mark the location she has Joshua on her GPS?" Campbell demanded. "You think she's going to label it 'hideout' or 'abandoned cabin'? She knows where it is, she's not going to mark it for anyone else."

Erin waited impatiently for it to finish booting up. It didn't have a lot of battery reserves. Probably it didn't hold a charge very well and Kim just kept it plugged into the cigarette lighter for power and used it while the car was running. But Erin didn't want to turn on the ignition. Kim might be nearby, and she just might recognize the sound of her car starting and wonder what the heck was going on.

The main menu finally appeared. Erin started tapping the menu choices with her fingernail, trying not to leave any fingerprints on the screen.

"She might not mark it in her favorites, but if she has bread-crumbs turned on..."

"What are breadcrumbs?" Mary Lou asked.

Campbell was looking thoughtful. He raised his eyebrows, nodding. "It's like Hansel and Gretel," he told his mother. "When they walked through the forest, they left a trail of breadcrumbs behind them so that they'd be able to find their way home again. Breadcrumbs on a GPS show you where you have been, so you can follow them back again."

Mary Lou watched Erin fiddling with the menu options. "Do all GPS's have that?"

"Most of them do. It's standard. I don't know how many are turned on by default..."

Erin was hoping they were. She finally drilled down through the menus and found 'previous tracks.' She paged through them. The hospital. The grocery store. Out to the city and back running errands. Out of town to the east, following a secondary road that didn't lead anywhere with a label.

She continued to page back, seeing the same routes repeated several times. She was out on that secondary road every day.

"Look at this," she commanded Campbell. "Memorize it for when we get back to the truck."

She zoomed in, and they both watched the screen intently as it took the route turn by turn, and then back to the house again. Erin tried to commit every inch of it to memory.

"Okay. Let's go."

～

"Should we take the night vision goggles with us?" Campbell asked. "We might not be able to see where we're going without them."

"No." Erin shook her head. "We have to leave everything exactly where we found it so that the police can collect it as evidence."

"How are we going to explain how we found the route out to... the cabin or whatever it is?"

"I don't know yet. That's not important. We need to get out there."

They closed everything up, leaving it the way they had found it, and walked back to the truck. Erin looked at the house several times as they passed, trying not to, but looking for any sign that Kim was in there. Sleeping before the next shift. Tucked away safely so that they didn't have to worry about her. Her car was still in the garage, so it wasn't like she was at the cabin waiting for them. The only person waiting for them at the cabin would be Joshua.

Hopefully.

Assuming she had no accomplice.

The lights on Terry's truck came on as soon as they opened the doors. Erin wished it were an older truck or had some kind of stealth mode. She felt like she was naked in the middle of a spotlight and everybody was looking at her.

She oriented the truck in the direction the car would have been traveling once Kim pulled it out of the garage and onto the street. She and Campbell watched for the curves in the road, the intersections, and the turns they needed to take to get out there.

Mary Lou sat in the back, silent, saying nothing to hurry them along or to stop them. Erin tapped the Bluetooth control and gave it the command to call Terry. He answered almost immediately.

"Are you on your way back?"

"No. We're going to another location, where we think Joshua was being held. You can follow your GPS. Have the sheriff drive you out this way. Call Detective Coleman and let him know where we're going."

"You'd better call him."

"I'm driving, trying to remember the way. You can give him our locations better, watching us on your GPS. I can't walk him through it while we're trying to navigate."

Terry grunted. "Fine. Do you want me to stay on the phone with you? Three-way call?"

"No. I need to focus."

"Do you remember what I told you about staying out of trouble and not chasing this person on your own?"

"She's at home in bed. Her car is in the garage. All the lights are off."

"She could have another vehicle. You don't know."

"There was no space for another vehicle in the garage. It was full of junk."

"That doesn't mean she doesn't have another vehicle. Where did you keep your car?"

"Well… on the street, because Clementine's Volkswagen is in the garage. But the car in her garage is her primary vehicle. We know that she—never mind. It's the vehicle she's been using. She's not somewhere else. She's a nurse. She probably has an early shift."

"You know a lot more than you did when you left here. I told you not to poke around."

"I think you should come out here. And I think you should call Detective Coleman."

"I will. You keep out of trouble and stay safe. Don't go into any more buildings. Just stay where you are and let the police department do their job."

"I will when we get there. I'll either wait for you or for him."

"It won't be me. He'll be closer and it's his jurisdiction. At least, I assume it's within his jurisdiction."

"Unless he tells you he won't come out until morning."

"He's not going to say that. Not with civilians about to get themselves into a boatload of trouble."

"Good," Erin acknowledged. "I'll talk to you when I see you."

She clicked the button to end the call.

Campbell smothered a laugh. "I knew you were trouble, Miss Erin, but I didn't realize just how stubborn you are."

"Joshua could be in danger. It isn't like we can sit around waiting. If I get in trouble for… hurrying things along a little… then I guess I get in trouble."

"That's one way to look at it."

They were all quiet, watching the road and trying to remember all of the turns. Erin had been afraid that she wouldn't be able to remember the entire route. The call with Terry had pushed many of the details out of her head altogether. But she remembered the highway number, so she watched for it on the road signs. Then they only had to find the right exit. That could be challenging at night, especially if it were only a trail. And Erin suspected it wasn't a paved road. Not with the mud that had been splashed onto Kim's car.

The miles clicked by. It seemed like it would take forever, but Erin knew that it was pretty close. As she had suspected, Kim couldn't take huge chunks out of her day to travel to and from the place where Joshua was being kept. It would be too inconvenient for her and too likely to be noticed.

Then she started to think that they must have gone too far. She slowed, and they watched for the turnoff or some sign that they had missed it and needed to go back.

"There," Campbell said, pointing. "That one is the right angle."

Even looking at it, Erin nearly missed it. She slowed some more and pulled onto the gravel road. "You're sure this is the one?"

"As sure as I can be." Campbell didn't sound too certain of himself, though. "This has to be it."

Erin went slower down the gravel road. She had to turn on her high beams to see far enough ahead on the road to be sure she wouldn't hit some animal or miss a switchback.

"Do you think she used the night vision here? So that she didn't have to turn on her lights? No one would even know someone was coming down this road, if they didn't have their lights on."

"Maybe," Campbell agreed.

Erin gripped the steering wheel tightly, the truck jouncing around over potholes. She noticed that Campbell was holding tightly to the door handle to keep himself still. "Sorry. Bit rough here."

And she was nervous. She was sure she wouldn't run into anyone out on that road, but what if she did? What if someone were guarding the cabin? What if Kim were out there in a secondary vehicle for some reason? Maybe she banged up the exhaust system on the pock-marked road and had to get a rental until she could afford to fix her car. There were a hundred other reasons she might not be home in bed like Erin had told Terry she would be.

She looked at the truck GPS, trying to discern whether the route on the GPS screen looked the same as what she had seen on the screen of the GPS in Kim's car. It was all muddled in her brain. She couldn't be sure. They could miss the cabin altogether and end up at some other farmhouse or dead end.

Erin remembered their drive out to Theresa's house and was immediately twice as anxious. They had been so confident going out there that it was the right thing to do, and that they would find Terry and Jack Ward out there.

Well, they had.

Eventually.

There had just been the intervening incident with Crazy Theresa and her gun and wildly jealous temper in between.

And Terry and Jack had not been in good condition when they had found them. So why was she repeating the process again? Why run that risk?

Because if they had waited until the next day, when they could have convinced the police to go out there and talk to Theresa, it would have been too late. For Jack Ward for sure. Maybe for Terry too.

She wasn't going to wait one more day to rescue Joshua either.

CHAPTER 47

"I think this is it," Campbell whispered.

Erin slowed still more and tried to make out shapes in the darkness ahead of them. There were ghostly buildings ahead of them. And yes, the end of the gravel road. They had reached their destination. Erin pulled the truck to a position as far to the right of the road and the clearing where the buildings were as possible and shut off the ignition.

They waited for all of the truck lights to turn off, and for their eyes to adjust to the dark. Erin wished that she had agreed to bring the night vision goggles. The pale buildings looked completely deserted. Like they had been deserted for decades. Who knew how old they were.

Was that where Deidre had lived when she had first been married? Had it been the homestead? Or was it just some random abandoned farm that Kim had picked out, something completely unrelated to her family? That would have been safer. Safer to use a place that had no connection with her and her people. Much harder to find that way.

Erin waited.

They didn't know how long it would be until Detective Coleman got there. If Terry had talked him into following Erin right away, he might only be five minutes behind. If Terry had left Bald Eagle Falls with the sheriff or another driver and used their lights and siren, they might only be another fifteen minutes behind.

They wouldn't have to wait for long. Terry would know that Erin had stopped. She had told him that they would wait. They wouldn't go rushing into any abandoned buildings and mess everything up. They wouldn't put themselves in danger.

There was no sign of a guard. If Kim had an accomplice, he must be at home asleep as well. Or heading to bed in the next couple of hours. There wasn't anyone inside, since there were no other vehicles in the clearing.

Though another vehicle could be parked just behind one of the pale old buildings, or even inside one of them.

Erin shifted restlessly. Campbell looked at her. She couldn't see his eyes in the dark, just his face pointed toward her. She imagined that his eyes were begging to be allowed out of the truck, to go start searching the buildings for Joshua. Erin wanted to. She didn't like sitting there waiting for someone else to come in and do the work. She wanted to be the one to discover Joshua and to bring him to safety.

"Should we—" Mary Lou started, and then stopped.

Erin could only imagine how excruciating it must be for Mary Lou. Knowing that her son was in one of those buildings, tied up, maybe hurt. Maybe dying. But she wasn't able to rush in and find him and give him everything he needed.

"Soon." Erin said. "They'll be here soon and we'll find him."

"Thank you for doing this, Erin. I know it has been at risk to yourself. And your relationship with Officer Piper."

Erin's mouth twisted into a grimace. She wondered how upset Terry was going to be with her for going ahead and doing what he had said not to do. Would he be able to forgive her? Or was that it for them?

She didn't know how long he could stay with someone who wouldn't do what she was told. He would be putting his own reputation and job at risk.

"I just want to find Joshua and for him to be okay."

"Me too," Mary Lou agreed.

"Me three," Campbell chimed in.

They waited. Erin stared up at the stars. It was a clear night, and it seemed like she could see every star in the Milky Way. The tiny pinpricks of light were so brilliant out in the middle of nowhere. Amazing to someone who had spent most of her life raised in urban neighborhoods.

~

Finally, lights were coming down the gravel road toward them.

Erin caught her breath and held it. There were no rotating police lights. Were the police arriving without lights, or was it someone else? Kim or an accomplice realizing that they were made or there to check on Joshua to make sure he was settled for the night?

The vehicle got closer and closer. Erin couldn't see any light bar on the top of it. She ducked down, as if the driver might not see the big black truck if Erin were low enough. She saw Campbell mirror the movement beside her. But whoever was driving clearly saw the truck parked there. The headlights came straight at them, swerving off at the last moment as the car pulled up beside them. It was a long, dark sedan, with rust, dents, and scratches around the lower portion —an old car, driven for years through all kinds of weather.

Erin grasped the steering wheel tightly, her body looking for a way to defend herself or to escape. She reached for the key. If it were somebody threatening, she could start the truck and drive away before he could reach them. If she waited until right before he reached the truck, he would be delayed getting back into his own vehicle.

Unless, of course, he rolled down his passenger window and shot them from there. But the sedan was much lower to the ground than the truck; he probably wouldn't be able to get a good angle on them from there.

The door of the car opened, and a dark figure climbed out. Stocky, not moving quickly. Erin blinked her eyes, hoping they would adjust to the dark faster. The light from his headlights left bright afterimages in the center of her vision. He was nearly to the truck before she could make out the figure clearly enough that she started to relax. As he covered the last few feet, she could finally see his face. The creased, leathered visage of Detective Coleman of the Whitewater Junction police department. Erin buzzed her window down.

"Miss Price." Coleman glowered. "Can I ask what the hell you are doing here?"

Erin swallowed. "Did Terry—Officer Piper—tell you about Joshua Cox?"

"I am aware that he is missing, yes. We received those reports when he disappeared. Piper said that he has not yet been found and you are off on some wild goose chase trying to find him, causing no end of trouble."

Erin wondered how much of that was Terry's actual words.

"We think the kidnapper was Kim Brandon," Erin said evenly. "And she has been coming out here every day for the past week. Kind of strange, don't you think?" Erin looked out at the abandoned buildings. "Why would she be out here?"

He shrugged. "I have no way of knowing. There's no law against going for a hike in the woods. She could be prospecting, sketching wildflowers, looking at buying the place. Fishing. She could be distilling moonshine. Lots of reasons other than kidnapping."

"Well… I suppose. But with night vision goggles? Duct tape and zip ties?"

Campbell gave her a warning look. She realized he didn't want her to give away that they had been snooping in Kim's trunk.

"I have only your word for that," Coleman said. "Hypothetically, that would be suspicious, but not conclusive."

"You could look into it."

"What would the evidence on the warrant be?"

Erin searched for words. "I… she has motive. She wants to inherit her grandma's prize money. Joshua was on the verge of showing that the contest had just been a money-laundering scheme. She might have lost everything."

"And your proof of this is…?"

"Officer Piper is putting that together. They're building the case right now."

"As they should be. And when they have it built, they can put in a request for us to get a warrant to search Miss Brandon's property. Until then, I don't have anything to show that she might have been involved in anything criminal. Even though she drives out to an abandoned property regularly."

"So you're just going to wait? When Joshua could be on this property now?"

Coleman patted his pockets and came up with a cigarette and lighter. He turned away from Erin as he lit the cigarette and looked at the abandoned buildings.

"If he's not going to go in, I am," Campbell said.

"Just wait... see what he decides."

After a few minutes of contemplation, Coleman went to his car to retrieve several items. Erin couldn't see what he was doing very well in the darkness. He switched on a powerful flashlight that made her wince and turn away. When she looked back, Coleman was shining it at the ground. He looked down for a long time, walking a step or two and studying the ground. Eventually, he straightened up and shone it around him. The strong flashlight reached all the way past the trees that encroached on the edges of the clearing. He swept it around 360 degrees, methodical. He shone it on the various buildings. A big barn. Other sheds and outbuildings that Erin wasn't sure of. Storage for tools? Maybe a dairy? There was a little cabin, probably one bedroom, a living room, and a kitchen. Tiny, but big enough for a family of a hundred years ago, especially if they'd only had one child. Or one who had survived to adulthood. There was no sign she could see that any of the buildings had been used for decades.

Coleman returned to Erin's window. "You folks stay right here. If I hear someone coming up on me, I'm going to shoot first and ask questions later. If you follow me in there, you're gonna get plugged."

Erin nodded. Coleman looked past her to Campbell. "Is that understood, young man?"

"Yes, sir."

"Good." His eyes went to Mary Lou in the back seat, and he decided he didn't need to repeat the warning.

CHAPTER 48

They all sat there while Coleman walked toward the buildings, his flashlight on the ground. He picked his way along slowly, and Erin wondered if he were following someone else's footprints in the dirt. At least she and the others hadn't rushed in and obscured that evidence. Coleman really couldn't criticize her for sitting in the car, calling it in, and then waiting for him to show up. He and Terry might not like her following up on leads on her own, but she hadn't done anything dangerous. And they hadn't destroyed any evidence. They had left everything just as they had found it.

Erin wanted to go in with him.

And she didn't.

She remembered only too clearly following Willie into the barn that day at Theresa's farm.

Moving restlessly beside her, Campbell was apparently even more eager than she was to get in there. Erin didn't imagine he would stay put, but for Coleman's warning that he would shoot anyone who came up behind him.

Had Coleman called for backup units? Or did he think that she was off her rocker and that there would be nothing to find?

He was at least armed. Erin had seen the gun on his hip when he had approached the truck the second time.

As they watched, Coleman detoured around one of the buildings. In a few seconds, he was out of sight.

"Why did he go around there?" Campbell demanded. "Why didn't he check out any of the buildings? Does he think there is a car back there? Or something else?" His voice was higher than usual, pulled tight like a rubber band.

"He was following a trail. I guess Kim went around another way. Maybe the front doors are booby-trapped."

"Huh." Campbell accepted this, maybe deciding that Coleman knew what he was doing more than Campbell did. Campbell would probably have just run in through the front door. And who knew what would have happened then. Kim had clearly prepared for the abduction. She had managed to capture Joshua without raising any alarms. She had somewhere to transport him to that was out of sight of anyone else. She had not been caught removing medications from the hospital. And hospitals were usually really uptight about that kind of thing, with lots of security protocols in place.

Erin was on the edge of her seat. How long was it going to take for Coleman to find Joshua? How long before he was back out, confirming that they had found Josh?

And that he was safe.

Erin couldn't imagine having to tell Mary Lou that they were too late. Coleman would have made notifications like that before, but it couldn't be easy. Death notifications were bad enough when the person was at the end of their life and expected to die. A kid like Joshua, just starting to come into his own...

She couldn't help the little twitch that her brain responded with. An involuntary shake of her head. She couldn't do it. But she didn't have to.

And hopefully, Coleman wouldn't either.

It seemed like they were sitting there for hours waiting. Erin was starting to get cold. Her butt was sore from sitting for too long. She needed to get out and get some fresh air and the chance to stretch her legs. They were all so twitchy, reacting every time one of them had to shift position or looked in a different direction.

Erin checked the road again for any new arrivals, but couldn't see any more headlights approaching.

When she looked back toward the buildings, she could see a slight halo of light. Coleman was returning.

He kept his flashlight on the ground and made an arc around the clearing to where the vehicles were parked. He made a grim nod to Erin.

"He's in there."

Mary Lou clutched at Erin's arm, holding on for dear life. Erin expected more details from Coleman, but he wasn't wasting his time talking with them. He reached into his car and grabbed the mike of a radio. They couldn't hear his words as he called for backup and described what he would need from them, what they were going to find when they got there.

He spoke for two minutes? Five minutes? Ten? Erin couldn't parse the time period anymore. She couldn't even hold the current time in her head when she looked at her phone. She didn't know how long they had been there or how long Coleman spoke to his people on the radio. Eventually, he replaced the mike in its holder in his car and returned to Erin's window.

"You folks have water?"

Erin looked into the back seat, where Terry normally kept a go bag and emergency rations. She pointed to the black soft-sided cooler. "In there," she told Mary Lou.

Mary Lou tried to unzip it, her hands shaking so badly that it took several tries to pull the tab back, keeping the zipper track straight so it wouldn't jam. She reached inside and felt the water bottles. She handed one forward to Erin, and Erin passed it to Coleman.

"Is he okay?"

Coleman just looked at her and didn't answer.

But he didn't crack the water bottle open and take a swig himself, so Erin had to assume it was for Joshua as he headed back around the buildings, out of their sight.

Mary Lou was sniffling. Campbell put his hand over the seat to hold hers. "It's going to be okay, Mom. They found him."

CHAPTER 49

*E*rin hoped Cam was right. All of them stayed put in the car, following Coleman's instructions, but it felt like they had been trapped there forever. Erin was like a wild animal pacing back and forth, looking for the opportunity to escape. Her heart hammered in her chest. She wanted the reassurance that Cam was giving Mary Lou. Joshua would recover and return home. Everything would go back to the way it had been before. The Cox family could, once again, start the healing process. And maybe this time, nothing bad would happen to them.

There were flashing lights on the road. Lots of flashing lights.

Even though they hurt Erin's eyes, she watched them eagerly, mentally encouraging them to hurry. Joshua needed the paramedics. Coleman needed the policemen to secure the scene. And somebody had to go back and arrest Kim before she knew that Joshua had been discovered.

Mary Lou was crying more freely as the ambulance pulled off of the road into the clearing. Even Campbell was wiping away tears.

Coleman emerged from the buildings once more. He motioned for the paramedics to stay where they were, and talked to the men in the police cars, gesturing as he spoke. Then he went to the ambulance and spoke with the paramedics. They got out of the ambulance and removed the gurney from the back.

"They're going to take care of him, Mom," Campbell assured her. "They'll get him all fixed up. Everything is going to be fine."

"Can't I go see him?" Mary Lou begged. Though, of course, he was the wrong person to ask. Coleman was the person to ask, and he clearly did not want anyone else contaminating his crime scene. He led the paramedics in, keeping them to the edges of the clearing.

The other policemen got out of their cars and were putting up big lights, marking evidence, and cordoning off the area with tape.

The paramedics appeared around the buildings, carefully navigating the gurney through the gravel and grass toward the ambulance. Erin and the others all leaned forward, straining to see what kind of shape he was in. Coleman appeared behind them, then walked quickly past them and toward the truck.

He pointed at them and then held up one finger. His meaning clear: only one person was allowed out of the truck to see him.

"Cam, do you want to…?" Mary Lou asked.

"Mom, he needs you. You go."

"Are you sure?"

"Go."

She struggled to release her seatbelt and fumbled for the door handle, scrabbling at the door in the dark. She managed to open the door to get out of the car. Erin held her breath, worried that Mary Lou's legs would give out the instant she hit the ground, but Mary Lou was strong. She steadied herself against the truck and waited until Coleman and the paramedics were close enough to talk to, then walked alongside the gurney as it was pushed over the bumpy ground to the ambulance.

She leaned over Joshua, getting very close to his face. She found his hand beside him and held it as she walked with them to the ambulance. Erin watched Mary Lou's face, trying to read everything from it. Was Joshua awake? Was he okay? Or was he gravely injured or ill?

Erin wanted desperately to get out of the car and see for herself, but she stayed where she was, watching and waiting.

Campbell was watching and waiting with her. He wiped at tears and tried not to sniffle in front of her. Erin gave his shoulder a squeeze.

"Quit being such a rock," she told him. "Your mom is with him now. You don't need to be strong for her."

He cleared his throat.

"And I, for one, don't care if you cry. I promise I'll never even mention it."

Campbell looked at her for an instant, uncertain.

Then he put both hands over his face and let go. He was, in the end, an eighteen-year-old boy who had just been through a terrible ordeal. Being the man of the family and supporting his mother through something that few people would ever experience or understand. He was just a boy.

Erin pulled him against her shoulder with a sideways hug. He put his face against her and sobbed.

In a few minutes, it was over. Campbell wiped his face the best he could with his shirt, sniffled a few times, and sat upright again. His throat worked, swallowing hard a few times.

"There's more water back there," Erin said, jerking her head to indicate the back seat. "Get yourself one and hand me one too, would you?"

He reached his long arm into the back and snagged a couple of bottles. They sat in the car, sniffling, watching the paramedics finally loading Joshua into the back of the ambulance and Mary Lou climbing in beside him.

"Erin!"

She hadn't seen Terry and the sheriff arrive, but there had been a lot going on to distract her. Terry hurried up to the truck, and Erin did the best she could to hug him through the window. K9 was beside him, and broke ranks to put his paws on the door, whining.

She wasn't sure whether he wanted to get into the truck or was worried about her.

"Get out," Terry told her, "I want to make sure you're okay."

"I'm fine. Coleman told us to stay put, so…"

"Sure, him you'll listen to?"

Erin laughed weakly. "Well, he did threaten to shoot us."

"Is that all it takes?"

They watched the ambulance pull away.

"How is he?" Terry asked soberly.

"I don't know. No one has talked to us. Still alive. That's all I know."

"I'll see what I can find out."

He circulated among the other cops, talking to them and seeking out Detective Coleman, who shot several poisonous glances in Erin's direction as they talked. Eventually, Terry returned.

"He's not in great shape. Dehydrated and weak. Has been bound the whole time. But no serious injuries, so hopefully…"

"He'll get better," Campbell filled in. "He can get over all of that."

Terry nodded. "Hopefully," he agreed cautiously.

Erin wanted to hear a resounding 'yes,' and she imagined that Campbell did too. She looked at Cam, then back at Terry, and changed the subject.

"Does Detective Coleman want us to stay here to talk to him, or can we go?"

Terry rubbed the back of his neck, thinking about it. "He's probably got enough to deal with here tonight and tomorrow morning. I don't know what he'll need from you. I'll talk to him. Suggest that we all stay in Whitewater tonight so that he can have access to you tomorrow."

"I want to go to the hospital," Campbell said immediately. "Are they taking him to the little one here or to the city?"

"To the city."

"Then I want to go there."

"Okay… I'll let him know that you'll be in the city with Joshua and Mary Lou. And Erin and I can stay here at the hotel."

Cam nodded. Terry went back over to Coleman to talk to him

again, then spoke with Sheriff Wilmot, who was watching the proceedings with interest. He returned to the truck. "Yeah. That's fine. Let's go back to Whitewater first and check in." His eyes met Erin's. "I'm sure Erin will want to stop at the hospital for a few minutes before we retire."

She nodded her agreement. She couldn't stop herself from yawning, suddenly realizing what a long day it had been.

"You move over," Terry instructed. "I'm driving. Cam, hop in the back."

They all swapped seats, and Terry climbed up into the driver's seat, where he painstakingly adjusted the seat, mirrors, and air vents. Erin melted back into the warm spot Cam had left in the passenger seat and closed her eyes. It wouldn't hurt to rest them while they drove to the hotel to check in.

CHAPTER 50

*E*rin awoke when the car stopped. She rubbed her eyes, opened them, and stretched. She felt remarkably refreshed after the brief nap. Terry looked over at her and smiled.

"Better?"

"Yeah. Much." Erin looked out the window and instead of seeing the hotel, saw the big red brick hospital. She blinked and frowned and turned back to him. "I thought we were going back to White-water to check in first."

He grinned. "We did."

"We did?"

"Well, I did. You snored."

Erin giggled, embarrassed. "I don't snore."

"Well, you make a cute little rumbling noise when you sleep. You must have caught Orange Blossom's purr."

Erin looked over the seat at Campbell to say something about how she didn't snore, and found him sprawled on the back seat, limbs in every direction, dead to the world.

"I guess I wasn't the only one who needed a nap."

"He probably hasn't had much sleep since Joshua was taken."

"Yeah. You're right." Erin undid her seatbelt and reached over the seat, having to climb halfway over to reach Campbell and give him a good shake. "Hey, sleepyhead. We're here."

Terry snickered at her calling Cam a sleepyhead. But at least she had woken up when they had stopped. Campbell hadn't.

Cam grunted, flailed, and sat up gasping, like he'd been holding his breath underwater. "What?" he sputtered.

He looked around. Gradually, the wild look left his eyes as everything came back to him. "We found him, right? Tell me that wasn't just a dream."

"We found him," Erin agreed.

"Thank goodness. Let's go in."

He had his seatbelt off and was out the door before Erin, striding toward the hospital's big front doors.

~

Joshua was in a private room in the ICU. Erin was anxious. She had assumed that since the only things wrong with Josh were that he hadn't had enough to drink or been able to move around, he would just be in a regular hospital room. Once he'd had a couple of glasses of water and the chance to get used to having his feet under him again, he would be fine.

But it was more serious than that. Mary Lou whispered to them while they gathered around his bedside. It was probably a violation of the visitor rules for the ICU for them all to be there, and K9 but, as a police officer, Terry tended to get a little leeway on some of the rules.

"They have him on an IV to rehydrate. The detective gave him some water, but it isn't enough. They have to do IV to get his blood volume back up as quickly as they can safely. That will boost his blood pressure and help his heart to work the right way. But they're worried about his kidneys too because he was so dehydrated. They'll have to watch his fluid output for a few days and make sure his kidneys can both function."

"Poor guy." Erin looked down at Joshua, who appeared to be sleeping peacefully. "Has he been awake? Has he said anything? Can he identify Kim?"

"He hasn't really been able to talk. He recognized me. The doctors said that's good, because being that dehydrated can cause brain damage too. When he starts to get better… He'll be able to talk to Detective Coleman and hopefully tell him everything he needs to know about Kim Brandon."

Erin looked at Terry. "They have enough to arrest her, don't they? I mean, the stuff that was in the trunk of her car…"

"They have to have enough evidence to get a warrant to search her car," Terry reminded her. "They can't just bust their way in there and look in it. And if she figures out that they've found Joshua, she could destroy everything and run before they get a chance to find anything. That's why you're supposed to wait and let the police do their job, so they can gather the evidence that will be needed to *convict* Kim. They can't just lock her away on your say-so."

"I know. But I thought…"

"Your eyewitness testimony, on breaking into the vehicle, is not enough to get a warrant. Coleman needs corroborating proof."

"But we have that."

"No. You were acting on a theory. One that could just as easily have been wrong."

"But it was right. We found Joshua." Erin looked down at him on the bed. He looked so small and young. So vulnerable. "I'm not sorry we did what we did. How much longer would he have lasted if we hadn't?"

She looked at Mary Lou, hoping that she agreed. She wouldn't be so intent on having Kim locked up forever that she would rather have waited another day or two, would she? She would rather have her son back than justice, if she had to choose between the two.

Mary Lou nodded. She stroked Joshua's hair.

"He didn't have much longer," Terry agreed. He didn't add that he still wasn't sure whether Joshua would recover, but Erin heard it in his voice. She hoped it wasn't true. Joshua would get better. He was young and healthy before the abduction. His kidneys would kick back in. He would do a little physio and be back on his feet again. Everything would go back to the way it was before the kidnapping.

"So… what are the police going to do?" Campbell asked.

With the work that he did with Beaver, he probably knew a good amount about police procedure. He wanted to hear how it was going to go down.

"I don't have all of those details," Terry said. "I'm not part of it, so I haven't been fully briefed. But I gather that they'll fall back tonight and put Kim Brandon under surveillance. They won't tip her off that anyone has been at that farm. They'll clean everything up so that it looks pristine, and wait to see if she goes back for Joshua."

"Assuming that it wasn't her plan to just leave him there to die," Cam said.

"She was going back every day or two," Erin pointed out. "According to the GPS. So she should go out there sometime today."

"As long as it doesn't hit the news," Terry advised. "They're trying to keep it all under wraps, but there was a lot of activity tonight. It's going to be hard to convince all of the neighbors to keep quiet until the police can make the announcement after they have Brandon in custody."

There were a lot of ifs. But Erin was confident that they would be able to catch Kim going back to the farm. It had to work.

"We're going to get her," she promised Cam.

CHAPTER 51

Of course, Erin couldn't be a part of the surveillance team watching Kim's house. And she couldn't be at the abandoned farm to watch the sting go down if Kim went back there.

She didn't even know what Kim looked like.

So after she woke up early the next morning—even when she wasn't working at the bakery and had been up most of the night, her body's internal alarm wouldn't let her sleep late—she moped around the hotel room, looking out the window, hoping to see some part of the takedown in progress.

But all was quiet on the streets of Whitewater, especially so early in the morning. Terry groaned at her a few times to go back to bed, but she wasn't going to be able to sleep and her tossing and turning would only keep him awake.

The only thing that she could see in downtown Whitewater that was open so early was a local coffee shop. Not one of the big chains that dominated the city, but an independent store. Like Auntie Clem's Bakery. She was happy to support a local, independent business, so she decided to go down and get herself a cup of coffee. And she could get Terry a coffee, which would hopefully stay hot enough in its insulated cup, and a danish for when he decided to wake up and join the land of the living.

She grabbed her purse and her card key and scribbled a note on the hotel stationery before leaving so that Terry would know where to find her if he woke up while she was still out. Which she thought was doubtful. She tiptoed around K9, who raised his head to look at her and then put it back down again and closed his eyes.

~

The air of the coffee shop was thick with the fragrance of fresh coffee and baking. They probably didn't make their own pastries on site, so there must be a bakery open somewhere close by, where bakers like Erin and Vic were following their usual morning routine to get all of their fresh breads, muffins, and pastries baked, making sure that the coffee shop got the first batch so that they would have warm, freshly baked goods ready for their early-morning traffic.

Erin had been planning to order only a cup of coffee. She didn't need any extra calories to pad her waist. She normally would just have a piece of toast and tea for her early breakfast, and then have something more substantial for her lunch. But the baking smelled so inviting that she couldn't resist. She didn't have any work to keep her hands busy and keep her mind off of eating deliciously high-calorie treats like she normally did. It was different being a customer, planning to just sit down and have a leisurely cup of coffee.

So she ordered a nice, healthy, low-calorie bran muffin. Then she canceled the muffin and went for a couple of danishes, one for her and one for Terry. She could go for a walk while waiting for him to wake up and burn off the extra calories.

She watched the other patrons. Most of them were known to the staff, who called them by name and knew their orders before they placed them. People didn't seem stressed out in the before-work rush. They were relaxed and enjoying their coffee rituals.

A couple of nurses in smocks walked in. Coming off of shift rather than going on, Erin thought. They weren't bright-eyed and ready to start their day. They looked ready for bed. They ordered a tea and a soft drink rather than caffeinated drinks, and a couple of muffins to eat as their before-bed snack. The one who had ordered tea turned around while she waited for it, scanning the other customers, maybe looking for another nurse who should be there. Erin smiled pleasantly at her, feeling friendly and full of well-being from the delicious danish pastry. The woman nodded an acknowledgment and continued to look around. She had a heart-shaped face, blond hair that was a little sweaty and tousled from her shift at the hospital, and friendly blue eyes.

Erin thought she had probably seen the woman before. Maybe during the cooking contest. She had met a lot of different people during the competition. It had been chaotic, lots of introductions, hands to shake, personal stories to listen to. Only a few of them stuck with her.

The heart-shaped face turned back to her and the woman's eyes went over Erin again. Maybe also remembering that they had been introduced during the cooking contest.

The barista was holding a cup out toward the nurse. "Kim? Kim? Miss Brandon?"

Kim didn't take it. She remembered who Erin was. And she knew that Erin didn't belong there in Whitewater. She turned and bolted out of the coffee shop, leaving her friend and the barista staring after her, mouths open.

Erin jumped to her feet and ran to the window to watch Kim go. There was no point in trying to chase her. What was she going to do? Put the woman under arrest? Based on evidence that the police still didn't have?

Kim ran down the street and turned, disappearing from sight. Back home, where her car was parked. If she'd been at the hospital on shift, why had she left the vehicle at home?

Maybe someone had picked her up. She had carpooled. Or she liked to walk over when the weather was pleasant. But whatever the reason she hadn't had the car with her at the hospital, she was on her way to get it now. And then she was going to run, and keep on running.

Erin fumbled with her phone. It took her several misplaced taps and swipes before she managed to search for Coleman's phone number. Then, her phone seemed to be taking an inordinate amount of time to filter down to his contact entry and display it on the screen. She tapped and waited for the call to go through. It rang and rang, going through to his voicemail.

Erin hung up and started walking toward the police station. She tapped his number again, hoping that if he saw her number come up twice in a row, he would realize that it was an urgent matter. Did Whitewater have 9-1-1 service? Should she try?

"Detective Coleman." His voice was a snap in her ear.

"It's Erin Price. I just saw Kim Brandon in the coffee shop and—"

"I thought you didn't know what she looked like."

"I didn't. But I heard the barista call her by name, and she was looking at me. She realized who I am and—"

He swore. "Did you talk to her?"

"No. She just saw me across the coffee shop. She ran away. Left her order there and just ran back to her house."

"Stay away from her. Don't follow her, do you understand?"

"Yes, but—"

"But nothing. I've heard how fast and loose you play with the law, and I want to make this clear. If you go after her, if you follow her even at a distance, you will find yourself in a jail cell."

"I didn't. She ran away and I called you. I'm walking toward the police station, in case I couldn't get you on the phone."

"Okay. I'm not there. I'll interview you later in the day. In the meantime, I need you to stay out of the way of my operation."

"I am."

"We have people watching her house and the farm. She's not going to get anywhere, but she might lead us to the evidence that we need."

"What if she destroys the evidence in her car?"

"I told you. We have eyes on her. If she throws something out, we'll see her do it and recover it. If she torches the car or something stupid like that, we'll have officers right there."

"And if she goes to the farm, then that's evidence that she is the one who kidnapped Joshua."

"Or at least, she knew about it. Each piece of evidence is only one part of the story. We need to add them all together before there will be enough to convict her of anything."

"Yeah." Erin took a deep breath. She stopped walking. There was no point in running to the police station when he wasn't there. She would go back to the hotel.

First, she would go back to the coffee shop and grab the food she had left on her table, assuming it hadn't already been cleared away.

"Do you have someone watching her grandma at the hospital too? I don't know if Kim was doing something to make Deidre sick or just waiting for nature to take its course, but... if she thinks that I'm on to her, I wouldn't want her to do anything desperate..."

"Killing her grandma wouldn't accomplish anything if she didn't get her inheritance before leaving town. But yes, I've got someone at the hospital, too. A little more tricky, since she knows the staff there."

"I guess it would be," Erin agreed. She wondered who they had there. Someone pretending to be janitorial staff? A fake patient or a visitor watching from behind a newspaper? "I guess I should let you go. Sorry, I wasn't trying to get in the middle of things... she just walked into the coffee shop and recognized me."

"No problem, Miss Price. And... thank you."

Erin nodded and hung up.

CHAPTER 52

*W*hen Coleman came calling, Terry was up, sipping his coffee and eating the danish Erin had managed to recover.

Coleman knocked on the hotel room door. Erin let him in. She looked around. There wasn't really anywhere for a sit-down meeting in the room. She sat on the bed and Terry moved from the one chair at the writing desk and motioned for Coleman to take it. He sat down with Erin on the bed, brushing flaky crumbs off of his face. K9 lay where he was in the middle of the floor, sighing loudly.

"Kim Brandon has been arrested for Joshua's kidnapping," Coleman announced.

Erin let out a breath of relief. "Oh, I'm so glad! Thank you!"

"We're still building the case against her, but we have enough to get the warrants we need to search her house and car, her workplace, and grandmother's hospital room. We've pretty much finished with the farm buildings, but we'll have evidence techs go over it one more time to be sure we've got everything."

"With what was in the car, you should have enough…?"

"We'll see. Nothing is ever one hundred percent, but there isn't much that would explain away a kidnap kit in the trunk. Especially with needles and prescription drugs stolen from the hospital to sedate him or keep him compliant."

"How did she get them?" Erin shook her head. "I thought those things were all inventoried and kept under lock and key."

"Of course they are. We're trying to sort out the details. But I would say that as a nurse, she found ways around the system. She had legitimate access to them, it was just a numbers game."

"So she took more than she was supposed to?"

"Maybe said that a patient needed a higher dosage than they did, and pocketed the extra."

"Devious." Terry shook his head.

"Whatever we can or cannot prove, I think we can agree she is that."

The drive back to Bald Eagle Falls was quiet. Too quiet. Erin could hear K9 panting in the back seat. She knew that Terry was not happy with her for taking the truck and going to Whitewater Junction when he had said not to. She had known that he and the sheriff didn't want her to investigate. She was just supposed to stay out of the way and let them sort everything else.

But Erin couldn't let a friend suffer while she stood back and waited for the police to go through the proper channels. She had risked derailing the investigation and the police not being able to file charges against Kim. But Joshua's life had to come first.

If they argued about it, they would just go around and around in circles. Erin knew that. Terry would be sure that he was right and she would be sure that she had done the right thing. She wouldn't be able to change his mind.

So they were both quiet. She waited for him to start lecturing and criticizing her for using his truck to do something ill-advised and illegal. But he didn't. They both knew that was something that could never be resolved between them. And Erin didn't know where that left them. Was Terry willing to accept that discord in their relationship? Could Erin?

Forever?

CHAPTER 53

*B*ack in Bald Eagle Falls, life was normal. Everyone was happy to hear that Joshua had been found and were confident that he would recover easily. Kids were resilient. They bounced back faster than you would think. Erin hoped that was the case. She had seen the damage neglect and confinement had done to kids younger than Joshua.

She went by Auntie Clem's Bakery in the afternoon to check in with Charley and Bella and make sure that everything was going all right. She updated her shopping and task lists as she walked around.

"Smooth sailing," Charley assured Erin. "We can hold things together when you have something you need to do."

"I'm so glad you found Josh," Bella said. "I was so scared... when it's been more than a day or two, you know that things don't look good..."

Erin nodded. She felt like she had come through a long, dark, tunnel. She had been very worried. Afraid to even hope that they would be able to find him alive. But she had come out the other end of the tunnel. She could breathe again.

"Were you going to take some more baking over to the Fosters?" Charley asked. "I set some things aside for them."

"Did you? That's a great idea. Yes, I'll take them over now. Have you heard anything? I think she was confined to bed."

Bella nodded. "I think this one has been pretty hard on her. But it's not supposed to be much longer."

"She's a great mom, but having that many young kids must be so hard."

"Some women really love having a full house. I'm not sure I'd be able to manage."

Charley shook her head. "I always wanted siblings growing up, but I think that's too many. She needs to take care of herself. Get Mr. Foster snipped."

Bella's eyes got big and round, shocked. Charley laughed.

"Okay... I'm going to take some bread over to them," Erin decided. Bella would have to fend for herself with Charley.

No children were playing in the yard this time. Erin rang the doorbell, and there wasn't a mad stampede for the door. It was opened a few minutes later by a man Erin didn't know. Mr. Foster, she presumed. He was unshaven, hair tousled, his wrinkled shirt and slightly sweaty odor testifying to the fact that she had probably woken him up. She didn't know if he were a shift worker. He hadn't been there when she had dropped by before.

"Hi," he said tiredly, looking her over.

"Hi, Mr. Foster. I'm Erin Price. I own the bakery?"

"Oh!" His eyes brightened. "You're a really good baker! I wouldn't believe that all of the things my wife brings home are gluten-free, except they don't make Peter sick, so I know they are. It's amazing what you can do."

Erin's face was hot. "Thank you so much! I love to bake for people, and Peter especially. He's such a great little guy."

Mr. Foster nodded his agreement.

Erin made a little motion with the box she was carrying. "I brought some more supplies."

"Sure." He reached for his wallet in his back pocket. "How much do I owe you?"

"Oh, this is just a gift to help your wife while she's indisposed. You don't owe me anything."

He paused, hand on his jeans pocket. "Are you sure?"

"Yes. Please. Don't worry about it."

"Okay." He took the box from her. "Would you like to come in and see the little guy?"

"Oh, she had the baby?"

He nodded, a warm smile spreading across his whiskery face. "Just a few hours ago."

"Wow! Yes, I'd love to see him. Him—it is a boy?"

"Yes."

"Peter must be tickled. Another boy in the family!"

"Believe me, he is. Come on in."

Erin followed him into the house. Everything was quiet. Maybe a neighbor had taken the kids after school, or they had all been up late with the arrival of the new baby and were now napping to catch up. Mr. Foster led Erin into the master bedroom. It was warm and dark and close. Mrs. Foster was propped up in the bed.

"It's Miss Price," Mr. Foster announced. "With another care package."

"You didn't have to do that," Mrs. Foster said softly. "But I can't tell you what a help it has been the last couple of weeks. Peter has been able to make sandwiches for the girls, or to warm up some soup with a roll. I couldn't be up and around at all."

"He told me that. I'm glad it helped."

Mr. Foster went to the bassinet beside the bed. He carefully lifted out a little bundle wrapped tightly in a light blanket. "And here's the new addition to the Foster family."

Erin received him in her arms. He was so small and so perfect. She always said she didn't know if she were ready for children, or if she ever wanted to be a mother but, in a moment like this, when she held a newborn in her arms, it was a totally different story. Her heart yearned for one of her own.

"Oh, he's so precious. Congratulations."

"Thank you," Mrs. Foster said.

Mr. Foster slipped out to put the box of baking in the kitchen. Erin stroked the downy hair on the top of the baby's head.

"Does he have a name yet?"

"We're thinking of Alan. But haven't decided yet. We'll see what fits in the next few days."

Erin swayed back and forth, rocking the baby.

"Come here." Mrs. Foster patted the edge of the bed. Erin sat down, holding the baby so that Mrs. Foster could take him back if she wanted to. Mrs. Foster just stroked his cheek and let Erin hold him.

"I can't imagine how hard it has been for Mary Lou Cox to go through what she has with Joshua. I don't know what I would do if someone took my baby away from me. Or any of my kids, of course. It must be an absolute nightmare. The poor woman."

Erin was happy to be able to report the good news. "We found him last night. The woman who kidnapped him was arrested this morning."

"And he's okay?" Mrs. Foster's eyes filled with tears.

"He's alive. He's in ICU today, and probably for a few days, while they get him back on his feet again."

"Oh." She let out a long breath. "I'm so glad. You said 'we' found him? You?"

"Me and Mary Lou and Campbell. We kind of figured out who it must have been, and we went to Whitewater, and we were lucky in a lot of ways…"

"That's fantastic news." Mrs. Foster shook her head. "I don't know how you do it. It really doesn't make any sense. You're not a policeman or even a private investigator. But you know, just by seeing things and listening to people, like with Peter…"

Erin nodded. "Yeah. I'm sorry about Peter. Sorry that he was involved in those last couple of cases. I know it bothered you."

Mrs. Foster had been quite clear about that fact. And she had stopped letting the children go with her to Auntie Clem's, despite how much they loved picking out their own cookies.

"Let's put it behind us," Mrs. Foster suggested. "I don't want to say don't ever involve him in a case again. I think that you do a lot of good, but I worry about what could happen to him. Especially looking at Joshua. If it's that easy to take a teenage boy, just think about how simple it would be to snatch Peter or one of the girls. But if you think one of them might know something... would you please come to me?"

Erin nodded. She could feel herself flushing and was glad that the room was dim so that Mrs. Foster couldn't see how red she got. "Of course. Yes. I'll try to do that. I don't expect to be investigating any other crimes, though."

Mrs. Foster laughed and shook her head. "Oh, sure. I'm sure that will be the last time."

CHAPTER 54

*E*rin knew that Joshua was out of the hospital. She hesitated on the front steps, taking a deep breath before ringing the bell. While things had eventually worked out with Mary Lou, she still wasn't sure whether she would be accepted when a family member's life wasn't on the line. Things might have gone back to the way they were before Joshua had disappeared. Mary Lou might accept that Erin hadn't had anything to do with Joshua's disappearance, and acknowledge that she had helped to find Joshua and bring him home safely, but that didn't necessarily mean that they were friends again.

The door opened. It was Campbell. He smiled and nodded. "Hi, Miss Erin. Come on in."

"Is it okay?" Erin asked, trying to see around him to make sure that it was really okay with Mary Lou.

"Come on," he repeated, stepping back and motioning Erin forward. Erin followed him a little reticently.

Joshua was sitting on the couch. Despite the fact that it was warm out, he was wrapped in a blanket. He pulled it closer to him as he turned to see who had come in. His tense expression relaxed a little when he saw Erin.

"Oh. Hi. Mom just went upstairs for something, but she'll be back in a minute."

Erin sat in one of the chairs. "How are you feeling?"

"Still pretty weak. They said I'll probably recover pretty quickly."

Erin nodded. He looked thin and pale. Who knew what kind of damage there was that they couldn't see? Not just to his organs, but to his mind.

It was hard for her to understand what it must have been like for him. She had been abandoned in a cave, and most of the time she had been unconscious. But to have an experience like that to go on for days... bound in the darkness, not knowing if his captor would come back again, or would ever let him go...

Joshua's eyes hovered on Erin for a few seconds, and then flitted around the room, anxious, looking for danger. Erin put her purse down slowly so that he wouldn't be startled by her movement.

"I'm sorry that it took us so long to find you. I should have been able to figure it all out sooner."

"You did your best. I'm glad that you guys did find me. She said that it wouldn't be much longer. And I didn't think she was going to let me go."

Erin's heart felt like it was being squeezed. She breathed through the pain. "You must have been terrified."

"I wasn't... I figured... it would be better to be dead."

"What an evil woman. I don't know how someone could hurt you like that. You never did anything to harm her."

"I guess... she thought I was going to. That I'd get all of her money taken away—or all of her grandma's money." He stared at the tree outside the window. "I never thought what I was doing might hurt anyone."

"You were just trying to find out the truth."

"But that has consequences." He shook his head. "I never thought of the people. I thought... reporters just *report*. I never thought that what they do actually makes a difference, changes things."

"But that doesn't make it wrong. If they were laundering money through the contest, then that's hurting people. That needs to be stopped."

"But taking the money from the people who thought they were

just getting prize money for submitting a recipe to a contest...? That's not really fair to them."

Erin didn't really have an answer to that.

"Are they going to lose their money?"

"I don't know. It's all going to be investigated. I don't know if they freeze everyone's assets while they do that."

Erin thought about the woman lying in the bed in the hospital. She was past caring about whether they froze the assets or not. Kim had been thinking of her own selfish desires, not her grandmother's.

She heard footsteps on the stairs and turned to watch Mary Lou descending.

"Oh, Erin. I thought I heard voices."

Erin rose partway out of her seat to greet Mary Lou, but the woman waved her down. "Make yourself comfortable. You're practically family here."

There was suddenly a big lump in Erin's throat. *Family?*

"You helped us find Joshua. You helped out when Campbell had his trouble. And you were one of the only ones who stood beside us when Roger... had to go away. Even though he had targeted you. I'd say that makes you part of the family."

Mary Lou put her hand on Erin's shoulder and gave it a little squeeze as she walked behind Erin to the other chair. She sat down.

"I need to apologize for the way that I treated you."

"You were worried about Joshua."

"That's no excuse. I let someone manipulate me and thought that you were my enemy instead of my friend. I should have known better from everything you have done in the past. I should have seen what was going on in front of my own eyes."

"It wasn't your fault."

"Oh, Erin. I'm trying to apologize."

Erin pressed her lips together and nodded. "Yeah. Sorry. I accept."

Mary Lou smiled. "Good. I won't ever let that happen again. I know who my friends are."

"What about Vic?"

"Yes, Miss Victoria too. I'm sorry for flying off the handle about that escapade in the city... I wish I had known at the time, but I'm glad I didn't. You were trying to protect Josh and help Cam, but... I wonder if there might have been a better way to go about it."

"I wouldn't doubt it," Erin admitted. "I don't always make the best choice."

"No..." Mary Lou's voice wobbled a little as she decided what to say. "But you always try."

Did you enjoy this book? Reviews and recommendations are vital to making a book successful.

Please leave a review at your favorite book store or review site and share it with your friends.

Don't miss the following bonus material:
Sign up for mailing list to get a free ebook
Read a sneak preview chapter
Other books by P.D. Workman
Learn more about the author

Sign up for my mailing list at pdworkman.com and get
Gluten-Free Murder for free!

JOIN MY MAILING LIST AND

*Download a sweet
mystery for free*

pdworkman.com

PREVIEW OF HOT ON THE TRAIL MIX

CHAPTER 1

*E*rin pushed Orange Blossom to the side with her foot, ignoring his meows of protest, so that she could get into the pantry cupboard for the food she had set aside for Vic. In order to keep him from getting into something that would make him sick Blossom was not allowed in the pantry, even though it had now been determined that he hadn't gotten sick from getting into something he shouldn't have, but had been intentionally poisoned. It was still safest if she only fed him cat food she knew to be safe. Or meat that she prepared for him while making her own meals.

"I made you some sandwiches too, they're in the fridge."

Vic, a slim transgender woman, Erin's best friend and employee at the bakery, opened the fridge. Orange Blossom hurried over to her to see if Vic would be more cooperative about feeding him. Erin grabbed what she needed and shut the pantry.

"I made these granola bars. See what you think. I made some of them with certified gluten-free rolled oats, and some with buckwheat flakes. So the people who can't tolerate oats still have an option as well. If you can't really tell the difference, I'll just make the buckwheat, so I don't have to make two different kinds."

Vic nodded. "They look good. No nuts?" Vic knew that Auntie

Clem's didn't sell anything containing nuts. But of course, granola bars frequently had nuts.

"No. I put in some pumpkin seeds and sunflower seeds. And some raisins and goji berries. And I made this trail mix." Erin put a baggie down on the counter. "Sunflower seeds, hemp seed, and chia —loads of protein."

Vic swept her long, blond hair out of her face as she leaned over and packed the goodies into her backpack. "Sounds great. This should be more than enough to get us through the day."

"Make sure you have plenty of water."

"We do." Vic pulled the zipper of the pack closed. "You sure you don't want to come along with us?" she teased.

Erin flashed back to being trapped underground—no light, no water, bound hand and foot with no idea how to get out of the labyrinthine caves. She had been terrified she was going to die there, injured and alone. No one would be able to find her. She wouldn't be able to find her own way out. The oxygen had been thin and she had been dehydrated.

"No," she told Vic firmly. "I am never going into a cave again."

Vic squeezed her arm. "And you never have to," she assured Erin. She gave Erin a mischievous smile. "But I'm going to keep asking. Spelunking is so much fun."

"It's just not for me."

It amazed Erin that Vic was still into spelunking. After having been trapped in a collapsed mine, Vic should have hated dark, enclosed spaces as much as Erin. But she had bounced back quickly, and as soon as she and Willie had their casts off, they were back at it again. Maybe it was because she was so young, just barely an adult, that she had bounced back so fast.

"You can keep asking. As long as you don't think I'm going to change my answer."

Vic nodded. She shouldered the pack. "We're off, then." She looked at the clock. While early, it wasn't nearly as early as when they usually had to get up to bake the day's goods and open up Auntie Clem's. Considering their usual schedule, it was a relaxed morning.

"Saw 'hi' to Willie for me."

"Will do."

~

Once Vic and Willie were on their way, Erin sat down to work on her plans for the day and consider the upcoming week. In an effort to get control over the clutter in her purse and on her desk, she had actually purchased a planner. It had been a lengthy process. First, looking over the planners available at the stationery store in the city and considering all of the possibilities of size, layout, and binding type. And, of course, the price point. She didn't want something that would become a craft, with all kinds of stickers and accessories and time required to decorate it. Just somewhere she could keep her lists, plans, and appointments together and organized.

After finally settling on a book that would fit in her purse, she had started to use it. Breaking the habit of years of writing on scrap pieces of paper, napkins, and an assortment of notepads was not easy. She had to train herself to reach for her book instead and write her lists and thoughts in the appropriate place. Where hopefully she would be able to find them again later when she wanted them.

But she was growing to love her little planner. She didn't waste as much time searching for lists and notes that she had written and then 'filed' in her purse, wallet, or pocket for later reference. Her purse, while still full, was a lot less cluttered.

Erin sat on the couch with her feet curled under her. In a few minutes, Orange Blossom jumped up beside her and cuddled up.

She enjoyed the peace and quiet of the morning. Terry was still sleeping and could continue to sleep for however long his body let him. He didn't go on shift until the afternoon. If he got up in good time, they would have some couples time together and maybe go out for lunch.

Everything was finally calm and peaceful in Erin's life.

CHAPTER 2

*W*hen Erin heard Terry stirring in the bedroom, she looked at the time on her phone. She had promised Vic that she would check on the new dog, Nilla, and make sure that he got a break and a bit of exercise. That would hopefully keep him from destroying Vic's loft apartment over the garage.

She went down to the bedroom and poked her head in to look at Terry. "Morning."

Terry stretched and groaned. He scratched the stubble on his cheek and smiled. Not enough to show the dimple in his cheek, but it warmed Erin's heart to see him happy in the morning instead of worn out and miserable because he hadn't been able to get any sleep and had a migraine.

"Mmm. Come here."

Erin obliged, going around to his side of the bed and giving him a good morning hug and kiss. His body was warm, his hair mussed, and he smelled faintly of sweat. Erin buried her face in the hollow of his shoulder, enjoying their closeness and the looseness of his body.

"I'm just popping out for a few minutes to take care of Nilla."

There was a whine from K9 in his kennel.

"Yes, you can come too," Erin agreed. "Come on."

K9 jumped out of his kennel, tail wagging excitedly. He stopped to give Terry a nuzzle and get his ears scratched, then headed out the bedroom door, leading the way for Erin.

"See you in a few minutes," Terry told her.

Erin blew him a kiss and followed K9 to the back door. She disabled the alarm and followed him out.

⁓

Once in the yard, Erin could hear a frantic yipping coming from the direction of Vic's apartment.

"Uh-oh."

K9 was on his way to his dog run in the corner of the yard. He looked back at Erin with a comical eye roll. Sometimes his expressions seemed very human. Erin left him to his business and went up the stairs to the loft apartment. She unlocked the door, calling out to the little dog.

"Nilla! Come here, boy! What's the matter?"

The apartment was a mess and Erin knew it wasn't because Vic had left it that way. When Nilla got into a mood, he could be a little tornado of destruction. Kind of like the Tasmanian devil in the cartoons.

The yipping continued. Erin tried to home in on him.

"Nilla? Where are you? What are you doing?"

She was afraid at first that he had gotten himself into trouble and was stuck somewhere. But she found him in Vic's bedroom, wrestling with a pair of leggings.

"Nilla! No!"

Nilla turned on her, growling. If he'd been a big dog, Erin might have been concerned, but the little white fluff-ball was not very intimidating. Although he threatened, when the critical point was reached, he would run, not attack.

"No," Erin repeated firmly and bent down to pick up the leggings. She didn't want to start a tug-of-war, which might cause worse damage to the clothes than just leaving them on the floor. "Shoo. Get back." She waved her hands at the dog. Nilla remained growling fiercely until the last minute, and then he ran away. Erin picked up the leggings and any other clothes that Nilla had pulled to the floor. She folded them and put them into the top drawer where they would be safe. She made sure to shut the drawer tightly so that he wouldn't be able to open it, and pushed the others closed, making sure they were all tight so that hopefully Nilla wouldn't be able to drag any more out.

"Do you want to go for a walk?" She called out to Nilla. "Outside? Walk?"

Nilla growled, but when Erin left the bedroom and headed back toward the front door, he immediately dropped all pretense of being threatening and jumped at the doorknob. It was amazing the height that the little dog could achieve.

There were scratches on the door already from the past few weeks that Nilla had lived there. Erin should probably have told Vic no, no pets allowed, but since Erin had taken in two pets of her own and K9 also spent most of the week there, it was pretty hard to deny Vic the privilege.

It wouldn't have been a problem if Nilla had been better behaved.

She thought about texting Vic to let her know that Nilla was causing problems once more, but decided against it. Vic wasn't likely to have cell coverage where she was. Even if she did, there wasn't anything she could do to fix the problem and Erin didn't want her worrying about it the whole time she was away.

Erin managed to hold Nilla still long enough to get his walking harness on him, then took him outside and down the stairs. She always worried with how hyper and excited Nilla got that he was going to end up getting hung falling down the stairs, or falling off the side through the railing. The dog seemed incapable of moving in a straight line. But using a harness instead of a collar helped allay her worries. He didn't have something around his neck that was going to strangle him.

She managed to get down the stairs without getting tangled up in the leash and gently encouraged him toward the dog run. Unlike K9, Nilla seemed resistant to the idea of training to one area of the yard and always wanted to sniff and pee everywhere.

"Come over here. Come on. This is where you're supposed to go.

Watch K9. He knows what to do. Don't you want to be a big dog like K9?"

By the time she got him over to the dog run, she suspected he was empty, but she stayed there with him for a little while, encouraging him to make use of the run.

K9 was sitting watching them patiently, but Erin knew he wanted to go for a walk to stretch his legs. He was a big dog and needed a lot of exercise.

"Okay, you done, Nilla? Let's walk."

Nilla allowed himself to be coaxed toward the gate. He knew that walking was next, and though he was slower than K9 and easily distractible, he was pretty good for his walks.

"Come on, K9," Erin called. K9 bounded after her, quickly falling in at her heel and showing the little dog proper behavior. Nilla gave him a little growl, pretending that he could take K9 on if he had to, and went on with his explorations, ranging out on the leash as far as Erin would let him go.

Even though Nilla was just a little dog, Erin was always tired after walking him. He pulled and moved erratically and she was always worried about what he was going to do next, so the emotional effort took more than the physical. Nilla was also tired, and Erin was able to pick him up and carry him up the steps so that she didn't have to worry about him shooting off the side or between the slats. She took him to his kennel and shunted him inside. She shut the door while she got him some food and water. He was chill enough after his walk that he didn't whine or try to get out. She gave him his bowls and left, locking up behind her.

Terry had already let K9 into the house, and he opened the door for Erin as she approached. "How was it?"

Erin shook her head. "About usual! I'm sure glad that K9 is so well-trained and calm."

"Yeah. Vic really needs to get that dog trained."

"She's trying. And I think he's improved in the time that she's had him. But Beryl obviously didn't know anything about training."

Terry nodded. "Some people shouldn't have pets. Did you put him in his kennel?"

"Yes. But Vic doesn't want him to be kenneled all day."

"Won't hurt him for a while."

"If he was better-behaved, then I would just bring him over here. He gets along with K9. They could hang out together and Nilla wouldn't be lonely."

"After seeing the destruction that little dog can cause, I would not want to see how he would treat a cat or a rabbit."

"They're both bigger than him. He would probably end up with the wrong end of the stick. But I don't want to try it. I don't want any of them to end up hurt."

"No," Terry agreed. "We can try introducing them gradually, but since Orange Blossom still hasn't made friends with K9, I don't know how that would go over."

Erin sighed. "They're as bad as people. I wish that everyone would just get along."

Hot on the Trail Mix, Book #15 of the Auntie Clem's Bakery series by P.D. Workman can be purchased at pdworkman.com

ABOUT THE AUTHOR

P.D. Workman is a USA Today Bestselling author, winner of several awards from Library Services for Youth in Custody and the InD'tale Magazine's Crowned Heart award, and has published over 90 mystery/suspense/thriller and young adult books, including stand alones and these series: Auntie Clem's Bakery cozy mysteries, Reg Rawlins Psychic Investigator paranormal mysteries, Zachary Goldman Mysteries (PI), Kenzie Kirsch Medical Thrillers, Parks Pat Mysteries (police procedural), and YA series: Tamara's Teardrops, Between the Cracks, and Breaking the Pattern.

Workman loves writing about the underdog, who the reader may love or hate. She has been praised for her realistic details, deep characterization, and sensitive handling of the serious social issues that appear in all of her stories, from light cozy mysteries through to darker, grittier young adult and mystery/suspense books.

P. D. Workman, does not shy from probing the deep psychological scars of childhood trauma, mental illness, and addiction. Also characteristic of this author, these extremely sensitive issues are explored with extensive empathy, described with incredible clarity, and portrayed with profound insight.

— —KIM, GOODREADS REVIEWER

Some of Workman's titles have been translated into Spanish, French, Portuguese, German, and Italian.

Workman began writing at an early age and is a prolific reader as well as writer. She is also passionate about teaching and learning, expresses her creativity through art and cooking, and loves exploring the Calgary parks and green spaces where the Parks Pat Mysteries are set. She was a legal assistant for many years and has done extensive charitable work.

Workman was born and raised in Alberta, Canada, and is married with one adult son.

~

Please visit P.D. Workman at pdworkman.com to see what else she is working on, to join her mailing list, and to link to her social networks.

~

If you enjoyed this book, please take the time to recommend it to other purchasers with a review or star rating and share it with your friends!

tiktok.com/@pdworkmanauthor
facebook.com/pdworkmanauthor
twitter.com/pdworkmanauthor
instagram.com/pdworkmanauthor
amazon.com/author/pdworkman
bookbub.com/authors/p-d-workman
goodreads.com/pdworkman
linkedin.com/in/pdworkman
pinterest.com/pdworkmanauthor
youtube.com/pdworkman

Find P.D. Workman's books at

PDWORKMAN.COM

Scan the QR code below

www.ingramcontent.com/pod-product-compliance
Lightning Source LLC
Chambersburg PA
CBHW020229260626
47156CB00002B/605